Also available from
B.J. Daniels
and HQN Books

Sterling's Montana

Stroke of Luck
Luck of the Draw

The Montana Cahills

Renegade's Pride
Outlaw's Honor
Cowboy's Legacy
Cowboy's Reckoning
Hero's Return
Rancher's Dream
Wrangler's Rescue

The Montana Hamiltons

Wild Horses
Lone Rider
Lucky Shot
Hard Rain
Into Dust
Honor Bound

Beartooth, Montana

Mercy
Atonement
Forsaken
Redemption
Unforgiven

B.J. DANIELS

NEW YORK TIMES BESTSELLING AUTHOR

LUCK *of the* DRAW

HQN™

HQN™

ISBN-13: 978-1-335-04103-6

Luck of the Draw

Recycling programs for this product may not exist in your area.

This book is dedicated to Jodi Lee, who bakes an amazing cake, organizes an amazing quilt party and always challenges me with her quilt ideas.

LUCK *of the* DRAW

CHAPTER ONE

GARRETT STERLING BROUGHT his horse up short as something across the deep ravine caught his eye. A fierce wind swayed the towering pines against the mountainside as he dug out his binoculars. He could smell the rain in the air. Dark clouds had gathered over the top of Whitefish Mountain. If he didn't turn back soon, he would get caught in the summer thunderstorm. Not that he minded it all that much, except the construction crew working at the guest ranch would be anxious for the weekend and their paychecks. Most in these parts didn't buy into auto deposit.

Even as the wind threatened to send his Stetson flying and he felt the first few drops of rain dampen his long-sleeved Western shirt, he couldn't help being curious about what he'd glimpsed. He'd seen something moving through the trees on the other side of the ravine.

He raised the binoculars to his eyes, waiting for them to focus. "What the hell?" When he'd caught movement, he'd been expecting elk or maybe a deer. If he was lucky, a bear. He hadn't seen a grizzly in this area in a long time, but it was always a good idea to know if one was around.

But what had caught his eye was human. He was too startled to breathe for a moment. A large man moved through the pines. He wasn't alone. He had hold of a woman's wrist in what appeared to be a death grip and was dragging her behind him. She seemed to be struggling to stay on her feet. It was what he saw in the man's other hand that had stolen his breath. A gun.

Garrett couldn't believe what he was seeing. Surely, he was wrong. Through the binoculars, he tried to keep track of the two. But he kept losing them as they moved through the thick pines. His pulse pounded as he considered what to do.

His options were limited. He was too far away to intervene and he had a steep ravine between him and the man with the gun. Nor could he call for help—as if help could arrive in time. There was no cell phone coverage this far back in the mountains outside of Whitefish, Montana.

Through the binoculars, he saw the woman burst out of the trees and realized that she'd managed to break away from the man. For a moment, Garrett thought she was going to get away. But the man was larger and faster and was on her quickly, catching her and jerking her around to face him. He hit her with the gun, then put the barrel to her head as he jerked her to him.

"No!" Garrett cried, the sound lost in the wind and crackle of thunder in the distance. Dropping the binoculars onto his saddle, he drew his sidearm from the holster at his hip and fired a shot into the air. It echoed across the wide ravine, startling his horse.

As he struggled to holster the pistol again and grab the binoculars, a shot from across the ravine filled the air, echoing back at him. And then another and another and another. Four shots, all in quick succession. He winced at each one as he hurriedly grabbed up the binoculars again and lifted them to his eyes. His hands shook as he tried to locate the spot on the mountainside across the ravine where he'd last seen the two people.

With dread, he saw what appeared to be a leg on the ground, sticking out of the tall grass, where the two had been only moments ago. He quickly looked around for the man. In the dense trees, he caught the blur of someone running back in the direction where he'd originally spotted the two.

He focused again on what he could see of the body on the ground. The leg hadn't moved.

In the distance, he heard the faint sound of a car engine roaring to life. He swung the binoculars to the end of the ridgeline and saw a dark blue SUV speeding away. It was too far away to get more than that. It quickly disappeared in the trees.

Garrett swore. At moments like this, he wished he had cell phone coverage on the mountain. But his father had always argued that being off the grid was the appeal of Sterling's Montana Guest Ranch. No cell phones, no TV, no internet. Nothing but remote, wild country.

Reining his horse around, he took off down the

trail back to the guest ranch lodge. It had begun to rain by the time he leaped off his horse and hurried inside.

He used the landline to call Sheriff Sid Anderson.

"I just witnessed a murder," he said when the sheriff came on the line. He quickly told him what he'd witnessed, including giving him what information he could about the SUV that he'd seen roaring away.

"You fired a shot into the air?" the sheriff asked. "So the killer saw you?"

He hadn't thought of that. "From across the ravine. I don't think the killer is concerned about me."

"Let's hope not," Sid said. "You think you can take me to the body?"

"Meet me where Red Meadow Road connects with the forest service property and I'll take you to the spot."

"Twenty minutes. I'll be there. But be careful," the sheriff warned. "The killer might not have gone far. Or he might be on the way to your guest ranch."

CHAPTER TWO

ALL THE WAY from Whitefish, Montana, up into the mountains, Sheriff Sid Anderson was mentally kicking himself. If he had retired last summer, it would be someone else driving up here now to investigate an alleged murder.

His days on the job were numbered. He had hoped to get through them without something like this. It was his own fault, he told himself as he drove. He'd been worried about who would become sheriff when he was gone. Several of the deputies were champing at the bit to take his place. But it was the undersheriff that he'd been worried about most.

Undersheriff Ward Farnsworth had run against Sid in the last election and lost. He was the wrong man for the job and the voting public knew it. But if Sid had retired, Farnsworth would have been acting sheriff until the election. Sid couldn't turn the county over to a man who liked to throw his weight around and hide behind his badge. Worse, since Ward was running for the election again this fall, he spent most of his time campaigning rather than doing his job. But soon, the undersheriff wouldn't be his problem. Let the voters decide, he thought.

As he neared the mountains, large drops of rain began to smack the windshield, sounding like distant gunfire. Sid turned on his wipers. He was rolling with lights and siren even though there wasn't any traffic on this road because of the thunderstorm. The rain would keep the tourists down in the valley today.

He hoped the rancher was mistaken about what he'd seen—and not just for selfish reasons. He didn't need a murder—not when he was so close to retiring and putting his lawman years behind him. Had it been anyone but Garrett Sterling, he would have been more skeptical. He'd known the Sterling family all his life, but over his many years in law enforcement, he'd found even the best of people often weren't sure what they'd actually seen when thrown into a stressful situation.

One of the reasons Sid was skeptical at all was that he knew the spot where the rancher had been when he'd seen what he thought was a murder. The ravine between him and where he'd seen the couple was deep and wide. Also Garrett hadn't seen the actual shooting—he'd only heard the shots and seen what he thought could be a body lying in the tall grass—and someone fleeing.

Not that Sid couldn't envision someone driving up to the end of the road to commit a murder. But there were better places to kill a person with so much wild country around the area. Why pick one so close to Sterling's Montana Guest Ranch?

As he turned onto Red Meadow Road, he swore at the thought of the position the rancher might have put himself in. It wouldn't be the first time Garrett had intervened in an attempt to save a life. He was that kind of man. But the killer now knew that he'd been seen. It wouldn't take much for him to find the guest ranch—and the rancher.

As Sid drove, he kept an eye out for the dark blue SUV that Garrett had seen racing away, even though he had little hope of seeing it. Enough time had passed for the alleged killer to make a clean getaway. Not to mention that this area was a honeycomb of mountain roads. If the person driving the SUV knew the area, they could disappear down any one of them and be long gone by now.

He'd hesitated to call an ambulance or get the coroner involved at this point. First he wanted to make sure there had been a murder. Once he could verify that there was a woman's body on the ridge, he'd call in the troops. As short-staffed as they always were, he didn't want to waste resources.

Ahead, the road dead-ended at a wide spot. There was just enough room to turn around. Garrett's pickup was parked off to one side of the road. The rancher was smart enough not to disturb any fresh tracks where the alleged killer must have turned around before making his escape.

He could see deep grooves in the dirt—now turning to mud—where someone had left in a hurry. The blue SUV? The ruts were now quickly filling with rainwater.

As he pulled up, Garrett hopped out of his truck and rushed through the driving rain to the patrol SUV. He opened the passenger side on a gust of wind and rain.

"Nice day for a murder," Sid said.

Garrett shook rain from his Stetson and slipped out of his coat to shake it before climbing in. "I'm sure you've seen worse."

True enough, he thought. "One of the reasons I'm hanging up my gun and badge soon. I'm looking forward to doing some woodworking in my garage. Might pick up a part-time job if I get too hungry." He grinned over at Garrett. "If you're right, this will hopefully be my last murder case before the election when someone else takes the job. I'm hoping you're wrong and that all of that is behind me."

He could see that Garrett was keyed up and tense. Sid asked for more details as to where it had happened as rain pounded the top of the SUV and ran down the windshield like a river. The last thing Sid wanted to do was go out in this thunderstorm let alone find a woman's body lying in the grass and have a killer on the loose.

But as long as he was wearing this star… "Let's do it," he said to the rancher. Cutting the engine, he pulled on his rain gear and climbed out. Garrett joined him, the rain a steady drumming on their Stetsons and coats.

As they began to work their way up the muddy path next to the road, Sid was reminded of another reason it was time to quit being a lawman. He was getting too old for this. He wanted to spend his time enjoying himself. He thought of Dorothea Brand and smiled. He had his retirement all planned out and if he was lucky, she was going to be a part of it.

Dorothea had worked for the Sterlings for the past

thirty years and had been like a mother to Garrett and his two brothers after their mother died.

The wind howled through the pines, branches rocking as the rain fell horizontally, pelting him like hurled pebbles. He felt the icy-cold liquid soak his jeans and run down into his boots. He thought about his warm workshop where he did his woodworking. A bolt of lightning splintered the bruise-colored sky over the mountain peaks. In answer the deep, chest-vibrating sound of thunder followed behind it.

Stopping to catch his breath, he looked through the rain into the dark of the forest and felt a chill. *You just have to live long enough to enjoy retirement.* Where had that thought come from? He shook it off and, ducking his head to the rain, started walking again.

Garrett, he noticed, had a grim look on his face. It wouldn't be the first murder the rancher had witnessed. But it wasn't like anything a man got used to, Sid reminded himself, thinking of his first murder scene.

Of course Garrett was shaken. It was a lot to handle for a man who wasn't used to violence. He was no doubt wondering, the same as Sid was, why here? Why on this particular mountain ridgeline? And why had he been there to witness it? Coincidence?

When something like this happened, you realized that if you had taken just a little longer over breakfast, you wouldn't have seen a thing. You might have heard distant shots, but you wouldn't have thought much about it. With the thunder and lightning, you might not even have heard someone being murdered.

Ahead of him, Garrett stopped under the bough

of a huge pine. Sid followed his gaze across the ravine, now shrouded in fog and rain, in the direction
of the guest ranch.

"It's right up here," the rancher said pointing to
an open area ahead, the lush grass tall and green. So
deep that it would be hard to find a body.

"DON'T TELL ME that you aren't aware that the sheriff
has a crush on you," the elderly Eleanor Franklin said
without looking up from her knitting. "The way Sid
acts when he's around you? You've got yourself an
admirer, Dorothea Brand. Mark my words."

Dorothea scoffed, but only for Eleanor's benefit.
She prided herself on her second sight. Not that she
was clairvoyant exactly. It was just that she sensed
things and had for most of her more than fifty years.
Her mother had been a witch, well, at least according
to *her*. She'd taught Dorothea to cast spells.

Admittedly the spells mother cast had never exactly worked, at least not in the way she'd hoped.
Henrietta Brand was often stirring up a love potion
or two on the postman, the butcher at the grocery
store, the mechanic at the shop down the street.

Dorothea had struggled with her own spell casting. But that didn't mean that she didn't have a sixth
sense—keen intuition anyway. She'd certainly been
right about what she'd felt coming more often than
not. Not that she'd been able to change events with
her spells or her sage or her candles.

Her mother always told her that sometimes other
forces were stronger than any potion or spell. That's

how her mother explained why the love spells she put on the postman, butcher or mechanic hadn't made them succumb to her.

"If Sheriff Sid Anderson had a crush on me, I'd know it," she told the other woman and kept her eyes on her knitting. *Of course she knew it.* It didn't take second sight to see how tongue-tied the sheriff got around her. Or how he nervously worked the brim of his Stetson in his fingers and looked at his boots when he talked to her.

"He tries to flirt with you every time he sees you," Eleanor was saying. "Surely you've noticed." The small, gray-haired woman kept knitting but looked up suddenly. "I actually thought that was why you joined our knitting group. You really didn't know he was a member?"

She wasn't about to admit anything as she labored over each stitch, repeating in her head "knit one, purl one, knit one, purl one." For almost half her life, she'd spent her spring, summer and fall up at Sterling's Montana Guest Ranch where she supervised pretty much everything to make sure the staff did their job. Or at least stuck her nose into everything. She couldn't imagine doing anything else—no matter what the sheriff might have in mind. She'd heard he was retiring soon.

"Crush or not, I doubt he'll get up the courage to ask you to marry him," Eleanor said. "His wife Adeline's been dead for years. Bless her soul. Sid's managed bachelorhood this long…"

"I could never leave the boys anyway," Dorothea said. The Sterling brothers, Will, Garrett and Shade, had pretty much adopted her after their mother died. She told herself that they wouldn't know what to do without her—and hoped it was true.

"Even if Sid got down on one knee and proposed?" Eleanor said, stopping knitting to narrow her eyes in disbelief.

"At our age, he'd be a fool to get down on one knee," Dorothea said. "He might not be able to get back up." She laughed and Eleanor joined in. "What would the sheriff see in me, anyway?" she asked, happy to set her knitting aside for a moment. It was true. She owned a mirror. She was a short, squat woman with a helmet of dark hair and piercing dark eyes that came across as a disconcerting glare. "I'm bossy, set in my ways and a butt-in-ski. At least that's what I've been told."

Eleanor chuckled in obvious agreement. Her needles began to clack away again as yarn magically turned into a sweater on her lap. "You can't kid me, Dorothea Brand. I've seen you giving the sheriff an assessing eye right back. Anyway, the boys, as you call them, are grown. Will's married now. Won't be long before the other two head to the post, I'd wager."

She realized the woman was right. The time was coming when they wouldn't need her anymore. On top of that, her heart always beat a little faster around the sheriff, making her feel like a girl again.

"Sid's not a bad-looking man for his age," Eleanor said. "The silver hair suits him. You could do worse."

She wasn't sure how to take that. She wanted to defend Sid, but she wasn't sure if the "you could do worse" was more about her rather than the sheriff, so she kept her mouth shut.

"He's a straight arrow though. He's the kind of man who'd want to get married if he does come a courtin'," Eleanor said, glancing over her dime-store glasses and pursing her lips. "You might be too much of a Bohemian for that."

Dorothea snorted. It wasn't as if she hadn't been asked before. That was back in her late teens before she'd taken the job at the guest ranch. She'd always told herself that the timing had been wrong, but she knew it was more than that. She hadn't wanted to be tied down at that age and wasn't sure she did at this age, either.

"Well, when he asks, I say go for it," the elderly Eleanor said. "It's not the worst thing, being married." She looked up. "Sid might put a smile on your face." The woman cackled, not missing a stitch.

COLD, WET AND CHILLED, Garrett stood under a large pine to wait out of the driving rain. He had no doubt what the sheriff would find. But he knew Sid was still hoping that this was a wild-goose chase. Anything but murder.

The scene kept playing over like a video in his head. He saw the two people, the man forcing the woman deeper into the woods, the man holding the gun to the woman's head. Even in his memory, he couldn't see their faces. He'd been focused on the gun in the man's hand, more than their faces.

But when he thought about it now, he recalled the wind whipping the woman's long dark hair around her face. He frowned and tried to see the man, but the killer had been wearing a hoodie, his face in shadow.

Shaking his head, he attempted to put the disturbing images out of his head as he watched Sid move carefully along the ridgeline through the rain toward the spot where the woman's body should be. Water poured off the brim of his Stetson, making it even harder to see ahead of him.

He shuddered against the cold, the rain, the shock, wishing he had been mistaken but knowing he wasn't.

As THE STORM howled around him, Sid stared into the swaying tall grass, looking for a body, but hoping not to see one.

"You should be getting close," Garrett called from where he'd left him.

Wind lay over the tall grass, making it look like waves moving across the side of the mountain. He squinted down over the ridge into the ravine. This time of year the wild grasses were tall and lush and could easily hide a body. If there was a body here. He still wasn't convinced he would find one.

He moved farther down the ridgeline. A gust of wind moved through the grass, keeling it over, as it rushed toward him. He was thinking of dry clothes and a hot cup of coffee when all his hopes of this being a mistake blew away in the cold icy gust. As the grass lay over, he saw what appeared to be part of a jeans-clad leg.

Sid motioned for Garrett to stay where he was before he began to slide in the mud and slick grass toward the body.

He caught a glimpse of a sneaker sole as he slid down to the spot, stopping just feet from the figure. He could see that the leg was twisted awkwardly under the body. Stepping closer, he saw more of the torso and thought again of what Garrett had said he'd seen. A man and a woman. The man dragging the woman by the arm into the woods. The man putting the gun to the woman's head.

Sid stepped closer until he could see the victim's jacket soaked in rain and blood. It appeared that all four shots had gone directly to the chest. Kneeling, he parted the tall grass to get a look at the face, no longer shocked by what he was seeing—but definitely surprised. He checked for a pulse, even though he knew he wouldn't find one. Four bullets to the chest would do that.

Rising, he glanced back up the mountain to where Garrett stood in the rain. The rancher hadn't moved, his expression even grimmer now that the body had been found.

The sheriff looked again at the deceased lying in the grass. Garrett Sterling had witnessed a murder all right. Except it hadn't been the woman who'd taken the four bullets.

Dead on the side of the mountain was a man, no doubt the man the rancher had seen. Lying in the grass beside the body was a pistol.

And the woman? Somewhere in a dark blue SUV probably trying to put as many miles behind her as she could.

CHAPTER THREE

FIGHTING TO SEE through the pouring rain, the woman took the curve in the narrow road too fast as she careened off the mountain in the dark blue SUV. The tall pines on each side of the road whipped past in a dizzying green blur. The wipers clacked frantically, losing the battle against the relentless rain that pounded like the pounding in her head.

She caught her reflection in the side mirror, wincing at her already bruised cheek where the man had hit her the first time. The blow had knocked her senseless and taken all of the fight out of her as he'd forced her into his SUV. She tried not to think about what had happened on the mountainside.

Her head ached, but she could feel adrenaline burning like a wild grass fire through her veins. She gripped the wheel to still her shaking hands, fighting to keep the vehicle on the road. She was driving too fast but she refused to let up off the gas even as her stomach heaved. She had to reach town and help as quickly as possible.

The dark, dismal day pressed down on her with a weight that made her claustrophobic. If she didn't get out of these trees, this rain and off this endless road soon she thought she'd lose her mind.

A blinding flash of lightning exploded in front of the SUV. She jumped and felt the rear of the vehicle begin to slide out of control on the muddy track. Seeing the wall of trees coming up fast, she corrected but not soon enough. A tree branch smacked the windshield and ripped off the side mirror. Through strength of will alone, she managed to keep the SUV on the road.

The clap of thunder that followed the flash of lightning felt like a gunshot to her chest. She shuddered and looked down. With a jolt she saw something that had escaped her attention before. There was dried blood on her hands and clothing. The man's blood. Her stomach roiled and the realization hit her harder than the man had. She literally had that man's blood on her hands. How many more men's blood would she have on her hands before this ended? That was if they didn't get her first.

She glanced in the rearview mirror even though she knew there was no way he could be following her. He was dead. Even if he wasn't, he didn't have a vehicle. She'd taken his. But there would be others after her. In fact they could already be on this mountain.

Her gaze shot to the rearview mirror again. Something flickered in the dull light behind her like the gleam of metal on a vehicle. In her mind's eye, she saw the car gaining behind her. She saw the man lean out, the gun in his hand as he fired. She felt the rear window explode in a shower of glass before the sickening thud of the bullet as it tore through the SUV to splatter her brains all over the windshield.

She blinked. There was nothing behind her but muddy road and rain hemmed in by pines. Tears welled in her eyes. She feared he'd hit her harder than she thought this last time with the gun. The gun she'd dropped at the scene, she realized.

She shook her head, running scared. She was imagining things, things that seemed so real because she'd felt that she'd been running for her life for so long. She tried to calm down, knowing what was at stake if she didn't get off this mountain in time.

Gripping the wheel harder, she concentrated on keeping the SUV on the rain-slick road, but her vision kept blurring. The blows to her head had left her dazed. Or was it her mind refusing to believe what had happened back there. Even as he was forcing her along the ridgeline, it hadn't seemed real.

Not until she heard the gunshot.

She wanted to rub her eyes, now dry and strained from staring through the rain, but she didn't dare take her hands off the wheel even if her hands hadn't been covered with the man's blood. She knew she should slow down. She was having trouble keeping her eyes open. Could she have a concussion? Was that what was wrong with her? Or was it the fear, the horror of what she'd done, the realization that all of this had been real? Someone had tried to killer her.

She blinked hard, gripping the wheel even tighter. It couldn't be that much farther to town and help. And yet this wasn't the road the man had taken her on earlier. If it had been, she would have reached town by now. She was lost. The thought filled her with panic.

Worse, what if she was already too late?

Feeling as if she might throw up, she almost clipped another pine tree. Ahead, there seemed to be nothing but more rain, more trees, more of the narrow snaking road against the backdrop of more mountains. The landscape, the rain, the speed she was traveling all had a dizzying effect as if none of this was real. She pushed down harder on the gas pedal, frantic to get out of these mountains to get…

If she was too late then nothing mattered. All of this would have been for nothing. Tears welled in her eyes again. She wiped at them with her sleeve, losing sight of the road for just a moment.

It was a moment too long.

NUMB WITH SHOCK and cold, Garrett repeated what he'd seen for the record as he and the sheriff waited in the patrol SUV for the coroner and forensics team to arrive. Sid had said he wanted to get it down while it was all still fresh in Garrett's mind.

Now he stared into the video camera and went over it again to the sound of rain thumping on the roof and the whir of the heater. The windows of the patrol SUV had fogged over from their wet clothing, making all of it seem even more surreal.

He couldn't help feeling scared and confused. He'd been so sure about what he'd seen. Now, after finding out that the body lying in the deep grass wasn't the woman's… He thought of the only other time he'd given a statement to law enforcement and cringed at the memory. It hadn't been a lie, not exactly. He'd had his reasons for withholding information that time. He'd been protecting someone else.

Shaking his head, he wondered why he was thinking of that now?

"You all right?" the sheriff asked.

"Still in shock."

"That's understandable. We're almost done here. Had you ever seen the man before?" Sid asked after Garrett had gone through his story once again.

He shook his head. "Like I said, I couldn't really see their faces. They were moving through the pines on the other side of the ravine. I kept losing sight of them. Then when they finally emerged from the trees... It all happened so fast." He frowned as he realized why he hadn't gotten a good look at them. "The woman had long dark hair that was whirling around her face and the man had the hood up on his jacket, shading his features."

The sheriff nodded. "But the dead man on the side of the mountain, was that the man you saw?"

"I would assume so," he said, recalling the sheriff asking him to slide down the mountainside to where the body had come to rest against a rock. "I honestly can't say definitively, but who else would it be? The man I saw was wearing a hooded dark jacket and so was the dead man. He has to be the man I saw from across the ravine."

He knew what the sheriff was getting at. If there was only the man and the woman and now the man was dead, then logically, the woman had to have killed him. But when Garrett had first seen the two, the man had been the aggressor. He had been the one with the gun. He had been forcing the woman deeper into the woods and threatening her with the weapon.

"You said at one point she got away, but the man caught up with her and hit her?" Sid asked.

Garrett nodded. "He hit her hard enough with the hand holding the gun that she would have fallen to the ground if he hadn't had hold of her wrist. I saw her sag as if the blow had almost knocked her out. Then he put the barrel of the gun to her head. At that point, it had certainly appeared that the man planned to use the weapon to kill her."

"That's when you fired the shot to let the man know he had been seen."

"I had to put down the binoculars to draw my pistol." So what had happened when he wasn't watching? Was it possible she'd gotten the gun away from him that quickly, shot him four times and then taken off before Garrett could holster his pistol and pick up the binoculars again?

Not just possible. The only conclusion he could come up with since a gun had been on the ground next to the man's body. Unless the woman had had a gun or... He rubbed his temples, his head aching.

"What else can you tell me about the woman?" the sheriff asked.

He thought for a moment. "Long dark hair. Slim. She was shorter than the man and probably fifty to seventy-five pounds lighter." He shook his head. "I'm sorry, that's the best I can do." He shivered from the cold, his clothing soaked to the skin, and the shock and confusion.

"It's all right," Sid said as he shut off the video camera. "If you remember anything else, let me know."

Garrett promised he would. As the sound of sirens filled the air, he climbed out into the rain to run to his pickup. Once behind the wheel, he considered driving back to the closed guest ranch. He'd been staying up there this summer while the construction work was being done and his brother Will was on his extended honeymoon with Poppy.

But after what he'd seen on the mountainside, he'd called his brother Shade to ask him to take care of the construction crew working up there since it was Friday and payday. Which meant given the hour, the crew would be gone. He would be all alone up on the mountainside. Normally, that would have appealed to him. But not this dark, late, rainy afternoon. Not after the day he'd had. He didn't feel like being alone tonight at the isolated guest ranch.

Deciding to head to the main ranch in the valley, he started the engine and backed out onto the road after the ambulance and sheriff's deputies patrol SUVs passed on their way up the mountain. Driving through the rain, he tried to quit going over what he'd seen earlier across that ravine. But it kept playing, over and over in his mind.

He was beginning to doubt everything he'd thought he'd seen.

THE SHERIFF LED the coroner and crime scene techs to the crime scene, before going back to his patrol SUV to make sure the area remained closed off. He doubted there would be hikers today, but he wasn't taking any chances. The tracks were still preserved as much as they could be in the rain. The techs might be able to get a useable print, once things dried out. But not if anyone drove over them.

All the way back to his rig, he'd thought about the shooting. Self-defense? Or something else? Maybe the woman was on her way to the sheriff's office right now. Or not.

Earlier, when he'd called for backup, he'd asked what deputies were in the area. Sid had Undersheriff Ward Farnsworth patrolling north of town. It was summer, tourist season, and the traffic was unbelievable this close to Glacier Park. There weren't enough law enforcement officers to cover a state as large as Montana, but they did the best they could with the help of other law enforcement as needed.

Ward had gone out on a rollover earlier today on the way to the national park. But even if he'd been in the area, Sid didn't want him on this case. The man was like a bull in a china closet. He couldn't even spell the word *subtle*. All he needed was Ward tromping around up on this mountainside in the rain thinking he could solve this case, make himself a hero and win the fall election for sheriff.

"Is Deputy Conners available?" he'd asked. "Great. Send her." She would do what needed to be done until the state crime team arrived.

Now as he reached the area he'd cordoned off with crime scene tape, he saw the deputy walking up the hill from where she'd parked her vehicle and couldn't help but smile. Ward Farnsworth would have driven up, lights and sirens blazing, and pulled right up to the crime scene tape—if he'd seen it in time. Otherwise, he'd have gone right through it.

Lizzy had parked down the road and walked up. "You wanted to see me, sir?" she said as she reached him.

He was always a little taken aback by this grown-up version of her. Elizabeth "Lizzy" Conners lived next door to him. He'd watched her grow up from the time she was a gap-toothed tomboy who'd climbed his trees and held her own with the neighbor boys.

He'd never dreamed she would go into law enforcement. But after the police academy, she'd shown up at his door asking for a job. She turned out to be the best hire he'd ever made.

"I need you to make sure this area isn't disturbed," he said.

She nodded. "Will do." Ward would have argued. Or asked a lot of questions. Lizzy just did as she was asked and did it well.

He'd heard that she planned to throw her hat into the ring for his job this fall. She was a little green, but she had a good head on her shoulders. And she might be able to win against Ward who hadn't made any friends during his years in law enforcement.

As he walked back up the ridgeline to where the crime techs were working, he smiled to himself. He would love nothing better than to have Lizzy become the next sheriff.

As GARRETT STARTED to push open the door to the large rambling ranch house, he realized he didn't even remember the drive down to the ranch, he'd been so distracted and upset. He feared that the moment he walked in, Dorothea would see it and demand to know what was going on before he was ready to tell her.

He needed a beer. He wasn't saying a word about it until he had one. Or two.

As he walked into the house and closed the door behind him, he realized he hadn't needed to worry. Dorothea Brand had other things on her mind as she stormed out of the kitchen. "Your brother is impossible," she said, hands on her ample hips.

"Which one?" He thought his brother Will and bride, Poppy, weren't back from their honeymoon yet.

"The only brother in our kitchen," Dorothea snapped.

Garrett had to smile. The squat woman with her cap of dark hair and intense gaze was like part of the furnishings and had been as far back as he could remember. She'd come to work at the guest ranch thirty years ago and never left. When the guest ranch closed up for the season, she moved into one of the wings of the main ranch house down here in the valley, taking over the housekeeping duties.

Now at over fifty, she oversaw the housekeeping duties and everything else related to the three brothers—whether they appreciated it or not. Hell, she'd practically raised them after they'd lost their mother. Dorothea had stepped into that role like the mother hen she was.

"What's Shade done now?" Garrett asked as he moved through the large living room headed for the kitchen, following a burnt smell that only increased in strength with each step.

The brothers batched most of the year, eating whatever one or the other of them cooked. Dorothea couldn't boil water. At least that was her story and she was sticking to it. During the guest ranch months, they hired Buckshot Brewster to cook. He cooked one note: chuckwagon, which meant beans and meat, usually slightly charred.

But even Buckshot didn't char meat like this. "What was it before you incinerated it?" he asked as he looked into the skillet his brother had pulled off the stove.

"Grouse. At least I think that's what it was. I found it in the freezer earlier," Shade said sheepishly as he fanned smoke out the open window. "We could order pizza."

"Fine with me." He opened the refrigerator and pulled out a beer, popping the top as he turned to look at his brother. "Shade, thanks for going up and paying the construction crew."

"What was up?" Shade asked. "You sounded strange on the phone."

He let out a sigh, knowing neither of them would forgive him if they heard from someone else. He took a long pull on the beer. It went down icy cold. "I spent most of the day with the sheriff." He looked up as Dorothea poked her head into the kitchen doorway.

"The *sheriff*?" she echoed.

He wondered if her interest was in crime or the

sheriff himself. It was no secret that there was something in the air when Dorothea and Sid were around each other. He took another long pull on his beer. It tasted wonderful. He felt himself begin to relax a little.

"Order us some pizza and I'll tell you all about it," he said.

It wasn't until they were seated in the living room that Garrett told his story once again, cutting it down to the basics. "I was on my usual afternoon horseback ride up on the mountain when I witnessed something. A man appeared to be forcing a woman into the pines at gunpoint." Dorothea sat, eyes wide, as she listened. "I had pulled out my binoculars. She got away for a moment, but he caught her, hit her and put the barrel of the gun to her head."

"Oh, my word," Dorothea said on a breath.

"I dropped the binoculars, quickly pulled my pistol and fired a shot in the air, thinking if the man knew they weren't alone…" Garrett sighed and took a long drink of his second beer. "But before I could pick up the binoculars again, I heard four shots, one right after another."

"He killed her?" Shade said.

"By the time I retrieved my binoculars and looked all I could see was part of a denim-clad leg in the deep grass. I got a glimpse of the vehicle as the killer escaped. A dark blue SUV. But I never got a good look at the woman's or the man's face."

"I can't believe this. He killed her even knowing you were watching them on the mountainside across from them?" Dorothea asked.

"That's what I thought, but when Sid and I reached the body, it wasn't the woman. It was the man."

"What?" Shade and Dorothea said almost in unison.

"I guess somehow when I fired the pistol it distracted him and she got the gun away from the man, shot him and then took off. It's the only thing that makes any sense. But she did it so quickly…" He shook his head.

Dorothea looked scared. "So what happened to the woman?"

Garrett shrugged. "Apparently she got away."

"She didn't go to the cops?" Shade asked.

"Apparently not."

Dorothea was studying him intently. "Why wouldn't she go to the authorities? She knew someone had seen them. It sounds like a case of self-defense unless there was some reason she couldn't go to the police."

He raised his hands in surrender. "You know as much as I do."

"You can bet this isn't the end of it," she said, sounding worried.

"Don't go putting salt along the threshold to my room," he warned her. "And no other spells, either." Dorothea fancied herself a witch. "I'm fine."

Shade grunted. "The killer saw you," his brother reminded him, as if he had to be reminded. "In this case, I think Dorothea might be right. If the woman realized where the shot had come from it wouldn't be that hard to find you. Maybe you shouldn't go back up to the guest ranch."

Garrett swore. "Seriously? The woman was simply defending herself," he argued with a whole lot less conviction than he felt. "The man is dead. So I really doubt anyone is coming after me." Even as he said it, he questioned what a jury would think about her shooting the man four times in the chest. How was she able to get the gun away from him to do that to begin with?

"Sounds like a woman who knows how to defend herself," Dorothea said as if she'd been thinking the same thing. "She might not be as…helpless as you thought she was."

"She isn't going to come after me, all right? Why would she?" Garrett said. "What I saw looked like self-defense and that's what I told the sheriff. Probably by now, she's sitting in the police station or sheriff's department confessing everything."

Neither said anything, but he could see what they were thinking. If not at the sheriff's department, then maybe she was on her way up to the guest ranch looking for him because nothing was like it seemed. And how hard would it be to find him since Sterling's Montana Guest Ranch was on the map—right across from the ridgeline where the killing had taken place?

"It's over and I'm fine." He got up to answer the knock at the door. "Shade, I hope you ordered sausage and pepperoni pizza and none of that girl pizza with pineapple on it." He was smiling as he said it because he knew Dorothea would take exception. Better to have her arguing about the pizza than worrying about some woman coming in the middle of the night to kill him.

SID WAS FOLLOWING the coroner's rig off the mountain with the body inside when he got the call about an accident on one of the logging roads in his area. A dark blue SUV had appeared to be traveling at a high rate of speed when it went off the road and crashed into the pines.

The description matched the vehicle Garrett had had seen. Also the logging road was one of the tributaries off this mountain. "The driver?" the sheriff asked.

"A woman. Unconscious. Taken to the hospital in Whitefish. Haven't gotten a status yet. But the deputy on duty ran the plates. The SUV she was driving was stolen."

"Any identification on her or in the car?"

"None that deputies could find."

"I'm on my way," he said and flipped on his lights and siren. The coroner pulled over to let him pass and minutes later he was walking into the hospital in the town of Whitefish.

"The woman who was brought in earlier from the car accident on the logging road to the north of town?" he asked at the nurses' station and was directed down the hallway.

He stopped in the doorway to her room when he saw the doctor changing her bandage. She lay in the bed, pale and bruised. He could see where a small part of her long, dark hair had been parted to sew stitches into her scalp. As he watched the doctor check her wound, and then put the bandage back in place, he waited for her to open her eyes. She didn't.

Sid stepped in and cleared his throat. "How is she doing?"

"Sheriff," Dr. Bullock said with a nod. "She's still unconscious, but stable. Right now, we have her listed as Jane Doe. Unless you have some identification on her."

"No, not yet. Was there anything with her clothing?"

Bullock shook his head.

He thought of Garrett. "There is someone I'd like to take a look at her." As he studied the woman in the bed, Sid was aware of a gut feeling he couldn't ignore. Since taking the job as sheriff, he'd gone with his gut and never regretted it. "In the meantime, I'd like her under protective custody." Did he really think someone might try to kill her again? His gut said it was a possibility and one risk he wasn't willing to take.

Also, he didn't want the woman going anywhere until he had a chance to talk to her. He would have felt better if, when she wrecked the stolen car she was driving, she had been headed toward town—and the sheriff's department. Instead, she was headed back into the mountains toward Glacier Park. Trying to get away? Or just turned around? Once she was conscious, he'd find out.

He texted Deputy Conners. "I'm going to put a deputy outside her door."

The doctor raised a brow.

"This woman is a person of interest." That's all he planned to tell the doctor or anyone else at this point. He wanted the woman's story first. In any shooting, even one that was allegedly self-defense, the woman would be arrested and arraigned while the investigation continued.

Dr. Bullock looked from the sheriff to the woman lying in the bed. She looked so damned innocent, he could see why the doctor had his doubts. Nor did she look capable of strong-arming a gun from a man half again her size and shooting him four times. But if Sid had learned anything, it was that appearances were often deceiving.

"Also forensics will be coming in to check for powder residue on her hands and clothing. I'm assuming you still have what she was wearing."

"It was about to be sent down to laundry," the doctor said. "I'll make sure it gets bagged for you. Anything else?"

"We'll also be taking a DNA sample to see if we can find out who she is," he said. "I'd just as soon we keep a lid on this for now," even though he knew everyone in the hospital would be speculating about her soon enough. "I want to speak to her about what happened before anyone else does. I'd appreciate it if you could give me a call as soon as she regains consciousness, no matter the hour."

"*If* she regains consciousness," Dr. Bullock said. "You never know with head injuries."

CHAPTER FOUR

ALISTAIR VANDERLIN HAD his secretary place the calls. He wasn't up to hearing the complaints he knew were coming. All he was doing was putting off the inevitable, he knew, but at least he could deal with them as a group, rather than one at a time.

He had his secretary tell each of them to come to the Seattle house on Capital Hill at six—early enough that he wouldn't have to offer them dinner. All three of them wouldn't turn down a drink, especially since he stocked only the good stuff, as they preferred to call it.

When he'd inherited the guardianship job, he'd thought he was only taking on one child, a five-year-old at the time. What he hadn't realized was that he would have more to take care of, all of them like baby birds with their mouths opening demanding more and more.

Sighing, he looked at his watch. Amethyst would show up first. She couldn't bear the thought that her brother, Peter, knew what was going on before she did. And of course her husband, Rance, would be trailing in her wake.

Alistair could barely tolerate the man. Clearly

Amethyst had married him for his blond good looks and not his personality or his ability to support himself. Oh, the man talked a good line about all the deals he had going—according to him, but Alistair knew better. The spineless Rance was in this for the money. Unfortunately, Amethyst had already gone through the bulk of her inheritance and was having trouble supporting her outrageous spending habit.

It boggled his mind to think how much money had run through her fingers like sand in a matter of years. If his friend Horace hadn't put some of his stepdaughter's inheritance in a trust with monthly allotments, she would be broke and Rance would already have moved on.

The doorbell rang. He braced himself as he waited for the maid to answer it. As he did, he looked around his wonderful home with its magnificent views of the Seattle area and knew that he wasn't the only one who had benefited by Horace's generosity. Also from his death.

Amethyst rushed to him in a flurry of expensive fabric and perfume as if propelled by a gust of wind. She looked a lot like her deceased mother. Tall and blonde with the face of a model. At thirty-eight, she was deeply involved in an ongoing battle against aging with the best pharmaceuticals that money could buy.

From a distance, she appeared stunning. But up close, it was clear that she was too thin, too pampered, too hungry. There was a jagged-edge brittleness about her that made a sensible person want to keep his distance.

"What has my stepsister done now?" she demanded before he could offer her a drink.

He looked behind her to see Rance chatting up the maid before he too entered the main living room.

"Drink?" he said to the man.

"I'll have what you're having," Rance said. Of course he would.

"And you?" he asked Amethyst.

She looked annoyed as she glanced around the room. "Peter isn't here yet? He just has to be late to annoy me."

"Amy, it's not even six yet," Rance said, calling her by a nickname that even Alistair knew she hated.

She shot her husband a withering look before turning her blue eyes on him again. "Gin and tonic. Make it a double," she said as if he were a bartender.

"Coming right up," Alistair said, relieved to be going to the bar as he heard the married couple begin to bicker.

He took his time making the drinks, thinking of his good friend Horace and the promise he'd made to look after his only biological child should something happen to him. He suspected Horace had known his life was in danger.

But Alistair had promised, thinking nothing would come of it. Little did he know that six months later, Horace and his new wife, Thea, would be murdered and he would become five-year-old Monica's guardian.

Amethyst had been thirteen, Peter eleven, at the time, children from Thea's other marriages before she'd thrown her net over widower Horace. Amethyst had gone to her grandmother's along with a comfortable monthly allowance and a very large inheritance when she turned thirty. Eight years later she was broke.

Peter had gone to an uncle with questionable means of support, who also received a substantial monthly allowance for his care, and had collected a generous inheritance when he turned thirty, as well. Horace had wanted his children to make something of themselves before they received their inheritances, not realizing that what they did was merely wait to be rich.

At least that was the case with his two stepchildren. Monica, Horace's flesh and blood from his first marriage, had been the exception. She hadn't cared about the money, often sending back the checks Alistair sent or forgetting to cash them. She preferred staying in hostels in Europe rather than luxury hotels. She was so much like her father, strong, determined, stubborn, independent, a rebel even at a young age. He often wondered though what she would have been like if her father had lived and if she hadn't witnessed his murder at such a tender age.

Not that she'd remembered what she'd seen. Her doctor said her memory loss was due to the trauma. The child didn't speak for weeks after it happened. Alistair had put her into counseling right away. She'd had a psychiatrist on retainer ever since.

It was part of what he'd promised Horace. That

Monica would receive everything she wanted or needed. No expense was to be spared and since there was no end to the money… The newspapers had termed her Poor Little Rich Girl. It was a title that had stuck—and was relevant even more now. In a matter of days, Monica would turn thirty and receive the bulk of her inheritance, which was nearly a hundred million dollars.

"That took long enough," Amethyst said when he returned with the drinks. She'd taken a seat on the sofa. Her husband stood by the window looking petulant, as usual.

Alistair had become used to being treated like a servant since he was sure that was how these people saw him. He doled out the money as well as the good and bad news. Just as he would be doing today.

As he handed a drink to Rance, he saw that he was fingering the leather on the couch as if to gauge its worth.

"Just tell us what is going on," Amethyst ordered. "I'm not in the mood to wait for—" The doorbell rang. "My brother," she finished.

A few moments later, Peter walked in. He was blond and blue-eyed like his sister. But where she was tall and willowy thin, he was athletically built. He'd definitely gotten his mother's good looks and he used them to his advantage living off wealthy women and squirreling his inheritance away as if for winter.

"Peter," Alistair said and handed him a beer, anticipating his arrival and his beverage of choice.

"Thanks, Al," he said and tipped the bottle at him in a salute.

What struck him was that this had become his family just as it had become Monica's. It wasn't the way he'd planned it. But his wife had died of cancer after the two of them had been unable to have a child of their own. They might have adopted, had she lived. And he might have remarried, had he not had Monica and all these others to take care of.

"So what's up?" Peter asked after taking a long pull on his beer.

He noticed that Rance had gulped his drink down and was now headed for the bar to make himself another one.

"It's about Monica."

"Oh, more drama," she groaned. "Big surprise."

Monica had definitely been the wild child. He'd had to get her out of numerous binds over the years. Her psychiatrist said her reckless behavior was due to witnessing the murders of her father and stepmother. That she didn't value life.

Alistair hoped she would outgrow it. She seemed to be a loner who liked to keep moving as she'd traveled the globe. Since she'd been back in the states, she'd continued to move around. Until recently.

He feared she was looking for something. Family? The three stepsiblings had never been close—since they were so far apart in age and other obvious reasons. The only time Amethyst and Peter seemed to acknowledge that Monica was part of their family was when they demanded updates on her. Where was she, what kind of trouble had she gotten into, how had she embarrassed them this time?

They got angry with him if he kept information from them, since he was considered the outsider.

"Apparently she's disappeared."

That got their attention. Monica would celebrate her thirtieth birthday soon and receive her inheritance.

"Disappeared?" Amethyst laughed. "More disappeared than she has been for years?" She shook her head. "She'll turn up soon. Probably at the last minute to pick up her money."

He cleared his throat. They would hear soon enough. "The last time I spoke with her, she said she doesn't want it and has made arrangements for all of it to go to charities."

Amethyst scoffed at that. "We'll see, won't we? She's just taunting us, trying to convince us that she's better than we are. Like she doesn't want the money." She let out an unladylike curse. "She's taken it for years, hasn't she?"

Alistair didn't answer. They'd all taken it for years, himself included. But that too was about to end. Once Monica turned thirty, it was all over and not just for her psychiatrist and her lawyer, but for him as well.

"I haven't seen her in over two years," Amethyst said and narrowed her eyes at him. "But you know where she's been, don't you?" When he didn't answer, she said, "So now you say she's disappeared? How interesting. Why now?"

"Why don't we cut to the chase?" Rance said.

"Is she alive or dead?" Peter said nothing as he finished his beer.

"I don't know," Alistair said. "I was hoping that one of you might have heard from her." He knew it was a long shot, but he had to ask. It wasn't the first time Monica had disappeared and he doubted it would be the last. As her psychiatrist, Dr. Neal Foster always said, "She's a troubled young woman who needs help." But Neal had also benefited greatly for the past twenty-five years from Monica's erratic behavior, thanks to Horace's gruesome death and Monica's "problems" following it.

The three shook their heads, muttering that they hadn't seen or heard from her.

"What if she's remembered?" Amethyst said, and exchanged a look with her husband. Her voice caught. "What if she's remembered who killed my mother?"

"Our mother," Peter corrected with a scowl at her. "And Monica's father. Our mother wasn't the only one to die that night."

The thought had never even occurred to him that Monica might have remembered that night. It was presumed that she'd seen the killer since, when she'd been found, she was covered in blood and hiding upstairs in a closet.

"I suppose she might have," Alistair said and nodded slowly. He saw that they all looked shell-shocked as each considered what this could mean to them. The murder would be in the news again.

"Wouldn't she have gone to the police if she had remembered?" Peter asked. No one spoke.

What if after twenty-five years her memory had come back? Hadn't doctors said it could happen? But now? Right before her thirtieth birthday?

THE WOMAN IN the hospital bed fought to open her eyes, coming up from the bottomless pit she'd fallen into. Instantly, she felt the pain in her head as she blinked in the dim light of the unfamiliar room. For a moment at the edge of consciousness, she felt only confusion and pain. Then the hospital room came into focus.

Her eyes flew all the way open. Panic filled her every cell. She tried to sit up but was too weak.

Oh God, don't let it be happening again.

A dream? She closed her eyes shut tightly, fighting to breathe. The image behind her closed eyelids was blood. So much blood.

But when she opened them, she was still in a hospital, still had the desperate feeling that something horrible had happened. But like all those years ago, her mind was a blank slate. She had no idea where she was or what had happened or maybe worse, how she'd gotten here. It was as if her memory had been wiped clean. *Again.*

She froze as, out of the corner of her eye, she saw her hands lying against the sterile white of the hospital bed sheets. *"No!"* The word came out a whimper. *"No, please no."* Feeling as if they were weighted by lead, she slowly raised her hands, willing her mind to be wrong.

Her heart rate spiked at the sight of the dried blood under her fingernails. She opened her mouth. *"No!"*

She hadn't realized she'd screamed until the nurse and doctor came running in. They rushed to her, trying to assure her that she was in the hospital and everything would be fine. But she knew better. Through the open hospital room door she saw a uniformed officer standing outside. The deputy's gaze caught hers for only a moment before she returned to the darkness.

It was happening again.

AFTER THE PIZZA and beer, Garrett was starting to relax a little. He'd convinced himself that as horrible as what he'd seen had been, it was over. He might never know what had happened on that mountainside. He'd done what he could to save the woman and apparently it had worked.

But a part of him wondered if he'd saved the wrong person.

He knew that was crazy thinking. It made him think of the other time he'd done what he'd thought was the right thing when he'd withheld information from the police. He'd helped out a woman only to find out later that he'd been wrong about her. Wrong about a lot of things.

Shoving those memories back into the dark corner where he'd left them, he tried to put today's events behind him. Dorothea and Shade seemed engrossed in the movie playing on the television, but every time a wind gust rattled a window, they all started.

It would have been funny, them all being jumpy, except for the fact that the sheriff hadn't called to say the woman from the mountainside had turned herself in. Only then could they all relax.

He tried to follow the television movie, but he was too distracted. He told himself he'd done the only thing he felt he could earlier today. Firing the shot in the air had given the woman the opportunity to turn the tables on the man. Clearly she must have feared for her life to put four bullets into him.

Still it nagged at him. How could she have gotten hold of the gun and shot the man four times in that narrow length of time? It seemed impossible unless as Dorothea had suggested, the woman had experience disarming a man and turning a gun on him. So who was this woman? A cop? Or a criminal? Or just a woman who'd been trained in self-defense?

That thought did nothing to reassure him. He shook his head, realizing he would probably never know. Whoever had been driving that dark blue SUV had gotten away. He assumed it was the woman but then again, he'd assumed it was the woman they would find dead on that mountainside. Maybe there had been someone waiting in the car. Why hadn't he thought of that before?

When his phone rang, they all jumped. He saw it was the sheriff and quickly picked up, hoping for some kind of closure, if not good news. At this point he wasn't sure what would constitute good news though.

"Garrett, would you mind coming down to the hospital?" the sheriff asked. "I need you to take a look at the woman who was driving what we believe to be the dark blue SUV you saw earlier."

He sat up in his chair. "Is she all right?" Shade muted the television.

"She rolled the vehicle and is unconscious but stable, according to the doctor," Sid said. "I know it's a long shot, but I'm just trying to connect the dots as best I can. Would you mind taking a look at her?"

"I'll be right there." He pocketed his phone as he rose from his chair. "That was the sheriff," he said to his brother and Dorothea who were both staring at him expectantly. "The woman he thinks is the one I saw leaving in the dark blue SUV apparently wrecked it and is in the hospital. He wants me to come down and see if I recognize her."

"I thought you didn't see her face," Dorothea said.

"I didn't, but I saw her hair and I could estimate her height and body build," he said. "Sid is sure it's the same woman I saw. He just wants me to verify it." He reached for his coat. "I shouldn't be long."

"Wait," Dorothea cried and rushed to him to grab his hand and press a small crystal stone into his palm. "Keep this with you at all times for your protection."

He groaned inwardly but had learned over the years that the best thing he could do was go along. "Got it." He made a show of putting the stone into his front jeans pocket and gave her a patient smile as he left.

In truth, he was nervous about IDing the woman— but also anxious to know the truth so he could finally put it all behind him.

THE SHERIFF WAS down the hall having a cup of vending machine coffee when the doctor joined him.

"She's drifting in and out of consciousness, which is a good sign," Dr. Bullock told him. "But I'd prefer that you put off questioning her, though, until she is fully conscious."

"Garrett Sterling is coming in. I need to see if he recognizes her. I can wait on questioning her. One of my deputies is outside her door. I don't want anyone but hospital personnel going into her room."

The doctor nodded but didn't look pleased. "If you really think that's necessary."

Somehow this woman had disarmed a man holding a gun to her head and killed him with what Sid was assuming was the man's own gun. He wouldn't know until he got the ballistics report. But he knew that a woman like that could easily walk out of a hospital without anyone noticing.

He mentioned that to the doctor.

"Without any clothing?" Dr. Bullock asked. "Hers was bagged for your forensics team, remember?"

The sheriff chuckled. "You really don't have a criminal mind, Doc. Finding something to wear would be the least of her problems."

At the sound of footfalls, they both turned to see Garrett Sterling headed for them. The rancher looked a bit haggard, but ready to see if he could ID the woman.

"Please just make this quick," the doctor said. "Suspect or not, the woman needs her rest." He walked off and Sid turned as Garrett joined him.

"You all right?" Sid asked.

Garrett nodded and swallowed. "You know I only saw her from a distance and not under the best circumstances."

"Got it. I just need to know if she could be the woman you saw."

"I can do that," the rancher said.

"Then let's get it over with."

They walked down the hall to the woman's room. Sid went in first. He wanted to see Garrett's reaction to the woman, not that he was expecting much. Garrett had just told him that he hadn't gotten a good look at her.

But the rancher should be able to tell from her size and shape and possibly the color of her long hair. Sid already knew that she was driving the stolen car that Garrett had described as the getaway car. Also the lab had found gunpowder residue on her hands and wrists as well as her clothing.

She *was* the woman, he was sure of that. But he liked to cover all his bases. With luck this one would tie up quickly. Once the woman told the same story Garrett had, it would be a case of self-defense and quickly off the books.

The sheriff was looking forward to retirement as he turned to watch the rancher come into the woman's room. Garrett glanced toward the bed and Sid was glad that he'd followed his instincts.

Otherwise, he might have missed the dumbstruck look on Garrett Sterling's face when he got a good look at the woman lying in the bed.

CHAPTER FIVE

GARRETT STUMBLED TO a stop only feet inside the hospital room door. He blinked, unable to believe what he was seeing. He stepped closer to the woman in the bed, telling himself that after the day he'd had, he couldn't trust himself.

The hair was a different color, darker like polished mahogany, but that face, even with part of it bandaged, wasn't one he was likely to forget. He stepped to the bed, reached out and caught a lock of her hair between his thumb and fingers.

A man also didn't forget the feel of a woman's hair he'd buried his fingers in. And that mouth. Oh, he knew that mouth so well it made him ache. The bowed curve of it, the full lips, the pale pink of a rose. He could almost taste her. Had he pulled back the covers, he would have known every inch of that body even after all this time. He knew this woman, intimately.

But how was this possible?

It wasn't. The woman in this bed, the same one he'd seen on the side of that mountain earlier, had to be a doppelgänger. A double. An identical twin. It couldn't be the woman he'd known. The woman he still knew on sight.

Her eyes fluttered open and he felt himself gasp as he looked into them. A glowing amber. Like a wild animal's. How many times had he lost himself in those eyes? She tried to focus on him for an instant and then the lids fell shut, the dark eyelashes relaxing against her pale skin.

His mouth had gone dry. All he could hear was the pounding of his pulse and the rain outside the hospital room window. He felt as if he needed to sit down and dropped into the chair next to her bed to put his face into his hands. How could she be the woman he'd seen earlier? The woman who'd almost gotten killed and had ended up killing her attacker?

Until the sheriff touched his shoulder, he'd forgotten Sid was even in the room. He raised his head to meet the man's gaze, still telling himself it couldn't be possible that he knew the woman—even though he knew there was only one Joslyn Charles.

He got to his feet and let the sheriff lead him away. But at the door, he stopped to look back, telling himself that only then would he realize how wrong he'd been. That he'd merely wanted to see Joslyn in that bed. That it wasn't her.

But even from a distance, he knew it was. No doppelgänger. No identical twin. It was Joslyn.

"Well?" Sid asked, after drawing him down the hallway away from her room and the deputy seated outside it.

Garrett hedged, wondering if he was trying to protect her. Or himself. He'd protected her once and look where that had gotten him. "I think she's the same woman I saw across the ravine."

"Garrett, I saw your reaction when you walked in there and saw her lying in that bed. You looked as if you'd seen a ghost."

He glanced at the closed hospital room door. "That's exactly what it was. A ghost from my past."

DR. BULLOCK PASSED THEM in the hallway, a stern look on his face. "Visiting hours are long over, Sheriff."

Sid nodded and considered taking the rancher down to his office to find out what had happened back there in that woman's room. But he didn't want to give Garrett that long to think about it.

"Let's talk in the waiting room," he said as he ushered a shaken Garrett Sterling into the nearest room. Neither spoke as he closed the door behind him. When he turned, he saw that Garrett was sitting in one of the waiting room chairs, his face in his hands again.

"Are you all right?" Sid asked, seeing that the man wasn't.

It took a moment before the rancher pulled himself together. There was a haunted look in his blue eyes when he finally looked up. It was clear that recognizing the woman had rocked the big cowboy, something that surprised Sid.

Garrett didn't rock easily. Earlier, after seeing what he believed was a murder, he'd been shocked and upset, but he'd kept his cool. The rancher had managed to take him right to the spot where he'd thought he'd last seen the couple—before he'd fired the warning shot. Before he'd heard the answering four shots and had seen what he thought was someone lying in the grass dead. Garrett had even managed to give him a pretty good description of the two people along with the SUV the woman had taken off in after the shooting.

But right now, the rancher looked as if a gust of wind would knock him over, which made Sid more than anxious to hear about his connection to the suspect lying in that hospital bed.

Garrett cleared his throat. "I don't know where to begin." He cleared his throat again. "You might remember. It was in all the papers. About two years ago? I'd been down in Missoula in law school. It was late at night." Garrett swallowed and met his gaze. "I had this sudden craving for chocolate milk." He shook his head. "I always wondered what would have happened if I hadn't walked into that convenience store that night."

Sid did remember now that Garrett had brought it up. He sat back in his chair, trying to understand what any of that though had to do with what was happening now. He could see that the rancher was still trying to make sense of all of this and struggling. Realizing he knew the woman had clearly been a blow, one he was still trying to absorb.

"I saw her when I walked into the convenience store. She had the kind of face that caught a man's attention. I went to the back, found a small container of chocolate milk and was on my way to the counter when I heard the man come in." Garrett grew quiet for a moment, a distant look in his eyes. "It still makes my heart pound when I think about it. The man had a gun, was visibly agitated and demanded that the young male clerk behind the counter empty the money from the cash register into a bag and then open the safe."

Sid was trying to remember if he'd heard anything about a woman in the store that night. "Where was she?"

"She'd been about to check out when the robber came in, so only a few feet away. She'd frozen, just like me. The maybe nineteen-year-old behind the counter was all thumbs trying to open the cash register and swearing he didn't know how to open the safe. I honestly didn't know what to do. I was wondering how much money I had in my wallet and if I could talk the robber down."

Sid groaned inwardly, having dealt with what sounded like a junkie or at least a very nervous criminal. Reasoning with them wasn't usually a viable option.

"The robber was getting more upset and nervous by the moment. Before I could move, he grabbed the woman, held the gun to her head, and told the clerk that he would kill her, then everyone else in the place, if he didn't open the safe."

"You saved her," Sid said, realizing that's all that could have happened since he was guessing that the woman was alive and now in a hospital room down the hall. The convenience-store robbery had brought Garrett fifteen minutes of fame as a hero two years ago, but six months after that the rancher had dropped out of law school. Sid had always wondered if the trauma of what had happened had made him change his mind about working in a profession where he would be brushing elbows with criminals.

"The robber hadn't seen me behind him," Garrett said, continuing his story. "I took one hell of a risk with that woman's life, but I cold-cocked the guy—"

"With a can of beans." That part had definitely made the news.

Garrett nodded. "The robber dropped to the floor, but he'd fired a shot and pulled the woman down with him. They were both lying at my feet. I couldn't tell if the woman was hit or not. I knelt down to shove the robber's gun out of the way and see if she was all right when the convenience store door opened and the second one came in armed and just as agitated. He had apparently been waiting outside in the getaway car but had rushed in when he heard the shot. The young clerk behind the counter had hit an alarm when the first robber came in because I heard sirens as all hell broke out. It all happened so fast. I leaned over the woman to protect her. I heard the shots and had assumed it was the second robber killing the clerk."

"But it turned out that the clerk had a gun behind the counter, drew it and emptied the pistol into the second robber," Sid said, still waiting to see what this story had to do with the woman down the hall. "And the woman?" he prodded.

Garrett sighed. "I was still covering her when she whispered, 'Can you get me out of here before the police come? I can't be involved in this.' I realized that I hadn't seen her car outside when I'd pulled up so she must have walked. I handed her my pickup keys, whispered my apartment address, and she took off out the back. The young clerk didn't see any of it. He had dropped behind the counter and was bawling his eyes out. I stayed and talked to the police. The clerk and I both said we didn't know who the woman was, only that she had left, which was true. The cops just assumed she'd been terrified and had run."

Sid couldn't believe what he was hearing and said as much. "You lied to the police? Weren't you curious why she didn't want to deal with the cops?" He let out a bark of a laugh. "Hell, I would have been worried that I'd never see my pickup again—let alone that everything of value would have been cleaned out of my apartment by the time I got there."

Garrett chuckled. "It did cross my mind, but when I got to my apartment, she was waiting for me. She told me she was an undercover cop and had she not gotten out of that convenience store when she did, her cover would have been blown."

He stared at the rancher. "And you believed her?"

"I wanted to," Garrett said with a sheepish grin. "We'd both just gone through something terrifying together. We were both thankful to be alive and safe."

Sid knew what was coming, even though he found it hard to believe since Garrett seemed the most sensible of the Sterling brothers. "You became involved with her."

"I guess it wasn't surprising that we found comfort in each other that night. And the next and the next."

"How long did it last?"

"About five months. Amazing months. Then she disappeared as if she'd never existed. I tried to find her, worried since as far as I knew she was still an undercover cop."

"Let me guess, when you went down to the police station, they said they'd never heard of her."

Garrett let out a rueful chuckle. "They convinced me she wasn't an undercover cop and that I'd been conned. They'd never heard of anyone by the name of Joslyn Charles. I looked for her, even hired someone to find her." He shrugged. "It was as if she'd never existed. I never saw her again—until today."

CHAPTER SIX

STILL SHOCKED BY what Garrett had told him, Sid decided to hang around the hospital in the hopes that the woman regained consciousness—and could talk. He had no idea what had happened up on the mountainside but after the story Garrett had told him about her, he was definitely more interested in hearing her side of it.

That Garrett had known this woman in the biblical sense was crazy enough—add to it the way he'd met her and how she'd turned up in his life again. His gut told him it hadn't been a coincidence.

His cell phone rang, startling him from his thoughts. He saw that it was the coroner calling and picked right up.

"Sam, you're working late tonight," he said without preamble.

"You brought me an interesting case. I wasn't going to be able to sleep once I saw the body on my table." Possible homicides were rare in Whitefish. Sam Samuelson didn't get a lot of interesting cases, the sheriff knew.

"How so?" he asked.

"You probably didn't notice given that his body

was found in the pouring rain, but once the lab tech came in to take his fingerprints, I noticed something I hadn't seen before. Altered fingerprints."

The sheriff had heard of criminals attempting to keep their fingerprints from coming up on federal and state databases. The most common way was scarring by biting, cutting, sanding or burning with heat or a chemical.

"Looks like they were deliberately burned off. Trying to burn off his fingerprints had to be extremely painful and such a waste since we will probably be able to get an ID on him through his DNA," Sam was saying.

"Let's get his DNA to the lab as soon as possible. I want to know who this guy is." And how he ended up with the woman Garrett had known as Joslyn Charles on the mountain across from Sterling's Montana Guest Ranch. He was even more anxious to get the woman's DNA results.

WALKING OUT TO his pickup, Garrett still couldn't believe the woman he'd seen across the ravine was the same one he'd rescued at the convenience store two years ago. The same woman he'd known intimately. Worse, a woman he'd done more than think about marrying.

He realized after seeing her again, that he'd never gotten over her. There'd been a few women over the past twenty-four months, but none he'd been serious about. Joslyn had always been there, tucked away in the corner of his heart—the heart she'd broken when she disappeared without a word.

Her disappearing had been so abrupt. Their last night together hadn't been any different than any of the other nights they'd spent together. There'd been chemistry between them, a passion that had left him completely enamored. He'd thought that she'd felt the same way. Then she'd just taken off, leaving him with a lot of questions, no answers and a whole lot of pain.

The hardest part had been not knowing what had happened to her.

He'd checked the hospital, the police station, everywhere he could think to look. He'd watched the news, thinking she might have had an accident and was either dead or in a coma and couldn't call. He'd come up with all kinds of scenarios, all of them a fool's dream. Joslyn was fine. She was just gone.

Sliding behind the wheel, he sat in the cool of the pickup's cab, still shaken. Joslyn Charles. She'd dropped into his life just as crazily as she had the first time. Now, all his instincts told him it couldn't be a coincidence. Not again.

The rain outside had turned to drizzle and fog now moved like a ghost through the hospital parking lot. The pickup cab had begun to feel cold. He told himself he should go home. But what he wanted to do was go back into the hospital to Joslyn's room. He needed to talk to her.

Unfortunately the sheriff had a deputy outside her hospital room and he'd heard Sid give both the doctor and the deputy instructions that no one was to go into her room except hospital personnel.

When Garrett had said he needed to talk to her, the sheriff had been adamant. "I have a dead man over at the morgue with what appears to be four bullet holes in him. Maybe her name is Joslyn Charles. Maybe not. But the woman has some explaining to do and it's going to be to me first and foremost."

Oh, she certainly had some explaining to do, Garrett thought. Not that he had any idea what he would say to her at this point. What do you say to the woman who you had fallen in love with years ago who'd lied to you about everything and then had disappeared without so much as a goodbye note? How much of what he thought they'd had between them had been a lie? All of it?

He sat for a moment longer debating what to do before opening his pickup door and getting out again. He wouldn't try to talk to her. But if he could get another look at her… He had to know if he was mistaken. Maybe she just resembled Joslyn. After all, it had been two years. There must be a hundred, well, at least a dozen women with her bone structure. Even with her eyes. Even with her mouth.

All the way to her room, he tried to convince himself that he was wrong. The woman in that hospital bed was a stranger. She had to be because otherwise, the woman he'd known as Joslyn Charles had disarmed a man and shot him four times, killing him. What woman her size could physically do something like that? Not the woman he'd known.

He remembered how scared she'd been that night in the convenience store. She'd frozen in place—just as he had. That alone should have been a clue back then that she wasn't an undercover cop. Otherwise, wouldn't she have tried to disarm the man? Wouldn't she have had a weapon on her?

Pushing open the hospital door, he headed for her room. But as he came around the corner, he spotted the guard outside her room. The deputy saw him and stood as Garrett approached.

He tried to think of what he could say to get inside her room, but he needn't have bothered. Her hospital room door opened and Sheriff Anderson stepped out.

Garrett saw his expression and felt his heart drop to his boots. "Is she…?" He couldn't bring himself to say the word *dead*.

Sid quickly shook his head. "She's okay. What are you doing here again?" He sighed and motioned for them to step away from her door.

Garrett followed him down the hall, his mind racing. Had she confessed? Had she turned out to be someone else other than Joslyn Charles? Of course she had. But what had the woman in that room told the sheriff to make him react the way he was?

Sid stopped and turned to him. "She says she can't remember anything. Not even her name. Not *anything*."

For a moment Garrett was too stunned to speak. Was she lying? He thought about the blow to her head up on the mountainside and apparently another one that the doctor had mentioned from the car wreck. "But even if it's true, it's probably temporary, right?"

The sheriff shrugged. "Doc says maybe, maybe not. I'm waiting on the autopsy report and ballistic results, but from the powder residue on her hands, she definitely fired a gun recently."

"Do you know who the man is yet?"

Sid shook his head.

Garrett raked a hand through his hair, his Stetson dangling from the fingertips of his other hand. He knew what was bothering him. "That man was so much larger and stronger than her. How could she—"

"You firing that shot had to have saved her life," the sheriff said as if he'd been giving it some thought as well. "You distracted him for a second, maybe she kicked him in the nuts, grabbed the gun still clutched in his hands, turned it enough to point the barrel at his chest and simply fired and kept firing." He shrugged. "Or she had her own weapon. Either way, she had to have gotten the jump on him because he was distracted just long enough at hearing your gunshot. I'd say you probably saved her life."

"I need to see her again." Sid started to make a disapproving face. "I just need to look at her. I swear it's Joslyn Charles but what if it just looks like her?" He could see that the sheriff was weakening. "I won't be able to sleep until I know for sure." Like he would be able to sleep anyway.

"Fine. Take a peek. You heard the doctor give specific orders that she was not to be disturbed for the rest of the night."

Garrett nodded and stepped to the door. He took a breath, let it out and pushed. The hospital room door swung open.

There was faint light coming in through the window enough that he could see her. She was lying on the bed, her head raised a little. Her long dark hair fanned out over the pillow like a dark, ominous wave. The white bandage on her head was as pale as her skin. It didn't seem possible, but she was more beautiful than he remembered.

Suddenly, her eyes flew open as if sensing him staring at her. Amber flashed and then focused—on him. And in that moment, Garrett saw something that stopped his heart.

Recognition. She *knew* him. Her eyes closed at once, the dark lashes dropping like a curtain back onto the pale skin of her cheeks.

Amnesia my ass, he thought. He stood, heart pounding, waiting for her to open her eyes again. No matter what she might call herself now, the woman who'd killed a man just hours ago was Joslyn Charles, a woman he'd saved two years ago and had foolishly fallen head over heels in love with.

CHAPTER SEVEN

GARRETT TRIED TO get his head around all of this. Joslyn Charles. How could it be after all this time? It made no sense, but none of that mattered. He remembered her—and *she* remembered him.

"Okay, that's enough," Dr. Bullock said, drawing him away from her hospital room. "Deputy, I don't want another person other than a nurse going into that room tonight. Is that understood?" He looked to the sheriff, then to Garrett. "You both need to leave."

Sid touched his arm. The last thing he wanted to do was leave. He wanted to see the woman again, but he knew that wasn't going to happen. At least not right now.

The sheriff walked him out. All the while, Garrett battled the thoughts whirling around in his head. He needed to tell Sid what he'd seen. The recognition in her gaze. She *knew* him. She was lying about not remembering anything. She was a liar—not that that news should have come as a surprise. But given what else had happened, that could be the least of it, he feared.

His mind was racing. Why would she lie about not remembering anything? Why would she lie about being an undercover cop two years ago? What else had she lied about?

By the time they reached their vehicles, Garrett had talked himself out of saying anything to the sheriff. Not yet. He needed to talk to Joslyn alone. He needed to be sure of a few things first. But how was he going to get a chance to talk to her with a guard outside her door?

"What will happen to her?" he asked, noticing that the rain had stopped. It wasn't even drizzling, but everything dripped and the air felt like the inside of a sauna.

"You mean when she's well enough to leave the hospital?" Sid asked. "She'll be arrested and arraigned. After that? It depends. From what you've told me, it was self-defense."

So he was about to save her again.

"Given her lack of memory, it could be a while before we know what happened on that mountainside—if we ever do," the sheriff said. "You aren't changing your story, are you?"

He shook his head. "I told you what I saw." At least what he thought he'd seen.

"It brings up some interesting questions though, doesn't it," Sid said. "Like why the man decided to haul her up that ridgeline so close to your guest ranch to kill her since, as it turns out, the two of you have a past."

Garrett had been thinking the same thing. "Have you fingerprinted her yet?"

"No match came up," the sheriff said.

"So she doesn't have a record. For all you know, the dead man abducted her and she is a victim in all this."

Sid was studying him. "It's possible. The SUV was stolen. But it doesn't mean she stole it."

He hadn't realized what he'd been thinking until he said the words. "She'll be getting out of the hospital soon, I would imagine, since her injuries don't seem to be life-threatening. If someone were to post bail for her once she's arraigned… I have plenty of room for her up at the guest ranch with us not open this summer. She could recuperate, get her memory back and when she does, if you haven't already solved the case, you'll get the answers before you retire."

He'd thought that he'd sold the idea fairly smoothly but the sheriff looked flabbergasted. "*You can't be serious.* After everything you know about this woman? If she even is the woman you knew two years ago. I think that's got to be the worst idea you've ever come up with—short of giving her your pickup keys during a convenience store holdup. You have no idea how dangerous this woman might be."

"I know if she hadn't disappeared back then, I would have asked her to marry me."

Sid shook his head. "Two years can be a long time. You have no idea where she's been or what she's done. You didn't know this woman then. You really don't know her now. What if you're wrong about her and have been from the start? We're talking about a woman who was involved in a killing. A killing damned close to your guest ranch. She knew about the ranch two years ago, right?"

"If you're asking if I took her there, no."

"But she knew."

He wasn't going to let the sheriff talk him out of this. "She's going to need somewhere to stay other than a jail cell while she regains her memory. I have an empty guest ranch. And since from everything I saw the shooting was self-defense. And if she can't remember any of it... What if I ask her if she wants to move into the guest ranch until she gets her memory back?"

The sheriff shook his head. "Why would she do that?"

He shrugged, pretending it didn't matter one way or another to him. Joslyn might refuse. There was always that chance. But he had a feeling... "If she agrees...then you'll know where to find her—if you should need her."

"You aren't worried about her skipping bail and leaving you holding the bag?"

It was a chance he'd have to take. If it meant getting her alone and getting the truth out of her, it would be worth every penny.

Sid was still shaking his head. "Sleep on it, Sterling," he said and swore. "Hopefully in the morning you'll have come to your senses." With that he turned and walked to his patrol SUV.

SID HAD PLANNED to go home and get some sleep himself. But he knew sleep wasn't likely until he settled something in his own mind. Garrett wasn't thinking straight. Not that he could blame him after the day he'd had. First witnessing what he thought was a woman's murder only to find out that she had survived—and was someone he'd obviously once cared about deeply only two years before.

That would send anyone into a tailspin. No wonder the man wanted answers, and thought that by taking the woman up to his closed guest ranch he could get them. Garrett seemed to have completely forgotten that his former lover still had the blood of the man she'd killed on her hands when she'd been taken to the hospital. Also she'd had the car accident because she'd been driving way too fast for the conditions, as if running from something more than a dead man.

Sid considered the story Garrett had told him about how they'd met. Whoever that woman was in the hospital bed, she'd lied from the start. She'd lied so she wouldn't have to face the police that night at the convenience store. And now she was probably lying to him as well.

Talk about a lot of red flags. The woman had gotten to the rancher once and Sid feared she'd never let go. It was why he couldn't let Garrett make a possibly deadly mistake by taking the woman up to the guest ranch with him.

Not that he could stop that from happening if the judge granted bail and Garrett paid it, and she agreed to go with him. Maybe the big question, the one his mind had been skirting around, was why, if the woman really remembered nothing, would she agree to go with a man she'd never met before? Unless even her amnesia was a lie.

It was obvious that Garrett needed closure from the old girlfriend he hadn't gotten over. Sid had seen it in the rancher's eyes. But Garrett also wanted to protect her. He saw her as a victim—two years ago and again now.

Sid had been in law enforcement for too long not to know that things weren't always the way they seemed. Maybe the deceased man had pulled the woman into the pines to kill her. Or maybe not. Maybe it had just looked like that from across the ravine. Because it was damned strange that the man was now dead and the woman was alive—and suffering from memory loss.

But what was going to cause Sid to lose sleep was the question of what she'd been doing so close to Sterling's Montana Guest Ranch. How convenient that Garrett had to save her once again—even if it meant putting his own life in danger.

Sid shook his head. Maybe Garrett thought he could get answers from the woman he'd known as Joslyn Charles. But the sheriff worried that it might get him killed instead.

Trying to convince him otherwise was a waste of breath, he realized. There was only one way to stop this. He had to find out who the woman was and just how dangerous she might be. It was a long shot that she'd told Garrett her real name, but he had to try.

In his office, he turned on the light and, stepping to his desk, booted up his computer. He typed in *Joslyn Charles*.

SLEEP? NOT LIKELY, Garrett thought. He lay in bed staring up at the ceiling, replaying all of it over again in his head. From spotting something moving through the trees on the ridgeline across the ravine to Joslyn meeting his gaze, he went through it, trying to see anywhere he might have made a mistake.

But in his heart, he knew. There was no mistake. The woman in the hospital bed was the Joslyn Charles he'd known. When she'd opened her eyes and seen him, that moment of recognition had felt like a bolt of lightning straight to his heart. It had rooted him to the floor, sent a shockwave through him. She *knew* him.

And he *knew* her.

That thought unsettled him. Because the truth was just as the sheriff had pointed out. He *didn't* know her. Didn't even know if her name was really Joslyn. He'd thought he'd known her from the months they'd spent together. He knew her laugh and her happy smile. He knew when she was worrying about something, although she'd always denied it.

He'd told himself when he'd had any doubts about her back then that she was the kind of woman a man could spend his whole life with and still not really know her. But he had been okay with that, more than okay. He didn't see anything wrong with a little mystery and had wanted to spend his life finding out her little secrets.

That thought made him laugh now. He had a bad feeling that Joslyn had a lot more than little secrets. Possibly deadly big secrets. Either that or she had a way of attracting men with guns who threatened to kill her.

He tried to remember if she'd told him anything about herself. They hadn't talked about their pasts as if they'd made a silent vow to live day to day after the convenience-store incident.

Or as if there was no tomorrow, he thought now with a curse.

She'd known she wasn't sticking around. There'd been a desperation in their lovemaking that he'd obviously mistaken for passion. Had he only thought there was amazing chemistry between them? Back then, all they'd had to do was look at each other and they'd be ripping off each other's clothing. Had that too been a lie?

He couldn't recall her ever talking about her family. Had she told him that her father was in the military or had he just assumed that because she seemed to have moved around a lot?

He had no idea what she'd done during the day while he'd been at law school during the time they were together. She'd said her law enforcement superiors were worried that her cover might have been blown and wanted her to lie low for a while.

She'd moved in after their first night together. It wasn't something they'd discussed. It was just a given since they couldn't keep their hands off each other. He didn't question the fact that she didn't seem to have many belongings to move in. Just as he hadn't questioned her story about working as an undercover cop. There was something strong and determined about her. She seemed street smart and that made him believe her. He'd thought back then that it was part of her charm.

Also she had seemed to like being secretive as if she had a whole bagful of tricks yet to bring out. Thinking of her so-called amnesia, he suspected she still did.

Sighing, he closed his eyes. She'd lied to him two years ago. She was lying now about her memory loss—and possibly the man she'd killed was also part of a lie.

And still, he felt her pull. He wasn't finished with her. Maybe he never would be. He'd been in love with her. So much so that he'd planned to ask her to marry him and had even bought the engagement ring. A ring he never got the chance to give her.

SID TRIED VARIATIONS on the name Joslyn. Joslin. Joslynn. There was no Joslyn Charles the right age when Garrett met her while attending law school. She hadn't been a cop, but he'd thought she might have been a student and lied about her age. He went to the university directory. He found Garrett Sterling. But no one by any spelling of the name Joslyn, last name Charles, had ever attended the university.

He rubbed his eyes, tired and frustrated. Even more confused and worried, he realized how late it was and shut off his computer. He thought about calling Garrett, waking him up, trying to solve yet another mystery surrounding this killing on the mountainside.

Pushing to his feet, he started to leave his office, but changed his mind and picked up his phone. If he couldn't sleep, then why should Garrett?

"Hello?" The rancher answered on the second ring, sounding wide awake.

"How do you spell her name?" Sid asked without preamble.

Garrett answered as if there had never been a break in their conversation earlier. "Joslyn Charles." He spelled it out. "Why?"

"I've been on my computer since I last saw you. There is no Joslyn Charles anywhere near the right age that I can find." He could hear what sounded like Garrett sitting up in bed, turning on a lamp, feet hitting the floor.

"So she definitely lied about her name and you said her prints turned up nothing either, right?"

"Right. Are you going to be able to get any sleep?"

Garrett chuckled. "Probably not. I keep going over everything."

"You're still sure about what you saw on the mountainside across the ravine, though."

"Yes."

"Well, I hope this changes your mind about asking her to come stay at your guest ranch."

"No. You and I both want answers. Eventually, she's going to be freed since you can't send her to prison when I witnessed enough to swear it was self-defense. When that happens and she disappears again, neither of us will ever know the truth."

He had a point there, Sid thought. "What makes

you so sure she'll come up to the guest ranch with you, a complete stranger, let alone tell you anything?"

"Just a feeling."

The sheriff shook his head. The man was besotted with the woman. "Well, let's see how you feel in the morning after a sleepless night." He was hoping they'd have more information by then to go on.

"You said she was driving the stolen SUV at a high rate of speed. Sounds to me like she was running from something—from someone. And it wasn't the man she'd just emptied four shots into. I'd say she needs protection."

Sid chuckled. "So this is altruistic on your part. You just want to protect her. Be her bodyguard. You sure that's what's going on here?"

"I'm not sure of anything except that she needs some place to stay and I want answers. Keeping her alive seems the only way I'm going to get them. Also you wouldn't have put a deputy outside her door unless you too think her life might be in danger."

"Well, if it is, then so is yours. You think you can't get any sleep now? Wait until you take the woman up to your isolated empty guest ranch. If I were you, I'd sleep with one eye open."

GARRETT HADN'T EVEN attempted sleep after that phone call from the sheriff. He got up, pulled on his jeans and padded into the kitchen. Opening the refrigerator, he started to take out a bottle of beer.

"Drinking this time of the night?" Dorothea asked

from the doorway. She wore a fuzzy thick pink robe over what appeared to be bear-print flannel pajamas.

He frowned. "You're right. If I'm going to drink, then I might as well have something a whole lot stronger. I definitely need it."

She followed him into the living room and sat down on the couch as he poured himself a shot of bourbon, downed it and poured another. "That's just going to give you a headache," she warned him.

"Then it will have to be on top of the one I already have." He groaned to himself as he dropped into a chair opposite her.

"I can understand how you might be upset over what you saw on that mountainside today."

"You don't know the half of it," he said as he studied the amber liquid in the glass. It reminded him of Joslyn's eyes. That thought did nothing for his disposition.

Dorothea was giving him one of her you're-holding-out-on-me looks. "What happened at the hospital?"

Garrett chuckled. He could feel the alcohol already racing through his bloodstream. He'd never been much of a drinker, but tonight he was going to make an exception. "The woman, the one who it appeared was about to be killed and ended up killing her attacker? I know her."

"What do you mean you *know* her?"

"I *know* her. Like in…*know* her."

"Okay, I get the picture. So is she someone I know?"

He shook his head. "I knew her two years ago

down in Missoula when I was going to law school." He took a sip of his drink, realizing that Dorothea would put the pieces together and know the real truth about why he dropped out of law school. But it no longer mattered.

"We were in love," he said, realizing he needed to talk to someone about this and Dorothea would get it out of him eventually anyway. "At least *I* was in love. There was this chemistry between us that was amazing and—"

Dorothea rolled her eyes. "I told you. I get it. You were lovers."

"Sorry. But here's where it gets crazy. I met her at a convenience store late one night."

"Well, I suppose that's better than a bar," she said.

He shook his head laughing. "Remember that convenience-store robbery?"

"Where you cold-cocked the robber with a can of beans?"

"That's the one. The woman the first robber was threatening to kill? Well, that was her. I helped her get out of there before the police came."

She was looking at him as if he'd lost his mind. "Why would you do that?"

"Because she asked me to. I handed her my pickup keys and sent her to my apartment."

Dorothea groaned. "What could have possibly gone wrong with that plan?"

"She was waiting at my apartment. She told me that she was an undercover cop and it would have blown her cover if she'd had to deal with the regular cops and her name ended up in the newspaper."

"Let me guess. She wasn't."

"Actually everything she ever told me was a lie—including her name." He looked down into his now empty glass. His voice dropped and broke. "I know it was fast, not quite six months together, but I was going to marry her. I can't tell you how close I came to asking her."

"This explains a lot," Dorothea said. "You dropping out of law school. You coming back looking like a kicked dog. I knew there had to be a woman. So this was the one who broke your heart and ruined you for all others."

He hated to hear her take on him even if it was true. "As if things aren't bad enough, I have you psychoanalyzing me." Getting up, he went to refill his glass.

She ignored that. "So why didn't you marry her?"

"We spent every minute I wasn't in law school together for those months. Then one day, she just… disappeared without a word. I looked for her. She was just gone."

"That's when you found out that she'd never really been an undercover cop," Dorothea said.

He sighed and, taking his fresh drink, plopped back down into his chair. "It wasn't just Joslyn that made me quit law school. I realized I was happiest working on the ranch. Anyway, it wasn't for me." He met her gaze and saw that she didn't believe a word of it.

"Joslyn, huh?"

"Joslyn Charles, but according to Sid, no one about the right age ever existed by that name. So I have no idea who I fell in love with or if any of it was real." He drained his drink, feeling it burn all the way down, and considered getting up for another, but suddenly he didn't have the energy. Also he was feeling the effects of the alcohol and knew he'd probably already overdone it.

"I was in love with a ghost," he said, his voice cracking.

Dorothea looked as if she didn't know what to say. This had to be a first, he thought.

"I don't think I've ever seen you speechless," he said and laughed.

"Why didn't you ever tell us?"

He gave her an are-you-kidding look. "It wasn't something I liked talking about."

She shook her head for a moment as if she'd never understand men, and then asked, "But if this woman in the hospital isn't Joslyn Charles, then who is she?"

"That is the million-dollar question, isn't it? And here's the kicker. Not even she knows—according to her. She's saying she can't remember a thing. But I looked right at her and she looked right at me and I swear, she recognized me. Whatever her name is, she knew me—and I certainly know her."

"You thought you knew her before she left, what, eighteen months ago?" Dorothea reminded him. "I think there are a few questions you should be asking yourself. One, why was she lying to you back then? Where has she been? And why has she shown up here now?"

He stared at the woman sitting across from him. It scared him when Dorothea made sense. "Those are just a few of the questions I plan to ask her."

"You can't think this is a coincidence that you witnessed what you did."

It might have been the bourbon. Or the lack of sleep. Or the shock of seeing Joslyn again. "Wait, what are you saying? You're starting to sound like Sid. You think there is some kind of preplanned plot?" He reminded himself who he was talking to. A woman who was constantly casting spells against perceived evil. A woman who saw conspiracy theories everywhere she looked.

"I don't believe in coincidence," Dorothea said. "Fate, sure. But this smacks of something else. She knew about the guest ranch, right?" He nodded. "And when someone is trying to kill her, it just happens to be nearby?"

He shook his head. "That is far-fetched even for you."

"Maybe. Who knows what she was up to in the months since you last saw her? But I really doubt it's a stroke of luck that she's turned up in your life again."

CHAPTER EIGHT

GARRETT WOKE ON the couch. He sat up confused and sporting a hangover. He smelled bourbon and saw an empty dirty glass on the floor at his feet. As he frowned down at it, his memory returned, making him swear. Not even when Joslyn had disappeared had he resorted to booze to get through it.

But this was a whole different rodeo, he reminded himself as he made his way to his part of the large, rambling ranch house. Turning on the shower, he stepped into the warm spray. Last night, even in his inebriated state, he'd realized that he'd have to be crazy to invite her to come stay at the closed guest ranch.

Even if she hadn't recently killed a man, he couldn't trust the woman as far as he could throw her. She had lied to him from the get-go. Neither he nor the sheriff knew just how dangerous this woman was. Also, she was lying about having amnesia. He'd trusted her once. But he liked to think that he wasn't stupid enough to do it again.

His head ached at the thought of all the things he'd never questioned during the time they'd spent together as he turned off the shower, grabbed a towel and stepped out. He'd believed Joslyn had been the woman she'd pretended to be. He'd wanted to believe it all, right down to whatever that had been between them that flashed like heat lightning when they touched.

He swore now, wondering at the depth of Joslyn's lies as he dressed. Still, at the back of his mind, he told himself that the chemistry between them hadn't been a lie, damn it. But there was only one way to prove it—no matter how dangerous.

Pulling on his jacket, he grabbed his keys and headed for the door.

IN HIS OFFICE, the sheriff looked at the photo he'd taken of the woman in the hospital when she'd still been unconscious. He'd run it through facial identifying systems, but had come up empty.

He had thought about having his deputies distribute her photo around town, thinking she might have been staying in one of the motels. It seemed like his best chance of getting an ID on her.

But it would be better to wait until the bandage came off. He needed to know who this woman was. She didn't have a record but that didn't mean anything. He knew what she was capable of. That was enough to be worried about. Not to mention her possibly going up to Garrett's closed guest ranch.

His hope was, after a sleepless night, Garrett had come to his senses and decided against asking her. Otherwise, he'd have to retain her in jail. Unless she made bail on her own and then she could take off and never be seen again.

Even if she didn't make bail, he still wouldn't be able to hold her for very long. Not when he had an eyewitness that swore the shooting had been in self-defense. The county attorney was up for reelection this fall. He'd already made it clear that he wanted this incident to go away as quickly as possible.

With a sigh, Sid rose. He had to get to the hospital and talk to the woman. If he knew Garrett, the rancher wouldn't have changed his mind. Even knowing the possible danger.

But what woman, after almost being killed and suffering from memory loss, would go to an isolated empty guest ranch in the mountains with a total stranger?

One who was lying, he thought.

So if Garrett was still set on inviting her to stay at the guest ranch... Sid was anxious to know her answer.

But as he started out of his office, his phone rang. He saw that it was a tech with the state crime lab who had been going through the wrecked blue SUV.

Sid felt his pulse jump. "What did you find?"

"A map. Wasn't in the car before it was stolen. The map was printed off the internet and shows how to get to the Sterling's Montana Guest Ranch."

GARRETT HAD HOPED that he would beat the sheriff to the hospital this morning. He wasn't sure how he'd get past the deputy posted outside Joslyn's door. He figured he'd come up with some way to get in. He had to see her. Had to talk to her.

But when he reached the hospital, the sheriff was standing outside her room talking to the young female deputy posted there.

He swore under his breath as he approached them. "What's up?"

Sid gave him a curious look. "You don't seem to have gotten any more sleep than I did. You know Deputy Conners?"

Garrett nodded and said hello to the young deputy. He was too nervous for small talk. Looking at the closed hospital room door, he asked, "Has her memory come back?"

The sheriff shook his head. "I wasn't sure I'd be seeing you here again." Garrett could tell he'd been sure of just the opposite. The sheriff had obviously been waiting for him.

"Doc says she can leave the hospital later this afternoon," Sid said, still studying him. "She will be taken to her arraignment where the judge will decide whether to grant bail and if so, under what restrictions. You have a change of heart?"

Garrett shook his head. "You find any evidence that would convince me otherwise?" Sid shook his head. He wasn't going to tell him that he'd talked himself out of it this morning in the shower only to reconsider. He was more anxious than ever to find out the truth about this woman. He couldn't let her go to jail, but he also couldn't let her figure out a way to disappear again. Not without at least an explanation.

"There's a chance she'll turn down your offer," the sheriff said.

He chuckled. "Doesn't seem to me that she has a lot of options. No money, no idea who she is, no way to leave town. Not even a change of clothing."

"None found in the SUV," Sid agreed. "Could be she'd been staying in a motel around the area. Or maybe with friends or family."

Garrett really doubted that.

"I was considering circulating her photo around town."

"I'd hold off on that. I have a feeling her memory is going to come back."

The sheriff seemed to consider him for a long moment. "Like I was saying, I was considering it. But then crime scene techs found something in the stolen car she'd been driving."

Garrett didn't like the sound of this. Whatever had been found, Sid clearly thought it was something that would change things. He waited.

"There was a printed internet map probably from your website showing how to get to the guest ranch," the sheriff said. "Whoever stole that car? They were headed for your guest ranch."

He felt the hairs on the back of his neck quill. So it was no coincidence that Joslyn and her would-be killer had been in the area.

"This changes things," Sid said.

"Not really. If anything, it proves that I'm already involved. Aren't you curious who printed out that map and why?"

The sheriff let out a bark of a laugh. "A hardened criminal with a gun. Or the woman who killed him. Either way, I think you should reconsider asking her back to your guest ranch. For so many reasons, this is a bad idea."

"Probably," Garrett agreed. "But I'm willing to take my chances."

Sid shook his head. "Garrett, this woman might not be the Joslyn Charles you knew. It's been—"

"Eighteen months since I last saw her."

"A lot can happen in that length of time. You have no idea where she's been or what she's done. Not to mention, she wasn't who you thought she was even back then."

He couldn't agree more. Except he knew one thing. She was definitely the woman who'd broken his heart. "I think she needs protection. And ultimately it's up to her, right? You really don't want to put a woman with amnesia behind bars. The local press would have a field day with this, since the shooting was self-defense."

"Save it for the judge at the arraignment," Sid said with a disgusted shake of his head. "You sure this isn't about rekindling a long-lost love?"

Garrett laughed. "Not hardly given what I've already found out about her. So let's see if she wants to come stay at the guest ranch after I get her out on bail. She might say no." He was counting on just the opposite.

"You're right. There's only one way to find out,"

Sid said and then knocked and simultaneously pushed open her hospital room door.

Garrett stepped in behind the sheriff to see Joslyn standing at the window. She was wearing one of those hospital gowns that didn't hide much of anything. Add to that the fact that she was backlit by the sunshine streaming in the room…

The sheriff cleared his throat, making her turn. She quickly rushed to the bed, covering herself with the sheet. It appeared she'd just finished breakfast because the tray was still next to her bed.

Garrett noticed that her alleged lack of memory hadn't hurt her appetite. Also some color had returned to the flesh on her high cheekbones, although she didn't seem embarrassed to be caught half-naked staring out the window.

She had a smaller fresh bandage on her temple and she must have been given a brush and ribbon because her wild mane of dark hair was brushed, pulled to one side and tied with a ribbon. He was betting the brush and ribbon were the nurse's doing.

The overall effect made her look younger—and much like the woman Garrett had known intimately. It also gave her an innocence that belied the fact that she'd killed a man not all that long ago.

Garrett stepped to the window to look out, curious about what had had her attention before they'd walked in. The view was of the parking lot. He studied the cars parked there, not sure what he was looking for since he didn't see anyone down there. But he did notice his pickup and as he turned back to the bed, he realized she had probably seen him arrive and had known he would be walking into her room minutes later.

He studied her with interest. She was looking at the sheriff and appearing to nervously knead the edge of the sheet in her fingers. Was it possible she was as nervous as he was? He didn't believe it. This woman hadn't been embarrassed to be caught standing half-naked at that window any more than she couldn't remember him—or what had happened on that mountain.

"How are you feeling?" the sheriff asked her.

"Better," she said and smiled.

Oh, Garrett remembered that smile only too well. It made his stomach churn and brought back memories he'd thought he'd packed away over a year ago. He waited for her to look at him. He wanted to gaze deeply into those amber eyes again, desperately wanting to see what she had hidden in their depths. But she kept her attention on the sheriff.

"I was hoping you were going to tell me that at least some of your memory has returned since we last talked," the sheriff said.

She gave him a sad shake of her head. "I'm afraid not."

Sid cleared his voice. "Well, here's the dilemma we have. You don't remember your name or how you ended up here. Nor did you have any identification on you or in the vehicle. Also I have reason to believe your life might be in danger."

Her gaze never left the sheriff's face. She appeared to be waiting expectantly. There was a vulnerability to her expression that would have fooled anyone. Just not him, Garrett thought. Not anymore.

The sheriff continued, "Doc says you can leave the hospital if you continue to take it easy and come back for checkups. Because you were involved in a shooting in which a man died—" those amber eyes widened in what looked like true surprise "—I am going to have to arrest you until the incident can be thoroughly investigated."

Her lips moved, but no sound came out, as tears filled her eyes. "You're arresting me? But I don't remember anything."

"I'm sorry," Sid said, sounding like he meant it. "But even under the circumstances, I have to follow procedure." He quickly read her her rights.

She blinked as if to hold back tears, but several broke free and cascaded down her porcelain cheeks. When he finished, she finally spoke. The words came out a whisper. "This is all so…unbelievable. I don't know what to say. And you think my life is in danger?"

"We have an eyewitness that will swear your life was in danger at the time of the shooting and that you acted in self-defense. It would certainly help your case, if you could remember what happened. I have a psychologist coming in before you leave to ask you a few questions that might trigger your memory if you don't mind."

"Of course not," she said quickly. Clearly she thought she could fool a psychologist. She'd already fooled the doctor and the sheriff.

"It's important that you remember what happened since your arraignment is this afternoon" Sid was saying. "But I have what might be good news." The sheriff glanced back at him as he continued. "Garrett Sterling, a local rancher, has offered to speak for you at the arraignment, and should bail be required for your release he has offered to post it."

Finally, she turned those eyes on him. Garrett looked into the glowing pit of them as if he was looking into the fires of hell. No recognition. This time she knew the sheriff would be watching her. This time, she'd been ready.

"I'm sorry," she said as if confused. "That is very nice of you, but I don't understand why you would make such an offer. You don't know me."

So that was the way they were going to play this?

Before he could answer, the sheriff spoke up. "I believe Garrett saved your life." She looked surprised—and interested—as she shifted her gaze back to the sheriff.

"Garrett and his family own a guest ranch in the mountains not far from here. He's offered you a place to stay until your memory returns or your family or friends come looking for you or until your trial."

"That is definitely generous of him, but I still don't understand why he would—"

"Mr. Sterling was there at the time of the shooting. Because of his quick thinking I believe he saved your life. He is also the eyewitness who's testified that the shooting was in self-defense."

She frowned and glanced at him again. "Really?"

He saw her eyes widen a little. "It seems I owe you my life, Mr. Sterling. Thank you. I'm sorry I can't remember, but I'm glad you apparently came along when you did."

He just bet she was.

"You can certainly say no to his offer," the sheriff said. "But because we have been unable to identify you and you have no memory of who you are, I doubt the judge will release you on your own recognizance. If you don't take Mr. Sterling's offer you will more than likely spend the time behind bars."

"I'd be happy to accept his kind and generous offer, if it is all right," she said in a small voice he'd never heard before. "If he saved my life, how can I decline? And it is only until my memory comes back or someone comes looking for me, right? The nurse said there's a deputy outside my door? She's there because I'm in danger?"

Sid sighed. "That's why I agreed to talk to you about you staying at Sterling's Guest Ranch. It's closed right now for construction so you should be able to get some privacy up there. You should be safe under Mr. Sterling's care. I don't think you'll have to stay there long. I would imagine your family or friends are already looking for you. Once they contact me—"

"I'm sure I'll be in good hands until then," she said as she turned to look at Garrett again. "The doctor said my memory could come back at any time. Or I won't ever remember." Their gazes locked as if she was daring him to argue the point. "I don't know how I'll ever be able to thank you."

How about telling me the truth? he wanted to say, but instead, he smiled and told her not to worry about it. "I'll talk to the doctor now and see what time you'll be released for the arraignment," he said over his shoulder as he left. His encounter with her had left him shaking inside. The woman was lying through her teeth. He didn't believe any of it.

Outside in the hall, he stopped to calm himself. Deputy Conners gave him a quizzical look. Garrett shook his head. He'd known Joslyn would agree to go to the guest ranch, but now that she had… *What was he doing?*

Taking one hell of a risk not just with his life—but with his money. But what choice did he have? This might be his only chance to get to the truth. She couldn't keep pretending she didn't remember—just as she couldn't keep lying. It was only a matter of time before she came clean.

He knew it was dangerous. Who knew how many secrets this woman had? Or how many men there were out there who wanted her dead?

Garrett had put himself in the middle of it—just as he had that night at the convenience store, the first time he'd saved her. But there was no going back. He was taking her up in the mountains to an isolated empty guest ranch. The construction crew was finishing up the work. So it would be just the two of them.

That alone should have scared him. He didn't need

the sheriff to tell him that he was vulnerable when it came to this woman. Was it that hard to believe that she might have killed that man on the mountainside in cold blood?

As he started down the hall to find the doctor, Sid called after him to wait. When the sheriff caught up to him, he said, "I have to ask you—"

"I'm not changing my mind," Garrett said, even though he was far from sure about what he was doing. But what was the alternative? Let her go to jail and disappear the moment she got out?

Damned if he would let her do that if he could help it. He just wasn't sure how to play this yet.

Sid opened his mouth to say something, probably to give it one more attempt at talking him out of it, when the sheriff's cell phone rang. He held up a finger and took out his phone.

Garrett had been on his way to find the doctor, but he stayed where he was when he heard the sheriff swear and say, "You're already finished with the autopsy?"

CHAPTER NINE

SID GLANCED AT Garrett as the coroner said, "This was one unlucky bastard, I can tell you that. Four shots to the heart at close range? He never knew what hit him."

Self-defense? He'd convinced himself that when Garrett fired that shot into the air the woman got lucky, the distraction giving her the upper hand. Still, four shots to the heart? That would make her extremely lucky. Or skilled.

"I was hoping you might have found a slug in the body," the sheriff said. "My deputies are searching the mountainside where the man was killed, but have come up empty so far."

"Three of the bullets went clean through him," the coroner agreed. "But you're in luck. One careened off a rib and lodged in his spine. I dug it out for you and sent it over to ballistics."

"You're the best," Sid said. "Let me know if there is anything else," he said, disconnected and looked at Garrett as he pocketed his phone.

"Anything new?"

"We should know soon if the man was killed with the gun found at the scene," Sid said.

"No ID yet?"

Sid shook his head. "We're waiting to see if we get a DNA match. His prints had been…altered so we haven't been able to get a decent match apparently."

Garrett raised a brow. "Altered?"

"Apparently burned off with acid." It said something about the man that made him nervous. This wasn't some angry boyfriend or run-of-the-mill bad guy. This guy would have a criminal record—probably one as long as his arm.

It made this case even more worrisome since Garrett was up to his neck in it and determined to get in even deeper.

"Just another day at the office," Sid said. "Makes you wonder though if the woman was involved with this man and what that would say about her."

"You're wrong," Garrett said. "She's the victim in all this."

Sid shook his head. "What if *you're* the one who's wrong about her? The map indicates that one of them was headed for your guest ranch. My guess is that they missed the turnoff and ended up on the wrong road."

Garrett said nothing as if the thought had crossed his mind as well.

"You have to be questioning why after all this time she turns up—and in a most troubling way. And now here you are, involved in her life yet again. If you're not wondering about it, well I certainly am."

There were just too many *if*s. If Garrett hadn't come along at just the right moment… If he hadn't fired that shot… If he hadn't witnessed what he had… If it hadn't turned out that he just happened to know the woman…

He'd allow some coincidence. But given the map, it was no coincidence she was on that mountain because of him.

"You can change your mind," Sid said, wanting to give the rancher one more chance.

With the brim of his Stetson in the fingers of his left hand, Garrett raked his free hand through his hair. He looked as if he hadn't gotten any sleep last night. *Welcome to the club*, Sid thought, remembering tossing and turning most of the night as well.

The rancher shook his head.

"You were right about her agreeing to go with you," the sheriff said. "A complete stranger. Got to make you wonder. It sure does me." What he couldn't shake was the feeling that Garrett knew more than he was telling him.

The rancher looked down at his hat for a moment before putting his Stetson back on his thick head of ash-blond hair. He could see what the woman had seen in Garrett Sterling. He was a big handsome cowboy with a cattle ranch and a guest ranch resort. That would look good to any woman. But for the one lying in that hospital bed? For her, maybe add to that the fact that he was also naive about the world after growing up in Montana.

"I need to talk to Doc to see what time she's going to be released," Garrett said. "Then I'm going to pick up something for her to wear to the arraignment."

Sid nodded, giving up. "I'll be driving up to the guest ranch to check on you."

Garrett smiled. "I'm sure you will. But don't worry about me. I know what I'm up against. I can take care of myself."

"Let's hope so." He wished he felt better about this, but there was nothing he could do legally. "Good luck… I fear you're going to need it." He watched Garrett leave before going back down the hall to the woman's hospital room.

She was sitting up in the bed when he pushed open the door. He wanted to catch her off guard and he had, because earlier she'd seemed so different from the woman who'd been brought into the hospital. When he'd talked to her after she'd regained consciousness, she'd been scared although she said she couldn't remember what had happened.

This woman seemed…in control. She no longer seemed overly upset about not being able to remember who she was. And she'd just agreed to go with a man she didn't know from Adam. On top of that, he'd startled her. She hadn't been expecting him to come back. But he saw that her guard had now gone back up.

"I just wanted to tell you a little more about this guest ranch Sterling owns, in case you're having second thoughts. It's up in the mountains, pretty isolated, no cell phones or internet or television. There won't be any other guests since they had a couple of fires back in March and some of the buildings had to be replaced. There will be a small construction crew around maybe another day or so, if that long. You two will be alone up there." He saw that she was smiling as if amused. "What I'm saying is that you can change your mind."

"Thank you, Sheriff. But the guest ranch sounds perfect. No distractions. Just fresh air and sunshine. Certainly an upgrade over a jail cell." Her smile faded. "Unless you don't trust Garrett Sterling." She blinked those unusual amber-colored eyes of hers. "You aren't questioning that he saved my life?"

"No, I still believe that's what he did. And Garrett is the kind of man who will risk his life to keep you safe." Wasn't that one of the things that worried him? Protecting this woman could get the rancher killed, since he had no doubt that trouble would be knocking at her door and probably sooner than later.

"Then it's settled," she said and gave him a smile.

"And it's just until your memory comes back."

"Yes," she said, her smile slipping a little as if for a moment she'd forgotten.

"I'll come up to the guest ranch to check on you."

"I'm sure that won't be necessary, but I appreciate everything you've done. Thank you, Sheriff. I hope my memory returns soon so I can help you solve your case."

Yes, so did he. But he wasn't holding his breath.

GARRETT SLID THE key into the pickup's ignition and froze. He'd been thinking about the past, the woman he'd known and what he was about to do. The memory had come out of nowhere, blindsiding him. He'd boxed up his memories of Joslyn eighteen months ago. Seeing her again had been such a shock. It was no wonder that the memories were tumbling out.

They'd been together 24/7 for months when he suggested she move the rest of her things in with him. She'd seemed hesitant at first, but had agreed she might as well since she was spending so much time with him. He'd offered to help her move later than afternoon.

"I have so little and I've been staying in a furnished apartment, so it won't take me long," she'd said. *He'd never been to her apartment.*

"Wait and let me help you move out of your apartment after my last class," he'd said and pulled her to him to look into those amazing eyes of hers.

She'd nodded and they'd kissed. She really hadn't agreed. Another lie, he thought now. Because later that day after he left the university, he gave a friend a ride home and after dropping him off, had taken a different route toward his apartment. That's when he'd seen her. She was coming out of a duplex with a suitcase and heading toward her old sedan.

"I thought you were going to let me help you?" he said after pulling up next to her car and putting down the passenger side window.

He'd startled her and it showed. It was almost as if he could see the wheels in her mind turning as she tried to come up with a good excuse. Just then an older woman came out of the adjoining duplex. It was clear that the two knew each other. He'd pulled up and, parking in front of Joslyn's car, had gotten out.

As he'd approached her and the older woman, he had the distinct feeling that Joslyn didn't want to introduce her neighbor. "Hi, I'm Garrett Sterling," he'd said extending his hand to the woman.

"Devon Pierce." She had turned to Joslyn. "I didn't realize you were moving."

"I'm not moving, not that it is any of your business. I'm just taking a few things to the goodwill shop."

Garrett remembered being startled by the lie and her rudeness toward her neighbor.

Devon had lifted a brow, though not nearly as surprised it seemed by Joslyn's rudeness as he was. "Seems like you're taking a lot to give away."

Joslyn slammed the trunk on her car without comment. "I should get going. Good to see you, Garrett, but, like I told you, I didn't have so much that I needed your help." With that she got into her car and pulled away.

Devon turned to him with a pursed-lip look of disapproval. "Short on manners, that one, and a list of other...shortcomings. I'd keep my distance from her if I were you." She'd turned then to go back into her side of the duplex.

When he'd reached his apartment, he'd found Joslyn unloading the few things she had from the back of her car. "Are you mad at me? I know you said you didn't need my help. I just happened to see you packing your car and stopped."

"You just caught me at a bad time."

He hadn't known if she meant that day or since they'd met. But he hadn't wanted to touch that. "Are you always like that with your neighbor?"

She'd groaned, finally seeing that he'd been upset by her rudeness. "I didn't want that nosy woman knowing my business, that's all. I'm sorry. It is none of her concern where I'm moving or what I'm doing. I didn't want her knowing anything about us. She was always watching out the window to see when I came and went. She was especially curious about what I did for a living."

"You didn't tell her, I assume?"

Joslyn had laughed. "Not hardly. So who knows what kinds of stories she made up in her head about me."

"So when is your lease up?"

"The end of the month. I spent so little time there with my work that the place looks just like it did when I moved in. I'll let my landlord know I'm out." She'd moved to him, brushing against him. "I didn't mean to be rude back there. It's just that woman..."

He'd kissed her and put the whole thing out of his mind.

Until now.

He sat for a moment, thinking about other times that he'd been suspicious of Joslyn's behavior when they were together. Phone calls at all hours that she refused to answer, saying it was some old boyfriend. Now he questioned all of it—especially why she'd just up and disappeared without a word. And suddenly here she was again.

While he took most things Dorothea said with a grain of salt, he had to admit, Joslyn Charles turning up here and under these circumstances was more than suspicious. He needed to know. Had she printed the map? Was she on her way to him? If so, why after over a year? And what about the man who had wanted to kill her? The man who he believed *would* have killed her if he hadn't stepped in?

Glancing toward the hospital, he figured the sheriff would try to talk her out of going back to the guest ranch with him. Somehow, he didn't think she would change her mind because he couldn't shake the feeling that he had played right into Joslyn's hands.

He started the pickup's engine. His plan had been to do some clothes shopping for her. But since remembering Devon Pierce, he had something he wanted to do first. He drove over to Mitchell Investigations, parked in the alley and slipped in the back door.

"Someday coming in like that is going to get you shot," his best friend William "Billy" Mitchell said as he slipped his pistol back into his desk drawer.

"Maybe you should lock your back door," Garrett suggested as he pulled out a chair across the desk from his friend and sat down. Billy looked more like a ski bum than a PI. He was *the* all-American boy, from his shaggy blond hair to his blue eyes and angelic face. It didn't help that he dressed like an overgrown skateboarder. The man skateboarded to work. Also he spent good powder days in the winter up on the ski hill outside of town snowboarding. But when not living the Whitefish, Montana, laid-back life, Billy was apparently a damned good PI. It helped that he looked fairly harmless. Also he had a talent for being able to talk his way in and out of trouble, something Garrett recalled from their youth.

"I have a favor. Can you get on Facebook?"

Billy laughed. "Anyone can get on Facebook. Even someone like you. You don't need a PI to do it."

"I'm looking for someone."

"Aren't we all." His friend laughed as he sat up and touched his computer keys. "You really should consider joining the twenty-first century. No one is this techno-illiterate."

"I grew up on the back of a horse. No internet, remember? Shade takes care of the ranch and guest ranch website. I have no interest in social media and my cell phone is just a phone—when I can get enough of those bar things."

Billy shook his head as if there was no hope for him. "What's her name?"

"What makes you think it's a woman I'm looking for?"

His friend said nothing, merely waited patiently.

"Devon Pierce. She used to live in Missoula."

A few seconds of tapping the keys and Billy turned the computer screen so he could see. "Is she one of these?"

"Yes, the third one down. You amaze me," he said.

"Yes, that was an amazing feat all right," Billy

said sarcastically. His friend eyed him suspiciously. "Are you sure *this* is the woman you're looking for? She really doesn't look like your type. Grandmother of four. Still lives in Missoula it looks like. I hate to even ask why you're looking for this woman."

"I want to ask her some questions. How would I go about that?"

His friend shook his head. "It's like you just climbed out of a cave. I'll message her. What do you want to say?"

"Ask her if she remembers a neighbor of hers. Joslyn Charles. Cute, brunette who apparently kept odd hours and wasn't very friendly."

Billy's eyes widened. "*Your* Joslyn?"

"It's a long story."

His friend began to type. "You do understand that she might not answer right— Skip that. She says she remembers her. She says she was stuck-up and rude among other things."

"Ask if I can call her?"

Billy typed. "She wants to know who you are."

"Tell her I'm one of your clients who is trying to find Joslyn."

The PI typed, waited a beat and said, "You know more people should be careful about who they connect with through social media. Here's her number." He wrote it down, tore off the top sheet of the notepad and pushed it over to him.

"Tell her I'll call her."

His friend finished the conversation and leaned

back in his chair. "As one of my alleged clients, how about you tell me what's going on?"

Garrett got to his feet. "I can't right now, but I promise, when this is over…"

"You're scaring me, man."

"I'm scaring myself. Thanks. Want me to lock the back door on my way out?"

"Naw. The lock's broken."

Garrett shook his head as he left. He called Devon Pierce from his pickup.

"You're trying to find her?" the now elderly sounding woman asked.

"You remember her?"

Devon took a breath. He remembered what Joslyn had said about the woman being nosy. "How could I forget her? Always coming and going at all hours. Very secretive. And the men! I swear, I never knew who was going to drive up and usually in the middle of the night."

"There were a lot of men?"

"The one looked like a cop. And the arguments she had with him."

Garrett frowned. Cop? "What made you think he was a cop?"

"Oh, you know, the way he dressed. Short hair, suits or at least sport coats. Maybe not a cop. Maybe the FBI. It was clear that she was in some kind of trouble."

He thought about what Joslyn had said about Devon probably making up all kinds of stories about her. "You said there were arguments? Did you ever hear what was being said?"

"The walls in this duplex are paper-thin. I've complained for years, but the landlord is so cheap and always makes excuses for why—"

"So you could hear the arguments she had with the man?" he interrupted to get her back on track.

"It was clear that he was trying to get her to do something she didn't want to do. I never understood what it was. Maybe turn herself in. Who knows what she'd done. She looked innocent enough, but I could tell the first time I saw her that she was far from it."

"You said there were other men?"

The woman harrumphed. "Slimy man with a camera wanting to know everything I knew about her. Said he was a detective, but he didn't look like the other one so I think he was lying. I told her about him and she pretended she wasn't worried, but I could tell that she was."

Garrett let her go on for a little longer before he ended the call. The walls weren't so thin that Devon had been much help. That Joslyn had secrets didn't come as a surprise. Nor did he trust the older woman's judgment when it came to what cops or FBI agents looked like. Or what might have been going on next door.

He thought about Joslyn's original story about being an undercover cop. What if there had been some truth to it? The chief of police could have lied to him because Joslyn was still undercover. But if true, when Sid ran her fingerprints they would have come up. Unless she was in deep cover?

Shaking his head, he started his pickup and headed for a clothing store. There was only one way to find out the truth. He glanced at the time. It wouldn't be long before the arraignment. He felt confident he could get the judge to release her to him. All his instincts told him that he was headed for more trouble than he knew how to handle. But this was the woman he'd once planned to marry. Didn't he deserve the truth at any cost?

CHAPTER TEN

GARRETT WAS COMING OUT of the clothing store when his cell phone rang. He saw it was his brother Will and picked up. "How was the honeymoon?"

"Wonderful. But we have a problem at the valley ranch. Can you swing by?"

He checked his watch. "I don't have a lot of time, but sure. I'll be right there."

The moment he walked into the house, he saw what he recognized as an intervention and figured he knew who was to blame. He shot a look at Dorothea, who of course, pretended innocence. He'd been ambushed and he had a pretty good feeling he knew why.

"What were you thinking getting involved with this woman again, let alone inviting her to stay at the guest ranch?" his brother Will demanded and looked to their younger brother for his support.

"He's right," Shade said. "This is the craziest thing I've ever heard you come up with."

"The bank sent you an email to the ranch account," Will said. "You're posting bail for the woman? This woman who lied to you two years ago and is still lying since you're convinced she remembered you so she's lying about having amnesia?" Will took a breath. "Not to mention, she killed someone?"

"I'm not sure how much she actually remembers," Garrett said. "But I know what I'm doing."

Will shook his head. "Big brother, you're the one who always tries to talk sense into us when we come up with some stupid idea. Also, I understand that you have hired our attorney to defend her?"

He understood why they would be upset. Even the sheriff had his reservations about this. "I've given this a lot of thought and it's my own money," Garrett said, digging his heels in. "You need to trust me."

Will laughed. "If there is one thing I've learned— and recently—it's what a woman can do to a man's common sense. Admittedly, I never thought it would happen to you. We knew you'd gotten your heart broken in law school. Otherwise you wouldn't have quit. From what we've heard, this woman can't be trusted."

"I really don't have the time to get into this right now," Garrett said. Not that he planned to ever get into this with them. Once he and Joslyn were at the guest ranch... Well, he planned to get to the truth one way or another.

"Bro, that is messed up," Shade said. "And what a crazy way to break up with you all those years ago, just disappearing like that."

"You have no idea how dangerous this woman is," Will said. "Not to mention all of this feels...off. I agree with Dorothea. You witnessing the shooting feels like some kind of con."

"Exactly," Dorothea interjected. "This woman *knows* you. She knows you're the kind of cowboy who might suggest something like this to help her. This has disaster written all over it. One man is already dead. You could be next."

That Dorothea was making sense was enough to confuse him. "You don't need to remind me of that," Garrett said. "I think once we're alone, she'll open up to me. A woman who doesn't know you, isn't going to go with a complete stranger up to a secluded empty guest ranch to regain her memory even if she does believe I saved her life."

"I think it's his trusting face," Shade joked. "Sorry, I know this is serious, but clearly Garrett's in love. Nothing is going to stop him. Even I can see that. Of the three of us, he has always been the most stubborn. So nothing you say is going to change his mind. We'll just have to drive up there and check on him."

He shook his head adamantly. "I want the two of you to stay away and keep Dorothea away as well even if you have to hog-tie her." He shot her a look. She mugged a face at him. "There is no doubt that what I'm doing is risky. I'll be the first to admit it. But I'm not safe until I find out what's going on. For her to turn up like this after all these years, for me to witness what I thought was her almost being killed… I agree. There is more going on here and Joslyn is the key."

"I agree with Dorothea," Will said. "This woman is playing you like a fiddle. What if you're being set up, walking into some kind of trap? And all because of these old feelings for this woman? You don't have a clue what you're in for—or just how dangerous it could be."

"It's my choice. So stay away. If I need you, I'll call." With that, he walked out.

THE SHERIFF STOPPED BY the morgue on his way to the hospital. He'd hoped to have some evidence that would break this case wide open—and possibly keep Garrett Sterling from making the mistake of his life.

"Anything new?" he asked Sam.

The coroner pulled back the sheet to show the sheriff the dead man's prison tattoos. "I did go online and try to track the tattoos to one specific prison but didn't have any luck."

Sid had to smile. Only in small towns did everyone get so involved in a murder. "What about the altered fingerprints? That can't be common even with hardened criminals."

"The scars are old. I suspect they were done before the man realized that he could be identified through DNA." He pulled one of the man's hands out from under the sheet to show Sid. The sight made him wince.

"What I need is the connection between the woman and the dead man and I need it quickly," the sheriff said. "I need that DNA report."

"Do you have reason to believe the man and woman knew each other?"

"No. Nothing of hers was found in the stolen car."

Except for the printout of the map to the guest ranch. "I suppose it could have been a crime of opportunity on the man's part. He could have abducted her off the street not having a clue who she was." He didn't believe that. One of them had that map. Isn't that what tied them together? It would certainly explain what they were doing up in the mountains so near the guest ranch.

"You think she was abducted?"

Sid nodded. "She would have had a purse, some identification, on her. Unless she dropped her purse when she was taken." He shook his head. He was clutching at straws, but it felt as if the clock was ticking. Garrett would be taking clothes to the woman and Deputy Conners would be taking her to the arraignment where Garrett had the family attorney waiting.

"We'll know more once we get the DNA results," he told the coroner.

"The woman still hasn't remembered what happened?"

He shook his head. He couldn't shake the feeling that she was lying and Garrett knew it.

Sid glanced at the time. "I need to go. Let me know if you find out anything else." He got the call on the ballistics results as he was leaving.

"Thought you'd want to know about this as soon as possible. That .38 bullet used on the dead man? I got a match—and, are you sitting down? There's a local tie-in."

This was the last thing Sid had been expecting.

Still gripping the phone, he dropped into his chair behind his desk. "Local?" He hated the way his voice wavered. He had only a matter of weeks before he would hang up his star and gun. He did not want to go out with any open cases hanging over his head.

"Remember that convenience-store holdup a couple of years ago in Missoula? Garrett Sterling was involved. The shooter was the kid behind the counter, the night clerk."

"Right." Sid remembered only too well since Garrett had reminded him of it not that many hours ago. "The young clerk got trigger-happy when it was almost over and shot the driver of the getaway car when he came through the front door of the store. The other one Garrett had beamed with a can of beans. The getaway driver died. Wasn't he the robber's younger brother, as it turned out? But how is the gun used in this recent shooting connected?"

"The clerk had brought it in because he didn't feel safe working nights. At least that was his story. Who knows where he picked up the gun since it's unregistered and he said he couldn't remember, he thought maybe he'd bought it at a gun show. Frankie Rutledge went to prison for the robbery. His younger brother, George, died on the way to the hospital from his gunshot wounds. In the confusion that night, the gun used by the clerk disappeared. And now it's turned back up in your recent shooting."

"How is that possible?" Sid asked, scratching his head.

"There was a third brother—just a kid at the time.

Didn't Garrett say he saw a kid in the back but just assumed he'd left the store before the shooting? Nicky Rutledge had come in first, possibly to stake out the store and let his brother know it was empty. He would have been eight or nine. He could have picked up the gun from behind the counter after the clerk drilled his brother."

He'd heard about the Rutledge family. Four brothers, all bad news. A couple of them were dead, the one Garrett had cold-cocked was in prison—or at least he had been until now apparently, and the youngest, Nicky was on the lam, wanted by the law.

"Let's say the kid picked up the gun and held on to it," Sid said. "As far as we know, it wasn't involved in any other shootings or the ballistics would have come up when you got this match. So where has the gun been the past two years?"

"Who knows? But you have to admit, it's interesting."

Very, he thought as he disconnected. Even more interesting if you knew that the woman Garrett called Joslyn Charles was the woman in the convenience store that night. Wasn't it more possible that she'd picked up the gun as she was avoiding the cops— thanks to Garrett? That was even more interesting.

And more dangerous to the rancher who now wanted to take the woman high in the mountains to the isolated family guest ranch.

GARRETT RETURNED TO the hospital with several bags of clothing he'd picked up, sorry that his family was upset about what he was about to do. But it wasn't going to stop him.

He hadn't had to guess Joslyn's size since from what he'd seen of her earlier standing at that window confirmed that she hadn't changed much. She was a little fuller in the hips and breasts. Two years ago she hadn't been more than a handful.

He cursed that thought away, reminding himself that he might know this woman in the biblical sense, but otherwise, she was a complete stranger and one who couldn't be trusted on so many levels it boggled his mind.

The male deputy at the door just gave him a nod.

"What's this?" Joslyn asked when he tapped at her hospital room door and stepped in carrying the bags.

"I thought you might need something to wear out of here," he said. "As well as something to wear to your arraignment. I have an attorney who'll be representing you. I hope that's all right."

She looked amused. "Weren't you worried that I might change my mind?"

He wanted to laugh. "Why would you do that?"

"After we talked earlier, the sheriff came back and told me about your guest ranch. I got the feeling he had some reservations about me going with you."

Garrett set the bags on the end of her bed. He wasn't sure he could keep up this pretense for long. "Well, it's entirely up to you. Either way, I figured you'd need something to wear since I believe your clothing is still being held as evidence."

The word *evidence* wiped the smile off her face,

much like he had expected it would. She swallowed as she looked at the bags he'd put down. "How did you know my size?"

"I guessed."

She didn't meet his gaze. "Why are you being so nice to me?" she asked, her voice low.

He was asking himself the same thing. "I'm a nice guy. That's why I'm going to step out into the hall so you can change. Your doctor said he'd be by to release you soon." With that he turned and walked out, his heart hammering. He'd never been one to play games with women. What they saw was what they got. But clearly Joslyn or whatever her name was, was a master at the craft.

He questioned whether he was up to this as he went out into the hall to wait. Maybe his family was right and he was making the worst mistake of his life.

Garrett hadn't been in the hallway long when the sheriff showed up. The moment he saw Sid's expression, he knew something had happened.

"We need to talk," the sheriff said and motioned to a nearby waiting room.

SID RUBBED THE back of his neck after the door had closed behind them. Earlier, he'd had a psychologist try to help the woman remember what had happened before the arraignment. But the questions the psychologist asked hadn't sparked a memory apparently.

Which left him no choice but to tell Garrett the news. He got right to the point, knowing they didn't have much time. "I just got the call on the ballistics test. The gun used on that mountainside? It was the same one the clerk at the convenience store in Missoula shot and killed George Rutledge with two years ago."

Garrett stared at him, clearly in shock. "How is that possible?" he asked, sounding as stunned as Sid had been. He could see that the rancher was trying to wrap his head around it. "Where has the gun been all this time if not on some shelf in police evidence storage?"

"It went missing at the scene. We have two theories. That boy you thought you saw in the store and assumed had left before the robber came in? The cops identified him from the surveillance camera tape as Nicky Rutledge, the youngest Rutledge brother. He was about eight or nine at the time."

"A brother of the robbers. But I thought he left before the robbery," Garrett said.

"He might have just hidden in the back. He would have known his brothers planned to rob the place and could have been a part of it. Until everything went south. You didn't see him again?"

He shook his head. "But there was so much confusion… You think he picked up the gun?"

"It's one theory," the sheriff said. "It's the other theory that is more troubling, and that's that your girlfriend picked up the gun."

Garrett tried to hide what he was feeling. But Sid could tell that the news had shaken him to his core. If his Joslyn picked up the gun two years ago, the same one that she'd killed the man on the mountainside with, that put a whole new spin on this case.

"She is the most likely since she was definitely there and she could have pocketed the gun before you handed her your pickup keys so she could avoid the cops. She definitely wouldn't have wanted to get caught with the gun on her. She could also have been involved in the robbery. You testified that she was on the floor near the counter when the clerk dropped the gun."

Garrett cleared his throat. "I think that's a stretch."

Sid had known he would jump to her defense even as he knew Garrett's rational mind would be arguing that she was the most likely to have picked it up.

"If she was running scared that night, she might have seen an opportunity to arm herself," Sid said. "The question is what was she running from back then? The same thing she was running from when she killed a man, wrecked the car and ended up in the hospital here? There seems to be a pattern and damn it, Garrett, you are the common denominator."

GARRETT PULLED OFF his hat to rake his hand through his hair in frustration. This news had come as a shock. He couldn't deny it. What if she had picked up the gun that night? What did that say about her? He'd helped her get away. She'd played him for a sucker in so many ways. Was he really going to the isolated, empty guest ranch with this woman?

"If she was involved in the robbery, when it went bad..." Sid didn't need to finish his sentence. They both knew where Joslyn had gone to hide out for a few months to lay low before disappearing again. "I'm assuming you never saw her with the gun that night or during the time you were…close."

Garrett couldn't believe Sid actually thought Joslyn might be involved in the robbery. That had never crossed his mind and he wished it hadn't now. "I never saw the gun or her with it while she was living with me." But that didn't mean that she hadn't taken it. She said that she'd moved most of her things to his place, but he didn't know that for a fact since she'd kept her apartment. An apartment he'd never seen. Maybe the gun was only one of the reasons she hadn't wanted him to help her move that day.

"Maybe you saw the gun but don't remember. She told you she was an undercover cop. If that was true, then she'd have had a weapon."

Garrett sighed and looked down the hallway toward her hospital room door. "So what are you saying? That you really believe she was a cohort with the Rutledges?"

The sheriff frowned. "I find that hard to believe too, but I'm not ruling it out at this point. But I do think she has to be the one with the gun for it turn up now. It makes sense if she picked up the gun at the convenience store that night. She might have had it with her since we haven't been able to tie the dead man to the weapon."

Garrett couldn't believe this. "If true, then what was her motive?"

"You'd have to ask her that."

"I'll add it to my list," he said with a curse.

"If I'm right, she is a dangerous woman and I don't think you should be up there at the guest ranch with her."

"But then again, this is all only speculation."

"Except for the fact that it is the same gun, which ties the two shootings together and ties you and Joslyn together."

Garrett knew what else tied them together besides a gun and two crimes. "So what are you going to do about it, besides warn me?"

Sid looked away and he knew that the sheriff could try to convince the judge to lock her up and deny Garrett's request. "Sid, let me take her to the guest ranch. Let me try to get to the truth."

The sheriff was right about the night of the convenience store robbery. There had been confusion. Joslyn *could* have picked up the gun.

But then so could the Rutledge boy.

"I'm not changing my mind." He was committed and willing to see this through as long as it took. No matter what.

The sheriff nodded. "I don't like it, but you know that if you get into any trouble—"

"You'll be the first person I call," Garrett said.

"I guess I don't have to warn you again about her."

He let out a bitter laugh as they walked back toward her hospital room. "Not hardly."

The sheriff sighed. "Then I have to ask, why are you really doing this?"

Garrett thought about giving him a pat answer. He

was a nice guy. She was a woman in trouble. Instead he considered his motives for a moment. "You can bet she's up to her neck in something. I don't know about you, but I want to know what."

"How do you plan to find out?" Sid asked, sounding worried.

"Patience." He laughed. "If she's the one who'd had the map to the guest ranch and knew I would be there, then there was a reason she was coming up to see me."

"You think she has her own agenda?"

"It's definitely crossed my mind." He met the sheriff's gaze. "And Dorothea is convinced the woman is up to something."

Sid smiled at that. "Dorothea has a lot of…suspicions and superstitions. It's what makes her so unique. But I'm a lawman. I deal in evidence. You're that positive this woman is the same one you knew when you were in law school?"

"Without a doubt."

"You really think she's going to tell you the truth?"

He laughed again. "I doubt she could tell the truth if her life depended on it."

"Then how do you expect—" The hospital room door opened and the doctor exited following directly behind him by the woman Garrett had known as Joslyn Charles. She carried the bag of extra clothing he'd purchased for her.

She stepped out of the room and seeing them, did a model turn. The clothes fit perfectly—just as he'd known they would. She'd chosen the coral dress, the one he'd bought because that shade of peach had been her favorite.

"Mr. Sterling was kind enough to bring me something to wear," she said as she looked at the sheriff.

Sid nodded and then looked at Garrett as if to say, "I hope to hell you know what you're doing, Mr. Sterling."

"I don't know how I will ever be able to repay his kindness," she was saying.

He just bet. "You should call me Garrett."

"Garrett," she repeated as if the name was new on her tongue. Oh, that amazing tongue of hers. "Thank you." Her gaze lit on his for just long enough to send a jolt to his heart and lower. This woman had knocked him to his knees not all that long ago. This time she might very well kill him.

"And why don't I call you…" He pretended to give it some thought. He could feel the sheriff's gaze on him. "How about…Joslyn?"

She seemed to consider the name for a moment before she gave him a tight smile. "Why not?"

CHAPTER ELEVEN

ALISTAIR REALIZED HE was feeling his age. He closed his eyes for a moment as he listened to the man on the phone. For forty-eight hours, Monica had been missing. But now they knew where she was. She hadn't remembered who'd murdered her father and stepmother. On the contrary, she'd lost more of her memory.

He opened his eyes, took down the information and called the sheriff's department in Whitefish, Montana. Over the years Alistair had posted bail, bribed officials and thrown around what political clout he could to get Monica out of trouble.

He'd lived up to his promise to her father. He'd been paid handsomely for the job. But in days Monica would be turning thirty and on her own. For the past eighteen months, things had been quiet. He'd actually thought that she was adjusting. He'd stopped worrying about her not because he knew where she was, but because he didn't get one of these calls that she was in trouble again.

And now this.

The sheriff was out. He spoke to Undersheriff Ward Farnsworth before calling the hospital and being put through to a Dr. Bullock. After all that, he'd called both Monica's doctor and lawyer. They'd come right over since they only had one client and patient—Monica.

"If what you're telling me is true, then Monica needs medical attention," Dr. Neal Foster argued as he poured himself a drink from Alistair's good stuff.

"She received medical attention at the hospital in Montana and was discharged. She was arrested for shooting a man and was arraigned today. Apparently, the judge remanded her over to a local man, Garrett Sterling, until the investigation is over. They don't know yet if it will go to trial because apparently it was self-defense. She was in the hospital after getting a concussion in a car accident following the shooting and has lost her memory."

Neal shook his head. "She needs real medical attention, not the kind she received back in Montana." He took a sip of his drink, meeting Alistair's gaze over the rim of the crystal glass. "You asked for my professional opinion. Well, you're going to get it. This is a cry for help."

He wished he hadn't asked. But he had to admit, this time was much more serious. He was scared for Monica. According to the undersheriff, someone had tried to kill her. He related this to the two men.

"This girl has been nothing but trouble." Her family lawyer spoke up after telling Neal to make him a drink while he was at it. Attorney Benjamin Purdy lolled on the sofa, looking around at Alistair's home as if he'd never seen it before. Like Neal, the lawyer

was also on retainer and had been for twenty-five
years. That too was about to change though with
Monica's thirtieth birthday—unless she kept him
on, which was doubtful.

Or unless Neal was right and Monica was a danger to herself.

Alistair had to admit that Monica *had* been a
handful. She'd been willful and rebellious as far
back as he could remember. He'd spoiled her, there
was also no doubt about that. Poor little rich girl.
The title fit.

"We've all profited off this trouble for years," he
pointed out, forcing the other two to fall silent for a
moment. The gravy train was about to run out for all
of them in a matter of days, unless Neal had his way.

"What are you suggesting?" Alistair asked. "Com-
mitting her?"

"For her own good," Neal said and Ben jumped
in a little too quickly, making Alistair aware that the
two had talked about this prior to arriving. "Who
knows how she stumbled across this man who tried
to kill her. She's never been careful about the people
she's associated with, as you well know."

"This wouldn't have anything to do with her upcoming birthday, would it?" Alistair asked with a
sigh, unable to hide his suspicion. Both looked of-
fended. If she was committed, then they would all
still be in business, so to speak, himself included.

"The woman needs help," Neal argued. "Another
memory loss?" He shook his head. "I'm sincerely
worried about her or I wouldn't suggest this. I know

it seems drastic, but I need to run some tests on her.
You know she won't come in on her own. These
memory losses could be indicative of DID."

"DID?" Alistair asked skeptically.

"Dissociative identity disorder. Formerly known
as split personality."

He laughed, shaking his head as he made himself
a drink. "I wonder which Monica will inherit then."

"Laugh if you will but I brought you some information on DID." He dropped a sheaf of papers on
the coffee table. "I suggest you take a look. It's rare,
but a history of severe emotional trauma is a key
feature of DID. Also the early loss of a parent and
considering what we know Monica witnessed the
night her father and stepmother were murdered…
I think you're going to see why I'm concerned. We
care about Monica and want the best for her."

Alistair took a sip of his drink. Monica had almost been killed and now had no memory of it. He
could see a pattern, even though he didn't want to.

"This all goes back to seeing her father and stepmother killed," Neal said. "Maybe if she could remember…"

Alistair thought of the one time Neal had tried
hypnotism on her. She'd been ten, not legal age, so
he'd had to give his permission. It had been a fiasco
and he'd had to put an end to it when she became
hysterical. Remembering was too traumatic for her.

But because of that, he thought Neal might be
right. Maybe her behavior all stemmed from the murder. Maybe this latest memory loss was a symptom of

something much more serious. This time she'd had a car crash after escaping her killer. She'd nearly died not once but twice this time.

"All right," he said. "I'll go along with this as long as it is for observation. You run your tests. Then we'll see."

"If I'm right and she has DID, it's going to take intense treatment," Neal said. "But at least this is a place to start," he added quickly.

Monica had been through so much. He thought of his promise to Horace and hoped he was doing this for the right reasons.

JOSLYN MET GARRETT'S bright blue eyes, her heart a thunder in her chest as they walked toward the elevators. She couldn't believe what had just happened in that courtroom. Garrett had been so eloquent in his appeal to the judge that she hadn't been surprised that bail had been set and she'd been released with the condition that she would stay at the Sterling's Montana Guest Ranch under Garrett Sterling's protection until the investigation was concluded.

"You all right, Joslyn?" he asked as he pushed the down elevator button and looked over at her. It took all of her reserve not to react when he said the name Joslyn. She hadn't heard it on his lips in so long. It sparked feelings she'd had to pack away back then, feelings she had made a point of not unpacking since. It had been too painful.

She recalled how Garrett's eyes lit up when he realized why she'd chosen to wear the coral dress first.

His gaze, burning with accusation, had locked with hers. She'd had to drag her eyes away, determined not to let him get to her. Too much was at stake to let hurt feelings stop her now. Once they were alone…

Still she couldn't help being afraid. She knew she would have never come here unless…unless she'd had no other choice. So what had happened that she wasn't just here, but that Garrett had saved her life? The sheriff kept saying he wanted her to remember. If only she could.

All she knew was that she'd killed a man who'd apparently been planning to kill her. She was scared. She'd tried to remember. But some memories were locked in a deep dark hole. She knew that whatever was down there, it was far worse than this. And yet now she'd lost another chunk of her memory.

That alone terrified her. Hadn't she been warned that it could keep happening and it could have psychological consequences? The psychologist the sheriff had her see had tried to dig around in her memories, but nothing about what was going on now had come out.

And yet she remembered Garrett and everything they'd shared in detail. How did she explain that? But Garrett was *her* secret. The one thing she'd hung on to all these months. And now, here he was and she was headed to the family guest ranch that she'd heard so much about but had never gotten the chance to see. Just the two of them. But only if they could get away before—she needed to get him alone even though that frightened her more than she wanted to admit.

They stood waiting for the elevator, not looking at each other. "Thank you."

"Don't thank me, I'm just doing what anyone would do under the circumstances."

She knew the circumstances he was talking about but said nothing. She noticed that the sheriff had stopped to say something to one of the lawyers. She reminded herself that it was a small town, everyone knew everyone and his business. She willed the elevator to come, fighting to hide how nervous she was. She'd been here before. It was only a matter of time…

When the sheriff had told her earlier that he'd sent her photo out over the wire in case her family or friends had reported her missing and that he should be hearing something soon, she'd barely been able to breathe. He said he'd also taken her DNA. It meant they would find out—if they didn't already know. They would send someone to get her.

"Are you all right?" Garrett asked.

She nodded and smiled. But she wanted to take the stairs at a run. She couldn't help feeling anxious. The sheriff was clearly worried about her safety, but he had no idea. He'd tried to talk her out of going with Garrett even though he'd said that the cowboy had saved her life. Saved her life and then invited her to stay at the family guest ranch. No wonder he was suspicious.

The elevator door opened. She let out the breath she'd been holding and stepped in quickly. Garrett turned to look back as if to see if the sheriff had planned to join them. She wanted to scream. But then he finally stepped in and the door closed. She tried to relax but it was impossible. The elevator began to move, finally. Until they reached the isolated guest ranch, she would stay on needles and pins. Even after that, she would be watching and waiting.

In the confines of the elevator, she glanced over at Garrett. If anything he was more handsome. He appeared to be in even better shape than he'd been when he was attending law school at the university. He'd always been tall, broad-shouldered, slim at the hips, with those long legs. But now he looked more muscular, his skin tanned from the sun, his body hardened from physical labor.

There were a few laugh lines around his blue eyes and just the hint of silver at his temples, giving her a glimpse of how he would look in old age. The realization was bitterly painful since she'd once dreamed of being around to see that happen.

She wanted to reach out and cup his strong jaw. She ached to draw him to her, to kiss that mouth that she'd dreamed about for so long, to feel his arms around her again, holding her, promising that there was a chance for the two of them even when she knew there wasn't.

All her instincts told her that going with him was a mistake in so many ways. But as the sheriff had pointed out, her choices were limited and he didn't know the half of it. And it wasn't as if she hadn't made mistakes before. Certainly falling for Garrett had been her worst. That had almost gotten her killed. As it was, it had forced Joslyn Charles to die. And she'd always liked that name.

This time it was a matter of life and death. And not just hers. Because if she was in Whitefish, Montana, then it wasn't just her life that was in danger.

As Sid finished answering the lawyer's question, his cell phone rang. He picked up hoping for good news.

"Nothing on the DNA on the woman," the lab tech told him. "I saw you had a rush on it. Just wanted to let you know."

He disconnected, feeling relieved. As he started down the hallway, he saw that the hallway was empty. Garrett and the woman were gone.

It still worried the devil out of him, but the rancher thought he knew what he was doing. Sid sure hoped so. His cell phone rang again as he started toward the elevator. When he pulled out his phone, he saw that it was Lizzy and frowned.

"Deputy Conners," he said into the phone, already sensing that something was wrong—even before he heard her voice. She spoke quickly, urgently.

There'd been a response on the photo and description of the young unidentified woman he'd sent out over the wire. Also apparently her DNA sent up some red flags. A US Marshal had called, upset and demanding to speak with her.

Feds? Flagged DNA? US Marshal? He didn't like the sound of any of this. Who the hell was this woman?

"Her family has been notified and is sending

someone to pick her up." He was not to let the woman Garrett called Joslyn Charles out of his sight.

"I'm sorry, can you repeat that?" His heart pounded. He'd caught the words *psychological problems*. This sounded serious. He reminded himself that Garrett was now taking the woman to his guest ranch. Just the two of them alone on a mountainside over the weekend.

Sid rushed to the elevator and hit the down button, but immediately realized he couldn't wait. He turned and ran toward the stairs. His mind whirled like a pinwheel in the wind. Hadn't he suspected there was more to the story about the woman? Hadn't he worried that Garrett had no idea what he was getting into? Hadn't he questioned the woman's alleged memory loss?

He shoved open the door to the stairs. "Tell them I'm going to need to see that commitment order," he said into the phone. "All right. I'm at the courthouse now. Yes, I'll make sure she doesn't leave." *If I can catch her.* He hurried down the stairs, his mind racing. Garrett and the woman would have left the building by now. They could have already driven away. He'd known something was wrong.

And yet, as he took the stairs, flying down the levels to the ground floor, he'd never in his wildest dreams imagined this.

Sid retrieved his weapon from security and burst out of the stairwell on the ground floor and ran toward the exit. But as he shoved through the doors, he saw Garrett's pickup driving away.

"Garrett!" he called, but too late. All of the ranch-er's attention would be on the woman. A woman he was taking to his guest ranch in the mountains not knowing anything about her except for a few months of his life when he thought she was his future.

The pickup didn't slow as it left the parking lot and turned onto the street to disappear into the traf-fic.

Breathing hard, Sid watched Garrett and the woman disappear around the corner. He tried the rancher's cell phone. It went straight to voicemail. He didn't leave a message. He knew where he could find them.

CHAPTER TWELVE

JOSLYN. SHE TRIED out the name, a whisper on her lips that felt like a caress. And a lie. Lie or not, she was Garrett's Joslyn and always would be. Until she told him the truth. If she got the chance before someone tried to stop her.

He'd said nothing on the walk from the courthouse to his pickup. Nor had he said anything after opening the passenger-side door for her and helping her into the cab. Garrett, always a gentleman. He lived by the Code of the West. It was no wonder he'd been wearing a light gray Stetson the first time she saw him. She'd known he was one of the good guys. One look into his blue eyes and she'd known that she could trust him in a world where she had found few to trust.

The pickup cab looked as if it had recently been cleaned and she had to smile. He'd told her when they were together that he was a rancher and that it wasn't as glamorous a life as some thought.

"It's dirty work. Boots and trucks are going to get muddy with dirt and manure," he had said and laughed. "But it's a wonderful life if you're the kind of man who loves wide-open spaces, the smell of pine and campfires, the sound of cattle lowing in the night."

"But you're studying to be a lawyer?" she'd asked.

"I'm thinking I can do both. My brothers are both ranchers like my father and grandfather. I felt like I needed something more when I started law school, but there are a lot of days when I miss the ranch so much…" He had shaken his head and smiled his wonderful smile. "I'd love to show you the ranch and the family guest house. That's where I spent my summers."

It had sounded romantic to her. She could picture the old log cabins set back in the trees, the large lodge filled with family history and the trail rides, roasting marshmallows over the campfire, dances at the back of the lodge.

She had wanted to be a part of his life with such an ache that she'd ignored the danger. She'd stuck around that first night at his apartment to thank him for his help and had been charmed by him. So charmed that she'd stayed not just that night, but so many others. She would have stayed a lifetime with him, and that was what hurt the most because she'd known she couldn't. Because Garrett had been in the dark when it came to her and she'd kept him that way.

Still she'd fallen hard for the charming cowboy who'd saved her that night at the convenience store. He was all cowboy. She'd been captivated by the man from his Stetson to his boots and the way his Wranglers fit every inch of his backside and long legs. But it had been so much more than that. She'd fallen in love with him.

Now as he drove his pickup out of town toward the mountains and the family guest ranch, the hot July sun hung over the top of the pines. She shivered even though the inside of the cab was quite warm. Garrett reached over without a word and turned down the air conditioner.

She couldn't believe she was actually leaving with him, going to a guest ranch that was closed so when the construction workers finished it would just be her and Garrett alone together in their own private hell. She could feel his anger at her coming off him in waves—just like she'd once felt the heat of his desire.

What was he thinking right now? She would have given a small fortune to know and realized what she was thinking, groaned inwardly. Just the thought of how good they'd once been together sent heat rushing to her cheeks. She glanced away, her gaze going to the side mirror. She'd been watching for a tail since they'd left the hospital. She hadn't seen anyone who appeared to be following them, but that didn't mean they weren't. It was only a matter of time before they knew where she'd gone and they'd come for her.

She could feel the clock ticking. She had to remember what had happened in the days right before she ended up in the hospital. But the more she tried to remember, the darker that hole seemed to grow—along with her fear. Her head ached. Her heart ached even more. She'd never wanted Garrett involved. It was why she'd left eighteen months ago without telling him. She hadn't wanted to take him away from his family, his ranch, the life he loved, and she couldn't stay. She'd had no choice.

But from the look in his eyes back in her hospital room when he'd suggested she go by the name Joslyn, she knew he'd never be able to forgive her for leaving the way she had. She hadn't forgiven herself, either. A few days before she'd left, she'd found a diamond engagement ring in his bureau drawer in a pretty dark blue velvet box. Just the thought of it broke her heart all over again. Garrett had been planning to ask her to marry him.

That was when she'd known she had to leave before he could. Then she'd seen a man canvassing the neighborhood handing out flyers. Or at least pretending that was what he was doing. She'd known. He was looking for *her*.

She felt him watching her now out of the corner of his eye. Watching and waiting. They would be at the guest ranch before long. She would have to tell him everything. She couldn't keep her secret even to protect him. Not anymore. She had no idea what he would do, let alone how she would survive this. Since seeing him at the hospital she'd been fighting the memories of the two of them together and the feelings he evoked in her. Once she told him…

A memory pulled her from her reverie. As Garrett drove down a narrow tree-lined dirt road that wound up into the towering mountains, she felt something stir. Had she been on this road before? The doctor had said that her memory could come back at any time. She'd feared that she might never be able to retrieve those lost hours.

For a moment though, this road… The memory slipped away like smoke. She felt a stab of frustration. She had to remember. If she didn't, she wouldn't know who or what was coming for her. Coming for her—and Garrett, because it couldn't be a coincidence that she'd ended up in Whitefish. Her only hope was remembering. In the meantime, she had to make sure that Garrett was safe. At least by being with him, she might be able to recognize the danger before it struck.

Glancing over at the cowboy, she saw the determined set of his strong jaw. He must assume that she was lying about *everything*. She'd seen that look in his eyes when he'd realized that she remembered him. He knew she'd been lying to him two years ago. He just didn't know to what extent. Is that why he had invited her up to his guest ranch? Was this about getting even? Or getting to the truth? Either could be dangerous.

She closed her eyes and leaned back against the seat. Sunshine poured in through the pickup's windows, lulling her in its warmth. She thought of her shock at seeing him again. That look in his blue eyes… She'd known at that moment that she was dealing with a different man than the one she'd known. This one didn't trust her. This one was onto her.

She opened her eyes to see a blur of green. They were on a narrow road climbing higher into the mountains with tall shimmering pines on both sides. She looked up the road and felt a stab of fear along with that vague sense of memory. This was a mistake, she thought, feeling rising panic. Or had she already made the ultimate mistake—and that's why she was here?

Closing her eyes again, she told herself that she could do this. It was the only way to save Garrett.

GARRETT GLANCED OVER at her. She'd fallen asleep! Looking at her, you'd think that she didn't have a care in the world. She'd always been cool as a cucumber, as his mother used to say. It was part of her attraction, he could admit now.

Still, he couldn't believe that she had fallen asleep. Eyes still closed, face turned up in the sun, damn she was beautiful. He kicked that thought to the barrow pit, reminding himself that he couldn't trust this woman as far as he could throw her.

He wondered how much she really remembered. That she remembered him, had recognized him, was in his pickup right now headed to a remote, isolated guest ranch told him that she was lying about her memory loss. So why had she agreed to come up here with him? She didn't seem worried about being alone with him—even after what she'd done to him all those months ago. No doubt, she thought she could handle herself in most any situation. Maybe she could, he thought, reminding himself of what happened to the man who'd tried to kill her.

When he'd seen her on that mountain, she'd been in trouble. Of that, he was certain. But somehow she'd turned it around. With his help? The shot he'd fired? Or had she been in control of the situation the whole time?

"Something amusing?" she asked, taking him by surprise. He really had thought she was asleep.

"Just smiling to myself."

She nodded, not pushing it. That was another thing about her. He'd told her a lot about himself when they were dating. But she hadn't offered much in return. She'd never quizzed him about anything, especially old girlfriends like other women he'd dated. He'd thought it was because she was so secure in herself and their relationship.

Now he knew that it hadn't mattered because none of it had been real.

If he'd been smiling, he wasn't anymore. He concentrated on the road ahead and questioned if bringing her up to the isolated guest ranch would prove to be the stupidest thing he'd ever done—and maybe the last.

He reminded himself that he didn't just have this possible murderer to fear. She had been running for her life when she'd crashed the car she'd escaped in. So who else was after her and how long before yet another killer showed up?

In the meantime, his plan was to live long enough to get some answers. This woman had broken his heart. He deserved to know why.

WHEN ANOTHER CALL had come into the sheriff's department about the Jane Doe at the hospital, Undersheriff Ward Farnsworth had been visiting with the dispatcher.

"It's a call about the woman, the one in the hospital," the dispatcher told him. "He's asking for you, but the sheriff said—"

"Never mind what the sheriff said. The caller's asking for *me*. Put it through to my office," Ward said. He'd been following the case—not that the sheriff had let him get near it. As if he didn't know what Sid was up to. Sid felt threatened now that Ward had announced he would be running for sheriff in the fall. But whoever was on the line had asked for him. He'd known the moment he heard about the case that it was one that could get him the sheriff's job—if he could solve it first.

He smiled as he stepped into his office. When his phone rang, he picked up. "Undersheriff Ward Farnsworth, how can I help you?"

"I hope I'm talking to the right person," said the whispery voice on the other end of the line. "I'd been trying to reach the sheriff…"

"He's out, but I can help you," Ward said. He thought of the earlier caller who'd just wanted him to verify that the woman called Jane Doe, whose description had been put out over the wire, was still in custody. He'd verified that she was at her arraignment after being arrested and the caller had hung up.

He thought this was going to be the same kind of call, a law enforcement officer calling about their Jane Doe. But he equally realized, this call was different.

"I'm worried and need to know who and what I'm dealing with," the person said. "I did some asking around and was told that you were the person to talk to if I wanted answers."

"You bet."

"Can you tell me about Sheriff Sid Anderson? I know I'm putting you on the spot."

The undersheriff beamed. "Not at all. Can I be honest with you?" he asked, keeping his voice down. "Sid Anderson's got one foot out the door. He's been threatening to retire and is finally set to do it this fall."

"He's the one investigating this incident involving the Jane Doe you have in custody? I'm concerned because I spoke with someone at the courthouse and understood that she's been remanded over to the care of a man by the name of Garrett Sterling, a local rancher. That concerns me."

"It should. The sheriff goes by the book—except when it comes to his friends." He knew that wasn't quite true, but it had never stopped him before. "Garrett Sterling is one of his friends."

"I see. I can't tell you how much I appreciate your help. I understand that you're running for sheriff this fall."

Ward felt as if he was bursting with pride. This person really had done his or her homework. The voice was deep, throaty. Could be a woman or a man. "I figured this county needs someone they can rely on."

"I would like to contribute to your campaign fund."

It was only a hundred and eight dollars, the limit on his type of campaign, but it was the faith the person had in him that pleased him most. Maybe he could win this election. His luck was finally changing for the better. "Thank you."

"I'm happy to help. In the meantime, I hope you don't mind if I go through you instead of the sheriff."

"No, that's just fine."

"I'd appreciate it you could keep me apprised of things at your end. Let me give you my number."

He could understand the person's concern. The request didn't seem unreasonable. He'd found that Sid could be hard to work with. "I'd be happy to."

"Wonderful. I hope you don't mind if I have my campaign contribution sent by special courier and in cash."

"Not at all." He felt as if the buttons on his shirt would pop. He was going to be the next sheriff with supporters like this.

"I'd hoped you might not mind. So is there anything new with the investigation?"

"It appears to me that the sheriff's case has reached a dead end." It wasn't until he'd hung up that he realized the person had never given him a name. Probably better that way. He didn't let that worry him for long. He grinned to himself as he leaned back in his chair. "Sheriff Ward Farnsworth," he said, and liked the sound of it.

WHEN GARRETT HAD told her about Sterling's Montana Guest Ranch high in the mountains outside of

Whitefish, Montana, he hadn't done it justice. As they came over a rise, she got her first look at the historic log buildings set against the shimmering green of the pines.

It was so picturesque. Almost like a Western fairy tale. She fell in love with the place instantly. She had a fleeting image of her and Garrett's children growing up here in the summers. She could see them laughing and running, their skin lightly tanned, their faces lit with joy. She would have loved spending summers here as a girl.

The image dissolved as she reminded herself what she was doing here.

She put down her window and breathed in the day, as she tried to still her growing anxiety. What would happen when they reached the lodge? When she told him everything?

She thought of that moment at the hospital when she'd heard her room door open and she'd looked up. She hadn't been prepared to see Garrett Sterling standing there looking right at her. She'd met his blue gaze and felt her heart soar at just the sight of him—and drop just as quickly when she realized what it meant.

She'd hurriedly closed her eyes, but she'd seen his expression and seen in all that blue that he knew not all of her memory was gone. She'd remembered him. And he'd remembered her.

She'd thought he'd go to the sheriff. She'd been terrified. She'd learned the hard way that she couldn't trust anyone, even the law. She'd ridden it out, hoping she could make Garrett doubt what he'd seen in her eyes. She didn't want him involved and had foolishly thought she could protect him by lying once again.

Garrett hadn't told the sheriff, even though they seemed to know each other well. Because he couldn't be sure that she remembered him? Or because he was protecting her?

After what she'd done to him, why would he want to protect her? He'd protected her once and look where that had gotten him.

It hadn't been easy, pretending she didn't remember the two of them together each time he'd walked into her hospital room. But not knowing how she'd ended up in the hospital in Whitefish, Montana, and how Garrett was involved, she'd had to keep silent to protect him. At least that's what she told herself.

Seeing him though had transported her back to those wonderful months they'd spent together. She'd never been happier. She remembered his touch, his scent, his words whispered in the night as they lay entwined in his bed. She'd drawn on every ounce of strength she could being around him and not giving herself away. If she gave him any indication that what he'd seen had been real, that she'd recognized him—

When the sheriff told her that Garrett had saved her life, it had been all she could do not to scream. No. She'd left him all those months ago to keep him safe. She'd never wanted him involved in this part of her life. How was it possible that he was, suddenly after all this time?

It seemed like a bad dream. And just when she

was hoping to wake up, the sheriff had told her that
Garrett was offering her a place to stay. On the Sterling's Montana Guest Ranch she'd heard so much
about. She'd heard the love in his voice when he'd
described it to her back then. He had wanted her
to come with him once he was out of law school in
June. He was going to teach her how to ride a horse.

She stared straight ahead now, her heart in her
throat. Seeing the place, she couldn't bear to remember that agonizing time with him when she'd known
that none of that would ever happen because by June
she would be gone from his life forever.

Having heard so much about this guest ranch, she'd
wanted to decline his offer. But she couldn't say no.
She had to get him alone. She had to tell him the truth.
If she had any hope of keeping Garrett safe until she
remembered…

Not that she didn't know what Garrett was after—
answers. Well, so was she. She desperately needed to
know what had happened to her before she'd looked
up and seen him standing in her hospital doorway.
Just as she had to know what she'd done.

According to the sheriff, she'd been driving at
a high rate of speed before the accident. Running
after shooting a man she had no idea who he was?
She needed to know how she'd gotten to Whitefish,
Montana and why—since it was a place she'd sworn
she'd never go.

That this could get them both killed terrified her.
But Garrett was already in too deep. She'd let the

sheriff believe that she couldn't remember anything. But she could never have forgotten Garrett Sterling.

"Well, here it is," he said as he stopped the pickup at the top of the rise to let her take in his family's guest ranch.

She could feel his intent gaze on her, knowing that he was looking for her reaction. "It's beautiful," she said truthfully. "You must love it." When he said nothing, she glanced over at him. He was smiling, his eyes shiny bright with the knowledge that she was a liar and probably worse.

CHAPTER THIRTEEN

GARRETT PULLED UP in front of the main lodge and cut the engine. Now that he was here, he wondered, what happened next. He'd told himself that once he got her up here and they were alone, he could get her to tell him the truth about everything. How exactly though, he had no idea.

He glanced over at the woman he'd thought he knew so well and saw her taking in the lodge. It was a large log structure with huge glass windows in the front and a towering rock chimney. To the right of the lodge were nine small log guest cabins set some distance apart in the pines.

"Will I be staying in one of the cabins?" Joslyn asked as she glanced in their direction.

"No, we'll be staying upstairs at the back of the lodge. There's an apartment up there and a series of smaller suites that the family uses." And of course, Dorothea, who was just like family, when she lived up here during the guest season. "I think you'll be quite comfortable in one of the suites."

She nodded and smiled. "I'm sure I will be. I don't see any men working today."

"It's the weekend. They're all off." In fact, he expected them to finish Monday and then they would be gone for good.

"I hadn't realized it was the weekend, I guess." She let out what could have been a nervous laugh—if he hadn't known her better.

"There are no guests now and probably won't be for the rest of the summer. We had two fires back in March." He wasn't going to get into what had happened. "The large old barn had burned and so had cabin five. The construction crew is still finishing up. I figure they should be gone soon. Is that going to be a problem?"

She turned to look at him. "Not for me."

"I thought you might say that," he said, opened his door and climbed out. She didn't give him a chance to come around to her side of the pickup to open her door. When he heard her exit, he headed up the steps and across the porch to the main lodge to unlock the door. Turning, he saw that she had stopped beside the pickup and was looking around. He watched her take it all in.

Her face seemed to soften, her eyes shiny and bright. She seemed enraptured by the place, making him recall all the times he told her stories about his summers growing up here. They would have been curled up in bed after making love, naked and sated and blissful.

He shook off that memory and reminded himself that none of that had been real. But as he watched her looking around, he would have loved to know what she was thinking.

Or maybe scheming. With this one, he couldn't tell. She'd agreed to come up here with him. She would have a plan. He would just have to wait to see what it was.

"Come on in," he said as if she were one of the guests. "Let me show you around, *Joslyn*."

SHE HEARD CONTEMPT in the word. *Joslyn*. But she realized she might as well get used to being called by that name—at least as long as she was going to be here.

The lodge was everything Garrett had told her and more, she thought as she took in the huge lounge area. An assortment of cozy leather furniture formed a half circle around the massive opening in the rock fireplace. All of it looked worn-soft and inviting.

Native American rugs dotted the hardwood floor and some of the walls. Other walls held antlers and animal heads, Western paintings and what looked like relics. She felt as if she was breathing in Garrett's past all the way back to his grandfather who had established the guest ranch here in the early part of the previous century.

"This is the heart of the place," Garrett said of the main lounge. She could feel him watching her, studying her reactions, trying to read her. It was disconcerting because he'd never been like this before. But then again, he'd never really known her, had he.

"I love it." She turned to him. "I hope we can have a fire even though it's July."

He chuckled. "July in the mountains of Montana,

you're going to want a fire, trust me." He seemed to realize what he'd said about trusting him. All humor left his face as he quickly added, "Then there is the dining room and kitchen."

She followed him through long log tables and chairs to what appeared to be a commercial kitchen. Everything sparkled. She loved how light and airy it was in here and said as much.

"I've had food delivered so the fridge and freezer are well stocked. Do you cook?" He chuckled. "That's right, you don't remember. Well, you're in luck because I'm the only one in my family who can boil water. I hope you like hard-boiled eggs."

"Sounds like we won't starve."

"I promise not to let you go hungry."

She thought about the meals he used to make for her during the months they were together. He could do a whole lot more than boil eggs and they both knew it.

He stood in the kitchen studying her in that bright light. She tried not to flinch under those laser-like blue eyes. Was he remembering their barbecues at night on his tiny porch? The two of them had been ravenous after lovemaking. She thought about the way they enjoyed the food and each other as they ate before cuddling up on his bed to watch a movie or listen to music on the nights he had to study. Her heart ached to go back. To do things differently, even though she knew it was impossible. She'd done the only thing she could have when she'd left him. But she doubted he would see it that way.

Garrett cleared his throat as if he had remembered the two of them and the way it used to be. His blue gaze had warmed, then cooled again as he said, "I should show you to your suite."

She followed him back through the dining room and lounge and up the wide log-railed staircase to the hallway. Her room was only two doors down. He opened a door and gave her a slight bow. "See if this is going to work for you."

She stepped in, taking in the largest of the rooms at a glance. It was a sitting area with a flowered couch and chairs, everything much more feminine than she'd been expecting. There was a bookcase stacked with books and a reading lamp by the large comfy-looking floral print chair.

"The bathroom is to your far left, bedroom right through that door." She glanced in to see a queen-sized bed covered with a pretty star quilt. She took a peek into the bathroom. There was a claw-foot tub but also a shower behind glass doors. Everything looked updated and sparkling clean. She swallowed the lump in her throat. This was so much more than she deserved and they both knew it.

Smiling she turned to him. "This is…" Her voice broke. "Thank you. It's all…wonderful."

He nodded as if he doubted that was true. "You will notice there's a phone but it only calls within the ranch. There's a phone downstairs for calls outside the compound, but you shouldn't need that since you have no one to call, right?" He continued without waiting for a reply. "There's no television, no internet, no cell phone service. The idea of the guest ranch is to unplug, disconnect, get back to another time."

"Then it's an ideal place for me to get my memory back, isn't it."

He smiled at that, making it clear that he thought that too was a lie. That all of it had been a lie. She saw the bitterness, the hurt, the naked pain in his expression before he quickly hid it.

"I'll let you freshen up. I'm going down to the kitchen and make us something for dinner. I'd ask you if you're allergic to anything or if there was anything you didn't like—"

"But what would be the point," she said, tired of his sarcasm. She wanted to blurt it out, tell him everything. But she knew that when she did, that would be the end of it. The end.

Selfishly, she wanted this time with him, even if she couldn't touch him, kiss him, make love with him. Even if he stayed angry with her. No matter how long it was, she wanted—needed—to be near him. They would come for her soon enough. Until then, couldn't she just enjoy being this close to him for a little while? What would it hurt?

She knew the answer to that. There might not be time to tell him the truth. Or worse, not time to warn him.

As much as she wanted this, she wasn't sure how long she could go without telling him that, of course, she remembered him. She could never have forgotten him or stopped mourning the loss of him. She hadn't been able to bear leaving him. Nor had she been able to leave a note. What could she have possibly said?

If only she could open her heart to him. But if she told him that she remembered everything about the two of them, why would he believe that her real memory loss was only of the days before her accident? Why would he believe anything she said, given all her lies? She only had herself to blame for her lack of credibility.

Take this time with him. Once you remember why you're in Montana to begin with... As long as she remembered before it was too late.

In the kitchen, Garrett was stewing over the woman upstairs when he realized she was right behind him. He had warned himself not to turn his back on her once he got her to the ranch. And here he was, busy grating cheese, both hands busy. He felt himself freeze. At her light touch on his shoulder, he flinched in spite of himself.

"What smells so good?" she asked, seeming to ignore his reaction to her touch.

He wanted to say, "I'm making your favorite," but in truth, he wasn't sure even that hadn't been a lie when they'd been together. "Chili and corn bread."

"It smells delicious. Is it your own recipe?"

He smiled. She knew damn well that it was. He sobered though before turning to look over his shoulder at her. He wouldn't have been surprised to see her holding one of the kitchen's butcher knives. That thought was so messed up, he knew he had to stop thinking this way. Who knew how long they would be here together.

"As a matter of fact, it is my own recipe," he said. "It used to be one of the only things I knew how to make. You like to cook?" He pretended to catch himself. "Sorry."

"Is there anything I can do to help?"

"You can set the table." He pointed to the cabinet. "Dishes over there. Silverware in that drawer. I thought we'd eat in front of the fire at that large square coffee table."

"When I came downstairs, I saw that you'd made a fire. Thank you. Eating in front of it sounds wonderful. That room is so huge and yet so cozy. I'm dying to sink into one of those leather chairs out there. Well, maybe not dying."

He ignored that, wondering if this was as uncomfortable for her as it was for him. He doubted it. She had the upper hand because she knew what was going on. He was stumbling around in the dark. "You're about to get your chance to try out the furniture while you're here."

He turned back to what he'd been doing, fighting hard not to remember the two of them on his apartment furniture in Missoula. It was college-student furnished, which had been fine with him. He wondered if she remembered the night they'd broken the bed.

They'd tumbled to the floor, naked and still in the throes of passion to uncouple in throes of laughter before they'd finished making love on the floor.

Behind him now, he heard her getting bowls and plates out, then silverware. At the sound of her retreating footsteps, he tried to relax. But when the timer went off on the oven, he jumped. Laughing, he shook his head. He reminded himself that he was going to be staying just down the hall from her for who knew how long.

Who could blame him for being jumpy though? Add to his total lack of trust in this woman the fact that she'd just killed a man. Still, he had to stop being so paranoid. He suspected she might take some satisfaction in his being skittish of her. And satisfaction was the last thing he wanted to give her.

DEEP IN ONE of the leather chairs in front of the fire at the guest ranch, Joslyn had been so mesmerized by the flames that she hadn't heard Garrett approach. Nor had she realized that she was unconsciously rubbing her hand along the smooth leather arm of the chair.

When he cleared his throat, she started and she saw that it amused him. He didn't want to be the only one edgy in this situation, she thought. He already knew she was a liar. She hated to think what else he thought her capable of. She was sure he would lock his door tonight. Maybe even keep a gun next to his bed.

She thought of the bed they'd shared in his apartment just off campus. The bed had sagged badly, making them both end up wrapped in each other's arms in the middle. She'd loved that bed. It had been one of the hardest things she'd ever done when she'd left it—and Garrett—behind. She hadn't had a good night's sleep since.

"I hope you're hungry." He put down a large pot of chili, her favorite, and a pan of corn bread on two trivets on the table. "Not the fanciest meal you've ever had, I'm sure."

"The smell alone is making my stomach growl," she said, sitting up as he filled her bowl and handed it to her. He scooped out a large piece of corn bread and put it on a plate for her. When she'd gotten down the dishes and utensils, she'd dug the butter out of the refrigerator and honey from a cabinet, knowing how much he liked both on his corn bread.

Now she saw him eye the honey before his gaze rose to meet hers.

"I saw the honey and butter after you said *corn bread*. I hope it's all right," she said, realizing her mistake. She shrugged. "It just seemed like a good idea."

"Great idea," he said as he took a seat. "It's how I like my corn bread, but then you would have no way of knowing that."

She watched him lather his corn bread with butter, then drizzle honey on it. "I would imagine you aren't the only one who likes it that way." He pushed the butter over to her, then the honey. She didn't like either on hers and he would know that. Which explained why he was waiting to see what she did.

Buttering her corn bread and then following his example, she drizzled honey over it. She took a bite and gave him her biggest smile. It was too sweet and, to her, spoiled the taste of the corn bread, but she would eat every bite. "Delicious."

He smiled back, humor sparkling in his gaze. He was enjoying this. How long were they going to play this game? Was he waiting for her to confess?

She took a spoonful of the chili. It tasted exactly like it had when he'd made it for her two years ago. "Oh, this is so good."

"Thanks. Like I said, it used to be one of the only things I knew how to make. So I ate a lot of chili in college and law school."

She frowned. "The sheriff said you were a rancher, but you're also a lawyer? You seemed so comfortable in the courtroom today."

He shook his head, his gaze holding hers. "I quit law school. Long story. I fell in love with a woman I met. After she left me…" His words were like a knife to her heart. "I lost interest in the law. So now I'm just a rancher."

She swallowed and fought back the tears that burned her eyes. "I'm sorry. But you must love what you do."

He nodded and she had to drag her gaze away. "I guess I've always been a cowboy at heart." They fell into an uncomfortable silence with the only sound the occasional pop of the logs burning in the fireplace.

"I thought you might want to go for a walk around the ranch after we eat," he said as they were finishing. "That's if you feel up to it."

"I would love to." She'd heard so many stories

about his growing up here. She realized that she wanted to see it all, experience as much of it as she could with what little time she was here.

WHEN THE GUEST RANCH landline rang, Garrett figured it would be the sheriff. He almost didn't get up to answer it. But he was afraid that would send Sid racing up here and that was the last thing he wanted.

Before he could say more than hello, the sheriff began to talk quickly.

"Is she in the room? Don't say anything, just listen."

He glanced toward Joslyn. She hadn't moved. She seemed to be staring into the flames, but he knew she would be listening.

"I heard from her family."

Joslyn's? He shot her a glance, surprised it had happened so quickly. Maybe more surprised to hear that she had family. She'd never mentioned any. But then again, he had to remind himself that everything about their time together had probably been a lie.

"They're flying in to take her home in the morning. Do me a favor. Don't lose her between now and then."

Was Sid serious? "I wouldn't dream of it." Her family? He had less time than he thought to get the answers he so desperately needed.

"You aren't safe with her so don't let your guard down. She isn't the woman you think she is. They say she isn't well, mentally. When her family comes in tomorrow, they are taking her back to Seattle for observation at a psychiatric medical facility back in Washington."

Okay, that was news.

"Also, her real name is Monica Wilmington and there is a whole lot more to her story. Am I getting through to you?"

Loud and clear. He glanced over at the woman sitting in front of the fire. The golden light illuminated her beautiful face. She looked…peaceful. And certainly not dangerous. Certainly not mentally unstable. But what did he know? Nothing.

"Right. Look, I'm busy. We can talk about this some other time."

"Just don't do anything more stupid than you already have," Sid said.

Garrett hung up the phone and looked in Joslyn's direction. No matter her real name, she would always be Joslyn to him. She seemed to be intent on the fire crackling next to her. Her family had already turned up? That was quick. They thought she was mentally ill and needed "observation"? He didn't believe it for a moment, did he?

He shook his head. Joslyn was sharp as a tack, as his dad used to say. She knew exactly what was going on. But why would the family think otherwise? Because of her accident? Well, he would find out in the morning. Which meant that he might have only tonight with her. As he stepped back toward her, Joslyn seemed to come out of the trance she'd been in. She rose and began to pick up their dirty dishes.

"Let me do that," he said.

Shaking her head, she said, "Please, you made dinner. It's the least I can do."

He considered that—and the sharp knives in the wooden block in the kitchen. "Why don't we do it together?" As long as he kept her away from anything sharp, it should be safe enough, he told himself. "That was the sheriff on the phone. He said he had some new information. He's coming up in the morning. Is there anything you want to tell me before then?" he asked as they carried the dishes into the kitchen and began loading the dishwasher.

"If you're asking if I have miraculously gotten my memory back..." She met his gaze. "Believe me, I want to remember what happened on that mountainside more than you do."

"I wonder about that." He stared at her intently, looking into all that amber the way she'd been staring into the flames of the fire. He wondered what she'd been thinking about. Did she think about the past, the two of them? Or was she working on a new plot, one that would leave him even more devastated than before?

"I don't blame you for doubting me." She looked away. "You have no reason to trust me."

You could say that again.

"I'm trying to remember. The more I try though..." She shook her head. "But when I remember, you'll be the first to know. As for the sheriff, I'm as interested as you are in what he's found out."

If so, then why did her voice quiver just a little? She was scared and so was he. *Joslyn, oh Joslyn, what are you keeping from me?*

CHAPTER FOURTEEN

GARRETT WAS LOOKING at her as if he could see into her soul. "If you're thinking about taking off—"

"Why would I leave?" Even as she said it, she wondered if that wouldn't be the kindest thing she could do. Just disappear again. But she'd left before to protect him. This time, she feared the only way she could keep him safe was to stay.

He didn't answer, just gave her an impatient look. "We're a long way from anything. This is rugged country and the chance of you getting lost—"

"I agreed to come up here with you. I know you don't trust me and think I'm lying about not remembering how I ended up on that mountain with that… man." She shook her head. "I'm sorry. I hope you're not regretting asking me to come up here with you. Unless you decide you don't want me here, I'm not going anywhere."

They stood, gazes locked in a challenge that she knew neither of them would win tonight. She was tired. She would tell him everything in the morning before the sheriff came. With luck she would have remembered what she was doing back in Montana by then. She would know how much trouble they were both in.

"It's getting late," they said in unison.

Garrett smiled as if he too remembered when they used to do that all the time as if they were that connected. Two lost souls that had found each other. At least for a while.

She looked into his handsome face. It was all she could do not to touch him. She remembered the feel of his slightly stubbled jaw against her fingertips, against her more tender skin, and felt a shiver.

"Cold?" he asked. He missed little.

"Maybe someone just walked across my grave. I think I'm a little too tired for a tour of the ranch tonight." She touched the small bandage on her head. "I think I'll go up to bed. Thank you again for dinner. It was delicious."

As if she was going to be able to sleep, Joslyn thought as she closed her suite room door behind her. She locked it although she couldn't imagine whom she thought it would keep out. Garrett wouldn't be trying her door tonight.

What she'd seen in his eyes earlier... She shuddered, hating that it had come to this. Where there had once been love, there was now bitterness and mistrust, anger and resentment. It broke her heart all over again.

As she moved deeper into the room, she told herself she couldn't think about that now. The sheriff had learned something that had him driving up in the morning. Whatever it was, it was important enough that he didn't want to discuss it on the phone. She tried to imagine what it could be. Had he found out the truth about her? That was the worst part. She had no idea.

She glanced around the room, telling herself she could run even when she knew she couldn't. And not just because of her memory loss, or lack of money or means. Even if there had been somewhere to run, she couldn't leave Garrett.

It couldn't be a coincidence that their lives had crossed paths again. Someone was setting them both up. All her instincts told her that the answer was here on this guest ranch. Or would be soon. All she had to do was wait.

She'd do whatever she had to when the time came to save Garrett. She couldn't let him pay for the mistakes she'd made. If she was right he was in danger. He needed to disappear for a while until…until whatever was going on, blew over.

But that was the problem. She knew Garrett Sterling. He wouldn't run. He wouldn't leave the ranch. She'd known that two years ago. It was why she'd had to leave him instead.

As much as she hated doing it and as dangerous as it was, she knew what she had to do. She'd just have to wait until Garrett was asleep.

GARRETT COULDN'T SLEEP after he'd made the call from his room to his friend Billy. He'd lied about the only phone with an outside line being the one downstairs. He'd recently had the line added with the other construction changes going on at the resort. This was one call he hadn't wanted her to overhear.

"Do me a favor?" he'd asked when his friend answered.

The PI had chuckled. "I can hardly wait."

"Find out everything you can about a woman named Monica Wilmington."

"Age?" Billy had asked.

"Late twenties, early thirties. Beautiful with amber eyes and long dark hair."

"How soon do you need this?"

"Since it's possible she's a murderess and she's staying down the hall at my guest ranch, sooner might be better than later."

He was too antsy to sleep. Giving up, he went downstairs, grabbed his jacket and stepped out into the summer night. This high up in the mountains of Montana it was often cold at night even at the end of July. A sliver of moon and a trillion stars lit the midnight blue sky overhead, casting shadows across the landscape. A breeze whispered in the tops of the tall pines as he walked down the trail that led along the front of the row of nine cabins.

He'd been raised here, spending his summers saddling horses, helping with guests, even making beds in the cabins when some of the staff quit before the end of the season. He hadn't minded it since there were a lot of girls who came up with their families. He and his brothers danced with them, taught them how to ride, showed them how to toast marshmallows over the fire, took them down to the creek to swim.

There were a lot of good memories connected to this place, he thought as he reached the end of the cabins, each tucked back into the pines some distance from the others. He could hear the creek below him. He'd never been afraid here, not of the bears that often passed through or an occasional mountain lion.

But tonight, he felt the hair rise on the back of his neck. Not far down this trail he'd witnessed a shooting. And he'd foolishly brought the shooter back to his mountain with him. A woman named Monica Wilmington. The sheriff had been right. He didn't know this woman, probably never had. What had he been thinking bringing her here?

Worse, he felt time running out. Her family was coming up tomorrow to take her back. Back to Seattle to get her help. Could he be wrong about her? Why hadn't he pressed her harder to tell the truth tonight? It was probably his only chance. By morning, she would be gone. He might never know why she'd left him all those years ago. Or if any of it had been real.

But did he really want the truth?

"Couldn't sleep either?"

He spun around, clearly startled to find the woman standing within feet of him. He saw her smile in the starlight. Amused that she'd scared him?

"I didn't mean to sneak up on you like that."

Garrett just bet. "I was lost in thought."

"I noticed." She looked away from him, to the edge of the path where the mountain fell away. She stood silhouetted there against the night sky. "It's beautiful here. Just as I pictured it."

He cocked his head, waiting for her to say more.

She wore jeans and a T-shirt and now hugged herself. He realized that she must have heard him leave and didn't want to take the time to grab a jacket. Slipping off his, he stepped to her and wrapped it around her.

She looked up at him, her gaze softening, those amber eyes suddenly like a warm, inviting fire. "Now you're going to be cold."

"Why don't you tell me why you followed me out here," he said.

"I couldn't sleep."

"Guilty conscience?"

Joslyn gave him an impatient look. "You're so angry with me. I can't imagine why you'd invite me to stay here."

"Can't you?"

She looked away again. "I'm not lying about not remembering why I was in that vehicle when it crashed. I don't know how many times I have to tell you that." Her gaze shifted back to his. An owl hooted from a nearby tree. The breeze lifted her hair. She tucked a stray lock behind one ear. She looked so young. So vulnerable. "I'm trying to remember."

He sighed. "I've already heard this story."

"That's what I'm trying to tell you. It's true."

"And I should believe you, why exactly?"

She shook her head and let out a short, frustrated laugh. "You're right. Why should you believe me? It isn't like we know one another. It isn't like you have any reason to believe anything I tell you. I'm sorry to have bothered you."

Joslyn started to turn away, but he grabbed her

arm and pulled her hard against him. His mouth dropped to hers in a searing kiss. He heard her gasp, then sigh as her lips parted. Her body melted into his. He'd yearned for the feel of her in his arms. His pulse thundered in his ears. Desire sparked and set fire to a longing in him that he'd thought he'd extinguished long ago.

He was never going to get over this woman. As he deepened the kiss, he feared that she would be the death of him.

For a long moment, he lost himself in the familiar feel of her. Memories, sweet as pure sugar, made him weak with wanting to rewrite the past. He didn't want to let her go any more than he had two years ago. His hand went to her breast. He could feel her hard nipple through the thin fabric of the T-shirt. She let out a moan against his lips.

A twig snapped nearby, startling them both as if hearing a gunshot.

Garrett let go, stepping back from her, feeling the memories slip away and reality step in. What the hell was he doing? He thought of the sheriff warning him not to do anything more stupid than he already had.

And yet he would have made love to this woman right out here in the starlight not knowing who he was making love to. He still yearned for the woman he remembered. Desire was like a spike through his heart. But this woman's name wasn't even Joslyn Charles. There was no Joslyn.

"Sorry." But he wasn't sorry. He still wanted her

and from the way she'd kissed him back, the way her body had reacted, she still wanted him as well.

He reminded himself that she'd lied to him, continued to lie to him and was dangerous in ways he apparently knew nothing about. She'd never even told him her real name. So why start now. He'd been a fool to bring her here. Had he really thought she'd tell him the truth about anything, maybe especially the two of them?

Or maybe her lies and leaving had said it all. He felt like a fool. A fool who'd fallen helplessly in love. This woman wasn't that woman. She never had been. He wouldn't make the mistake of forgetting that again, he told himself, knowing he was also lying to himself. "You should go in."

She nodded, slipped off his jacket and held it out to him. "Thank you," she said as he took it.

This time when she turned to leave, he let her go.

CHAPTER FIFTEEN

JOSLYN HUGGED HERSELF, chilled even in the warmth of her room back at the lodge. When she'd come back, she had locked her door and leaned against it as she'd tried to catch her breath and not cry. Being in his arms again...

She scrubbed at her face, hating the burn of the tears. She wanted to fall on the bed and sob until she couldn't cry anymore. But she'd already done that when she'd left him. Why hadn't she realized how unbearable this would be? She couldn't keep lying to him.

Trembling from the shock and power of the kiss, she moved deeper into the room. She could still feel his hand where it had been on her breast, her nipples both aching. If he had any doubt that she remembered him, he didn't anymore. She'd wanted him so badly that she would have made love with him right there in the pines. It wouldn't have been the first time they'd made love in the woods.

Without turning on a lamp, she moved to the window to look out on the summer night. He was still out there, hands deep into the pockets of his jacket as he walked toward the barn now under construction.

She suspected that like her, he was having trouble sleeping. Probably because of who he'd let under his roof, she told herself.

She touched her lips with her trembling fingers, remembering his kiss, the taste and feel of him. Garrett knew her intimately. What they'd shared was like a brand on her heart. She'd never been able to get over Garrett even though she'd tried. She ached to be in his arms again. She thought of their lovemaking, the nights lying naked in that sagging bed of his, their bodies molded perfectly together like two pieces of a puzzle, and felt more hot tears cascade down her cheeks.

Below her window, he turned then as if sensing her. His gaze shot to her window. She froze, wondering if he could see her. If he was thinking about what had almost happened tonight. Or thinking about the past. Thinking how much she'd hurt him.

Dropping his head, he turned back toward the lodge. She stood listening for his boots on the hardwood floor of the hallway. She didn't dare move until he'd passed her door. She hadn't realized that she'd been holding her breath until she heard his door close at the end of the hall.

Tonight, she'd come so close to telling him the truth but for all the wrong reasons. She couldn't bear the anger she'd seen in his gaze. The pain. The frustration. The suspicion. But that would be nothing compared to how he would feel when he learned what she'd been doing when they'd met.

Lying down on the bed fully clothed, she cried

until she was exhausted and the well of tears had gone dry. She listened. The lodge creaked and groaned, but she heard nothing from Garrett's end of the hallway.

It was time. With the sheriff coming in the morning, she had no choice. She had to know what was going on, how she'd gotten to Whitefish to begin with and why. And she had to find out tonight as soon as she was sure Garrett was asleep.

She lay in the dark listening. It had been several hours since he'd gone down to his room for the night. Was he asleep? She remembered how easily he used to nod off. A clear conscience, she thought with a grimace. She, on the other hand, had spent long hours lying beside him, listening to his steady restful breaths, while she thought about her life and the mess she'd made of it before Garrett.

Refusing to let herself wallow in those memories now, she rose from the bed and padded barefoot across the cool hardwood to the door. Listening, she heard nothing. The utter silence of this place was unnerving. She'd spent too many years in a city with the sound of sirens and the roar of traffic at all hours of the day and night. Because large cities were safer for her. She could disappear into the crowds.

Gripping the knob, she eased open the door. The hallway was dark. She listened to the absolute silence for a few moments before she stepped out and quietly closed the door behind her.

For a moment, she stood in the dark and listened, waiting. Garrett was staying at the end of the hallway. She stared at his closed door for a moment longer, then turned and padded silently down the stairs.

Moonlight shone in the lodge, lighting the stairway as she quickly descended. She'd spotted the phone earlier—a large old black one sitting on a small table near the door to what Garrett had said was his office.

She went straight to the phone, picked it up and was relieved to hear a dial tone. Garrett had said it was the only outside line at the lodge so she didn't have to worry about him picking up an extension in his room to listen, did she?

It was a chance she'd have to take. Still, she hesitated. She had desperately wanted to make a call from the hospital. But a woman who said she couldn't remember anything wouldn't have anyone to call— just as Garrett had pointed out earlier. She hadn't been able to take the chance at the hospital anyway. Just as she couldn't chance telling the sheriff the truth. She never knew who she could trust so she trusted no one. Until Garrett.

She knew that once she made the call, it would be traced. They would know where she was—if they didn't already. Taking a breath, she dialed the number that had become engraved on her memory.

The line began to ring. It was even later back east, but she didn't care. This might be her only chance. The phone rang again. She held her breath and waited, not sure what she hoped he would tell her when he answered.

By the fourth ring, she was starting to worry.

What if something had happened? What if he was somewhere off the grid? What if a lot more than her piddling life had been compromised? Or what if he was on his way to Montana?

In the middle of the fifth ring, he picked up. "Hello?" He sounded half asleep.

"It's me."

She heard him stir, covers being thrown back, feet hitting the floor. He swore. "Do you have any idea how much trouble you're in?"

She didn't. "I was in a car wreck. I ended up in the hospital. I can't remember the days right before that."

He swore. She could imagine him raking a hand through his hair. She'd put him through so much. "I know," he said, sounding less angry. "Your DNA was flagged. When it came up and I saw you'd been arrested for shooting someone. Why did you run?"

"I don't know that I did. I don't remember anything about the days before I woke up in a hospital. I don't remember killing anyone."

"Where are you? I can send someone to pick you up."

"I need to know what I'm doing in Montana. Did you—"

"I didn't contact you."

A memory, sharp and painful, flashed in her mind. A photograph of her and Garrett. But when she tried to hang on to the memory, it quickly slipped away. Had someone sent her the photo? The room seemed to sway for a moment before she said, "My cover—"

"Was fine until you ran." He swore. "Krystal, what were you thinking taking off?"

"My name isn't Krystal," she snapped.

"Call yourself whatever you want, your life is in danger if they find you. You know this. We've been through this before. If you had just stayed—"

"I can't do this anymore." Her voice wavered, but she knew she'd never spoken more truer words. "I'm done."

He swore and when he spoke it was through gritted teeth. "You know that you weren't really eligible for the program. I stuck my neck out—"

"How did you get me in then?" she asked now, suddenly suspicious and wondering why she hadn't been before. "My father and stepmother's killer is behind bars. You never needed me to testify."

He sighed. "Yes, your father's associate, Harvey Mattson, went down for the murders, but it's more complicated than that. If you remembered who you saw that night—"

"I haven't."

"But we believe that whoever has been trying to kill you is afraid you will and there is a chance that you will remember and we can tie up all the loose ends on your father's case. But now you're going to have to be given a new identity once we pick you up and straighten out all your legal problems."

His words sent ice up her spine. "I'm telling you I wouldn't have run. My cover must have been blown."

"If that's true, then they already have come for

you again. Where are you? You need to come back in. We'll set you up—"

"No." Not again, she thought. She could barely remember who she'd once been. She was sick of living one lie after another. Her pulse pounded in her ears. "My cover was blown before I headed to Montana. Wait, there was a photo someone stuck under my door." It was of her and Garrett.

"When I went by your place I did see a photograph of you with a cowboy. Is that what you're talking about?"

Her heart leaped to her throat. She'd been right. Someone had found her. They'd wanted her back in Montana. They'd known she'd go to him to warn him. The threat had been clear.

"Look, it doesn't matter. You can't do this alone. You've already tried that."

No, she couldn't. "I'm serious. I'm done with all of it." She hung up and thought about taking the phone off the hook. She waited a few minutes, but he didn't call back. He was probably relieved to be rid of her. Either that or he was already on the phone to Alistair—if he hadn't already called him. Because if she hadn't been eligible for the Federal Witness Protection Program, then there was only one person who could have gotten her into it. Her guardian.

They would be able to find her now. A US Marshal could get the number from the landline within minutes. But she'd confirmed what she'd feared. Garrett was also in danger. Someone had sent her a photo of the two of them. It had been a warning.

Which meant that not only had her cover in the program been compromised but they had known about her and Garrett. But who had known about them? She'd been so sure that Garrett was her special secret, that she'd left quickly enough that she hadn't put him in danger.

She felt sick to her stomach. The photo had been a warning that they didn't just know where she was. They knew about Garrett. She'd known then that she had to warn him. What had happened after that, she had no idea until she'd awakened in the hospital with blood under her fingernails.

Standing in the starlight-filled lodge, she knew there was only one thing to do. She couldn't put it off any longer. She had to tell Garrett everything tonight. She hurried up the stairs to her room to dress.

WHEN THE PHONE rang in his room, Garrett picked it up quickly before it would awaken Joslyn. He knew it was Billy calling and was anxious to hear what he'd found out.

"I would have gotten back to you sooner, but your line was busy," the PI said. Before Garrett would consider what that meant, his friend added, "Are you sitting down?"

He had been lying in bed still fully clothed staring at the ceiling, but now he sat up. "How bad is it?"

"I found an article entitled, Poor Little Rich Girl, Monica Wilmington. You want me to read it to you or just give you the gist of it?"

"The gist."

"She lost her mother at three and her father and stepmother in a brutal murder at five."

Garrett let out a curse.

"It gets worse. Monica is believed to have witnessed the carnage. She was found hiding in a closet covered in blood."

Garrett got to his feet to walk to the window. The dark summer night did nothing to chase away the chill he felt. What would something like that do to a child? Or even an adult?

Billy continued. "Insiders say that the girl didn't speak a word for weeks. The only witness to the murders, Monica isn't just not talking. Insiders say she claims no memory of the incident. After that, she was being cared for by her father's close friend and prominent businessman Alistair Vanderlin. He's still her guardian—until she turns thirty."

He didn't know what to say. She'd been through so much. Was that why her family thought she needed medical attention? "So no immediate family?" He murmured the question, but realized Billy wasn't listening.

"Wait until you hear this. Her father left behind a *fortune*. Some went to stepdaughter Amethyst, who was thirteen when her mother and stepfather were murdered and stepson Peter, who was eleven. The bulk will go to Monica when she turns thirty, which is only days away. Garrett, I'm talking about over a *hundred million dollars*."

He thought he must have heard wrong. He was

speechless. Couldn't be the same woman. His Jos-lyn couldn't be this poor little rich girl.

As if his friend was questioning the same thing, he said, "Monica Wilmington. Is she your Joslyn? The possible murderess down the hall?"

"Possibly."

"Wow," Billy said. "I found some photos of her on a yacht in the Mediterranean taken with a tele-photo lens, it looks like, when she was in her teens. A couple more paparazzi shots at nightclubs when she was a little older. But then nothing. This woman is drop-dead beautiful. If she is the same woman…"

He wasn't sure of anything. "According to the sheriff who plans to pay us a visit in the morning she is Monica Wilmington." He turned at the soft tap on his door. "I have to go. Thanks for doing this. I owe you." He hung up. There was another soft tap at his door, this one more insistent.

Still overwhelmed by what he'd learned, he walked to the door and opened it to find Joslyn stand-ing there. Her amber eyes were wide and shiny.

"Garrett," she said on a ragged whispered breath. "I think there's someone—" The sound of glass breaking downstairs cut off the rest of her words.

CHAPTER SIXTEEN

"STAY HERE. LOCK the door. Don't open it for anyone but me," Garrett said as he pushed past her and headed for the stairs.

"Be careful," she called after him.

He couldn't miss the irony. He'd thought the real person he had to fear was the one sleeping down the hall from him. The last thing he'd expected was to hear someone breaking in. A hardened criminal like the one who'd tried to kill her, would have come in like a stealth bomber—not making all this racket.

At the top of the stairs, he slowed. The night even with the starlight was too dark to see who had shattered the window in the large front door to reach inside. He could hear the person fumbling with the lock. Within moments, the intruder would be inside.

Garrett descended the stairs quickly, going straight to his office and opening his gun cabinet. The shotgun was kept there, always loaded. He stuffed the pistol into the back waistband of his jeans and tucked his shirt over it. Usually the shotgun was for scaring away bears—not human prowlers. He stepped back in the dark of the main lounge at the same time the large door swung open.

"You're sure no one is up here?" said a young female voice from the darkness. "I saw a pickup—"

"The place is closed for the summer," a male voice said a moment before the young man stepped in and reached for the light switch. "We have the place to ourselves."

The young female giggled. "You're going to get me into trouble."

"He sure is," Garrett said, snapping on a nearby lamp.

For a moment the two in the doorway were blinded by the light, their faces caught in shocked surprise. The young female let out a shriek of alarm. The young male stared at Garrett, then the shotgun in his hands. "We were just going to—"

"I know what you were going to do," Garrett said. "But why don't you tell it to the sheriff after he calls your parents."

The young man nodded, before turning and barreling into his date.

Both finally got their feet under them to run toward the car parked down by the barn. Garrett walked out on the porch and watched them go. He could call the sheriff, but no real harm was done except to the window. He could get that replaced. He'd been young once. Hell, he still felt as randy as a teenager, he thought, turning to see Joslyn standing partway down the stairs.

She was hugging herself, looking scared. Sometimes he forgot that just a day ago a man had dragged her into the woods to kill her. At least that's what he thought he'd witnessed.

"It was just a couple of kids," he said coming in from the night and closing the door behind him. Glass glittered on the floor below the door window. He could hear the rev of the car engine as the two roared away. He locked the door even though anyone could reach in now to open it. One more repair to add to the contractor's punch list, he thought.

Settling his gaze on Joslyn, he thought about what Billy had told him. Poor little rich girl. His heart went out to the child Monica Wilmington had been. He couldn't imagine the kind of scars that would leave on a person.

"Are you all right?" he asked.

She nodded mutely, but he could tell she was still frightened.

"I could make you a cup of hot cocoa." He used to make it for her when they were together. He knew back then that she'd had trouble sleeping. Guilt?

She gave him a sad, knowing smile. "Earlier, I was coming down to your room to talk to you when I heard someone breaking in." She glanced toward the fireplace.

"Since it appears we won't be sleeping anytime soon I can build a fire to go with the cocoa."

Her face brightened. "A fire would be wonderful, but no cocoa, thank you. If you aren't too tired, I really do need to talk to you."

He thought about what Billy had said about the line being busy the first time he'd tried to call back.

That could only mean one thing. She'd called some-one. And now she was ready to talk?

Isn't this what he'd been telling himself he wanted? Just an explanation for what happened two years ago. But he realized he wanted a whole lot more than that. His heart thudded deep in his chest as he stepped to the fireplace and began to pile logs onto the embers. Behind him, he heard her come all the way down the stairs.

By the time he got a blaze going, she was curled up on the couch under one of the lap quilts that had been folded on the back of a leather chair.

"You sure you don't want hot cocoa?" he asked.

She shook her head.

"I have a feeling that I'm going to need a stiff drink. Can I make you one?"

"No, thanks." She seemed to wait as he went to the bar and poured himself a shot of bourbon and downed it in one gulp. He poured himself another. He would have dragged the bottle back to the couch in front of the fire, except he knew he had to keep his wits about him. He hardly ever drank—until Joslyn had returned to his life, he realized.

The fire crackled and flashed brightly as he sat down at the opposite end of the large leather couch so he could face her. So he could face whatever was coming. He took a sip of his drink, waiting, wondering what she was about to tell him and dreading it. He'd thought this woman couldn't hurt him any worse than she had. But at this moment he knew that too had been a lie.

SHE STUDIED HIM in the firelight. He'd closed his eyes and leaned back on the couch, stretching out his long denim-covered legs to prop his boots on the large square coffee table. Her cowboy. That's how she'd always thought of him. The only person she'd ever told about him was a young woman she'd struck up a conversation with on the bus one day when she was at her weakest. She'd had to tell someone about Garrett. Otherwise, none of it seemed real.

"It sounds like a summer fling," the woman had said. "I had one of those. They're hard to forget. But if the two of you had really loved each other, the kind of love that lasts, wouldn't you still be with him?"

"I had to leave him for his own good. It was the hardest thing I've ever done."

The woman had smiled and hugged her. "But you have such luscious memories. Be thankful. Memories are often better than reality," she'd said with a laugh as she rose to get off the bus at her stop.

But reality looked awfully good right now, she thought, unable to look away from the cowboy. She wanted to memorize this moment in time, hold it close, tuck it away so it would always be there. She smiled to herself, remembering how she used to watch Garrett sleep, doing the same thing. Memorizing snapshots of him. Imagining what he'd been like, what he would be later in life, knowing she wouldn't be there. Had he fallen asleep here in front of the fire as a boy? When he got older? This place fit him just as his boots and jeans and Stetson did.

"There was a time we would have done this naked," he said, his eyes still closed.

She swallowed around the sudden lump in her throat. "I know."

His eyes opened slowly and focused on her. She stared into all that familiar blue and felt her heart break. "Your memory coming back?" he asked.

Her voice broke when she spoke. "I could never forget you."

He stared at her for a long moment before he took a sip of his drink. "So it was all a lie, what you told the sheriff, everything?"

She knew what he was asking. "No. It's true that I've lost the days before I ended up in the hospital. That wasn't a lie, still isn't. But before that…" She met his gaze and swallowed again. She felt tears blur her eyes. "I was afraid to tell the sheriff, afraid I couldn't trust him."

"Afraid you couldn't trust me?"

She shook her head adamantly. "No. I just didn't know how to tell you. I still don't."

"Why don't you start with that night at the convenience store." There was hurt in his voice overlaid with anger. His blue eyes were bright and hard, his body still and stiff. He was waiting, coiled for the blow he knew was coming.

"I wasn't lying that night. If I'd had to stay there and talk to the police, give them my name…"

"You lied about being an undercover cop."

She sighed. "I've made a lot of mistakes in my

life. You weren't one of them. Unfortunately, you came along at the wrong time."

He chuckled. "Wrong time? That's why you didn't leave a note when you left. That's why you couldn't even say goodbye? You had to know that I was in love with you."

Hot tears welled and spilled down her cheeks. "I knew."

His handsome face seemed to crumple as he downed his drink and set the glass on the coffee table where his boot heels had rested only moments before. Sitting up, he leaned toward her as if he wanted to reach across the distance between them. "You still left without a word." He shot to his feet to move away from her to stand in front of the fire, his back to her, his hands buried deep in the front pockets of his jeans. He stood away from her as if he didn't trust himself. "Why, Joslyn? Just tell me why."

She stared at his broad back. "There'd been threats against my life before I met you. I needed some place to hide until I decided what to do."

GARRETT SPUN AROUND to stare at her. Was this just another lie? "So you hid out with me for a few months before you ran again," he said, realizing that even if it wasn't a lie, he was only a convenient stopover.

"It began that way, I'll admit." She met his gaze and held it. "I hadn't planned to stay long but then… I didn't want to leave. I thought maybe you and I…" She shook her head. "I was just kidding myself. People were looking for me. They would have found me.

They would have found you. Once I saw the engagement ring you bought…"

"You saw it and you still left?" He let out a harsh laugh. "So you knew I wanted to marry you."

Tears filled her eyes again. "I can't tell you how badly I wanted that, too." Her voice broke and she looked away.

He didn't say anything for a few moments, his mind racing. "What happened to you after you left?"

"I called the person who was to be my contact with the witness protection program and said I was ready to come in. They picked me up and gave me a new name, a new town. Not Joslyn Charles since I'd used that name with you."

He shook his head. "You're telling me you went into the witness protection program?" Was any of this true? "Then how did you end up on the mountainside across from my family's guest ranch?"

She shook her head. "That's what I don't know. But I remembered something tonight. I received a photograph of the two of us. I realized my cover was blown but more important that if they knew about you…" She locked gazes with him again. "That you were in danger and I had to warn you."

"A photograph?" He didn't want to believe her and knew he was afraid to. But there had been a map to the guest ranch. "None was found in the car you wrecked before being brought to the hospital." He waited for her to say something about the map.

"I don't know where the photograph is. I don't even know how I ended up in that car with that man."

She got up, casting off the quilt and took a step toward him. "The last thing I wanted was you involved in all this but the only thing that makes any sense is that I had been headed here to warn you when I ended up in the hospital."

He studied her, looking for the truth. How much of this did he believe? She'd had plenty of time to come up with this story. "Who did you call tonight?"

She started. She hadn't thought he'd find out. "My handler, a US Marshal. Apparently the sheriff ran my DNA and it came up on a federal site. That's how he found out that I'd bolted."

"If any of this is true, then you should have told me back then," he said angrily, thinking of the time they'd lost and all the if-onlys. "I would have gone with you."

She shook her head as she moved to stand before him. "I couldn't take you away from the ranch, from Montana, from everything and everyone you loved—"

"Not *everyone* I loved," he said, glaring at her. "You should have given me the choice."

"To go live somewhere with another name, another career, another life, living a lie?" She wiped at her tears, torn apart at the pain she saw in his handsome face. "I've done it. I know what it's like to leave behind someone you love knowing you can never see them again without risking both of your lives."

He chewed at his cheek for a moment. She saw the

anger slowly ebb from his features. In its place, she saw an unbearable sadness. "And yet here we are."

Joslyn nodded solemnly. "When I realized that you were in danger…" She swallowed. "I didn't think anyone knew about you two years ago. You remember my neighbor, the old busybody who lived in the duplex next door?"

"Devon Pierce."

It surprised her that he remembered the woman's name. "Garrett, when I went back to move my things out of my apartment, she told me about the man who had come around asking about me. She described him. I knew then that whoever had tried to kill me and sent me on the run had found me again. I didn't think he knew about you. It's also why I didn't want Devon to know about you."

Garrett looked away for a moment, his jaw muscle taut again. "I could have protected you if you'd only told me."

She shook her head. "I couldn't risk your life. I was putting your clothes away after I'd washed our laundry one day and I saw the engagement ring." Tears were streaming down her face again, but she couldn't stop them. All the pain of the past year and a half welled up inside her again. She was looking into Garrett's bright blue eyes, seeing the pain, feeling it heart deep.

"That must have been the last straw. You were out of there," he said.

She shook her head. "There wasn't anything I wanted more than a life with you."

"Then you should have stayed and we would have worked something out."

"Like now? They will be coming for me, for us—if they aren't already. Your life is in danger because of me. Because I stayed with you as long as I did back then. You need to disappear."

He laughed. "No, that's your thing. Whatever is coming for me, I'm staying right here and fighting."

She wiped at her tears. "I knew you'd say that. It's why I'm here. I had to warn you. I wanted you to at least have a fighting chance."

"What about you? The program giving you a new identity?"

"They want to, but I said no."

"You'd risk your life for me?"

She heard the sarcasm in his words. "I already have."

His eyes widened. He bowed his head. "I'm sorry. Excuse me for not reacting well to all of this. But you should take the feds' deal."

She shook her head. "I'm tired of running. A year and a half ago I thought I was saving you. Now I want to stay and fight. The problem is that I don't know who we have to fear. There is so much you don't know about me."

He met her gaze in the firelight. "I might surprise you, Monica."

CHAPTER SEVENTEEN

THE SHERIFF GOT the call the next morning early that Alistair Vanderlin was waiting for him in his office. He hadn't expected that. He'd spoken with him on the phone last night and had to tell him that Monica Wilmington was no longer in the hospital or behind bars. When he'd refused to say where she was, it hadn't gone over well.

"You do understand a court order, don't you?" Vanderlin had demanded. Sid hadn't liked the man from the get-go. Alistair Vanderlin was the type who was so used to getting his own way. The man had seemed shocked that a small-town sheriff would buck him.

"If you don't honor the court order, you will find yourself behind bars, Sheriff." He hadn't liked the way the man had said *sheriff*, either.

"I wouldn't dream of not honoring a court order— especially if the woman in question really is a danger to herself or others," Sid had said carefully.

"Are you questioning me on that?"

"My job is to question anything that doesn't feel right to me, Mr. Vanderlin. I have no idea who you are let alone why I should hand this woman over to you. She's under arrest here in my little burg. Another court order let her go to a safe place for her to recuperate. I can lock her up and hold her pending the rest of my investigation, trumping your court order or at least holding it up until this whole thing can go before a judge. And I will if I think it is in her best interest."

Alistair Vanderlin laughed. "You don't want to play hardball with me, Sheriff. I have no doubt that you know where Monica is. Honor the court order. You don't want to spend your retirement in prison." The man had hung up, leaving Sid fuming.

Was the woman a danger to herself and others? Other than her alleged memory loss, she'd seemed fine. Not that he was a doctor. He knew, along with disliking Alistair Vanderlin the first moment the man spoke, he wanted to help Garrett and the woman. But while he might be able to stall Vanderlin, he was pretty sure that his hands were tied. He would have to honor the court order to turn her over for a medical evaluation.

Now, the man was waiting for him down at the sheriff's department, no doubt with said court order in hand. He was anxious to meet Alistair Vanderlin and find out as much as he could about the woman staying high in the mountains at Sterling's Montana Guest Ranch with Garrett. First and foremost he was a lawman—at least for a while longer.

When he'd called the rancher last night to warn him, Sid could tell Garrett hadn't believed any of it.

Neither did he. But maybe they were both blind when it came to the woman.

As he walked into his office, he found a distinguished gray-haired man in a dark suit waiting in a chair across from his desk. The man rose as he entered. "Sheriff Anderson? I'm Alistair Vanderlin, Ms. Wilmington's guardian."

ALISTAIR HAD ALREADY made up his mind that he wouldn't be as confrontational as he'd been on the phone the night before. He studied the very fit, silver-haired Western sheriff. Always before when Monica got in trouble, he'd dealt with younger men, police in larger cities around the world. Usually Monica's ability to look innocence and money did the trick.

One look at Sheriff Sid Anderson and he knew there was no bribing this man. He shook the man's hand, not surprised by his strong grip.

"I'm a little confused why a woman her age has a guardian," the sheriff said as he took his place behind his desk.

Vanderlin settled into the chair he'd been sitting in earlier. "I'm not sure what she's told you…" He hesitated, and seeing that the sheriff wasn't going to respond continued. "But Monica is a very troubled woman and has been for some time. I'm here to make sure she gets the help she needs."

"And what kind of help is that?"

"Her medical condition is privileged information."

The sheriff leaned back in his chair. "Oh, come on, you've already said it's mental. I have a judge here in town who will take a look at your commitment order and if it isn't spelled out—"

"It's more than the fact that she isn't behaving rationally, although that is cause for concern. She'd been doing so much better before this. All I can assume is that something sparked this latest…ordeal."

"Ordeal?" The lawman let out a bark of a laugh. "Excuse me, but not many people would be behaving rationally after someone tried to kill them. I have an eyewitness who saw the whole thing." Not quite accurate but close enough with this man. "You're her guardian, what was she doing in Montana?"

"Truthfully, I have no idea. I was led to believe that she simply took off from where she'd been living and was gainfully employed."

"Since the feds are involved, I'm assuming she was in the witness protection program?"

Vanderlin sighed. "As I understand it. I just know that she had a habit of disappearing for months at a time. I would send her checks and sometimes they would come back, *addressee unknown*. For over a year now, the checks have gone automatically into an account for her. A few days ago, I was notified that she no longer had that account. That's when I knew that she'd disappeared again. I won't know what happened until I speak with her."

"That could be a problem. She doesn't remember. After the shooting, she escaped in the man's vehicle, was in an accident and has a head injury, which the doctor says could explain her lack of memory."

"Yes, I spoke with her doctor at the hospital. He

told me about the memory loss." Vanderlin nodded. "It wouldn't be the first time she's lost her memory after...an incident. Her doctor wants her under observation back in Seattle. I've hired several attendants to take her by ambulance."

"What kind of hospital?"

"Not what you're imagining. It's much like a resort. Most of the patients are there for drugs or alcohol rehabilitation, unlike Monica."

"Privileged or not, I need to know what I'm dealing with here. I have a body in the morgue and your...ward killed him. She has information I need to close my case."

Alistair looked away for a moment before he settled his gaze on the sheriff again. He could see that butting heads with his man would get him nowhere. "Her psychiatrist is afraid that she suffers from DID, dissociative identity disorder, formerly known as a split personality."

SID SAT BACK after making a disbelieving sound. "You can't be serious."

"It's very rare, usually brought on by some form of trauma."

"What trauma brought hers on?"

He could see Alistair reining in his impatience. "Monica saw her father and stepmother murdered when she was five. Anyone would have been traumatized by something so horrific. She didn't speak at all for weeks after that and still claims to have no memory of the event. But unfortunately, she had begun to show symptoms of DID."

"How long ago was that?" Sid asked.

"Two years ago."

About the time Garrett met her.

"Like this time, she had taken off without a word. I hired a private investigator to find her. She was convinced her life was in danger and demanded help, calling the FBI without my knowledge. She believed that the man behind bars for her father's and stepmother's murders all those years ago had sent someone to kill her. She was the only eyewitness to their murders, but she couldn't testify at the trial because she had no memory of the crime."

Sid frowned. "So how was she able to get into the witness protection program?"

"I had to pull a few strings but since she was the only witness..."

He could just imagine what kind of strings the man had to pull.

"She believes that the man the police arrested, the man who claims to be innocent, isn't the real killer but that he holds her responsible for his being in prison because she is the only one who can clear him, if that makes any sense." Vanderlin shook his head.

"The feds must have believed her for them to allow her to go into the program even if you had to pull a few strings."

The man nodded. "You can see why I was upset to hear that she'd left it the way she had—and had immediately ended up in the hospital after an…incident."

"Wait. So you didn't even know where she was before this?" Sid asked.

"No. I didn't know if she was alive or dead, quite frankly. It wasn't until a US Marshal contacted me. He hadn't even known where she was until her DNA came through the system. Then I got a call from Seattle law enforcement. You sent her photo over the wire. They recognized her since there have been numerous stories about her and the murder over the years. That's how I found out she was in the hospital here." He shook his head as if the young woman had been a trial for years and that this was just more of the same.

Sid didn't know what to believe. "This memory loss—"

"A symptom of her dissociative identity disorder. The problem is that it seems to be getting worse. At this point, I fear for her safety. That's why I requested the judge's order to take her back for treatment. She will be safe there and available for future inquiries from you should this…incident go to trial."

Sid asked the question that had been nagging at him. "Did you know she was in Montana another time? Two years ago?"

The question seemed to take the attorney by surprise. "I was not aware of that. It couldn't have been for long. It isn't where the private investigator I hired said he found her." Vanderlin looked confused. "That's odd. You're sure she's been here before?"

Sid nodded, but didn't elaborate. "Not that it's important at this point. What is the treatment for DID?"

The guardian shook his head. "It varies, but the process is often very intensive and extensive."

"So you're saying that if she has this DID, that she could be locked up for a long time."

"I wish there were another way." Vanderlin got to his feet. "I have attendants standing by to take her back to Seattle as soon as possible. I had asked that she be kept at the hospital, but I was informed that she was released yesterday."

Sid also got to his feet. "I'm going to have to look into that judge's order."

The man scowled. "I had hoped it wouldn't come to this." Vanderlin had to know he was stalling and seemed about to put up a fight, but changed his mind. "That will be fine as long as you can assure me she is somewhere safe."

Sid nodded. "I'll wait to hear from the judge, but I'm curious. How did you become her legal guardian?"

"I was a close friend of her father's. He made me promise that if anything happened to him, I would take care of his daughter."

GARRETT WOKE TO the smell of bacon frying. At first he thought he was dreaming, but as he hurriedly dressed and went downstairs, he found Joslyn in the kitchen, cooking. He'd thought he might find her gone—just like the morning. He couldn't believe how late it was, almost noon.

They'd stayed up most of the night talking. She'd told him all about her childhood growing up, all the trouble she'd gotten into, all the time feeling as if at any moment her life could end.

"My doctor, Neal Foster, says that it stems from seeing my father and stepmother murdered," she'd said. "All I know is that I feel as if most of my life I've been running from something. That was until I met you. It was the first time I wanted to stay."

After everything she'd told him, he'd felt exhausted and unsure. He still didn't trust her. There'd been too many lies. Hell, he wasn't even sure she wasn't lying still.

"What are you doing?" he asked, unable to hide his surprise that she hadn't taken off without a word again—and that she was cooking. Joslyn had never been an early riser. After their late night, he couldn't imagine her up—even though it was almost noon—let alone cooking.

She jumped at the sound of his voice and spun around. He'd startled her. She'd apparently been lost in thought. "Is it all right if I make breakfast for lunch?"

The woman he knew couldn't make toast in a toaster. "I'm not sure. Can you cook?"

"Apparently," she said with a wave of her hand to indicate what she'd done so far.

His stomach rumbled at the sight of crisp bacon and a stack of fluffy-looking lightly browned pancakes. "That actually looks delicious." He couldn't help sounding skeptical though.

"You of so little faith," she said and laughed, but it lacked humor. They were both tentative with each other this morning. Not that he hadn't wanted to take her in his arms last night and make love to her. But he'd kept her at arm's length until he'd suggested they get what sleep they could and talk in the morning.

"Thank you for bringing me here," she'd said. "No matter what happens…"

He'd nodded. His head had been spinning with everything she'd told him and he'd been angry and hurt and unforgiving. She should have told him eighteen months ago. That she'd denied him the chance of going with her killed him inside.

Picking up one of the pancakes, he tore off a piece and popped it into his mouth. "Yum." Apparently she'd learned to cook. Or she'd been holding out on him back then. Another lie?

He pushed the thought away.

Clearly, he was still upset this morning. He wasn't sure how much he believed of what she'd told him. But last night's kiss had brought back way too many memories of the two of them and why he'd fallen in love with her to begin with. Why he'd also bought the engagement ring and had planned to marry her. Why when she'd disappeared the way she had, it had broken his heart and as Dorothea had pointed out, had ruined him for any other woman.

That Joslyn could still get to him like that with one kiss scared him. He'd told himself he wasn't susceptible to her charms. He really had to quit lying to himself.

Reaching into the cabinet, he pulled down a bottle of huckleberry syrup. He'd introduced her to huckleberry syrup two years ago. He wondered if she would remember that, as he set the table.

Joslyn seemed proud of herself as they took the food over and sat across from each other. If she was worried about what the sheriff had to tell them, she didn't show it. "Please, help yourself," she said, smiling.

Everything smelled delicious. He slathered butter on the pancakes, then syrup and took a bite. He felt his eyes widen in surprise. "Seriously, they're really good."

"I wish you'd quit sounding so surprised. They're pancakes. Anyone can make them with a recipe book and the right ingredients."

"You used a recipe book?"

"Actually, I made them from scratch. It's an old family recipe."

Garrett couldn't help staring at her. An old family recipe? He leaned an elbow on the table and rested his chin on it. "Let me get this straight. You said you didn't cook during the time we were together."

"I'd never cooked. It was true."

"Then how do you explain making these pancakes from an old family recipe?"

"I looked around for a cookbook, but couldn't find one. So I started putting ingredients together and as I did I remembered a recipe my favorite nanny used to make… It was *her* old family recipe. I must have watched her make it and remembered it. Strange, huh."

"Your mother didn't cook?"

"She died when I was two. I don't really remember her and I'm pretty sure my stepmother never cooked. Amethyst, my stepsister? She told me that we had staff that did all that."

He'd forgotten for a moment what Billy had told him about the woman being heir to a fortune. Joslyn hadn't mentioned it last night. The omission was not a lie exactly, right? "You had a favorite nanny?"

"Didn't everyone," she joked. "My father made a lot of money." She shrugged. "I honestly don't remember that part of my life."

"So your stepsister, Amethyst, is eight years older and your stepbrother is six years older."

She nodded. "We aren't close because of the age difference and probably the fact that we don't share a parent."

He wondered if that was all it was. "And your guardian?" he prompted.

"Alistair?" She smiled. "He's in his late sixties. He's always seemed old and stuffy to me. He wasn't like a father figure. His job was to make sure I was fed and clothed and educated."

"You went to college?"

"Several universities before I got kicked out." She stopped eating to look down at her plate. "I was a troubled young woman, he would tell you. Rebellious. I got kicked out of some of the best schools that money could buy."

He nodded and went back to eating, but his appetite was severely affected. She'd hinted at the wealth she'd grown up with again, but hadn't come out and told him. He thought of what Billy had read him. Poor little rich girl.

Joslyn looked up from her plate. "I didn't care about anything. Until I met you. Then I cared too much."

He held her gaze for a long moment, thinking about the two of them in front of the fire last night and what she'd told him. Had she thought by confessing everything that it would wipe out the hurt, the pain, the anger and disappointment he'd felt? When she'd left, he'd thought he would never see her again.

When he had... She had no idea how much he wanted to trust her. He would love to take up where they'd left off. Last night he'd ached to tear down the wall he'd built between them and carry her upstairs to his bedroom. But he'd known that making love to her wouldn't erase the pain and all the lies between them.

"Joslyn—"

They both turned at the sound of a vehicle pulling up out front. He recognized the sheriff's patrol car. He reminded himself that the sheriff said he would be bringing her family, but the only person in the patrol car was Sid.

"I should have told you last night," he said as his gaze returned to her. She wasn't the only one keeping secrets, he realized. "The sheriff said that your family was coming up this morning to take you back home."

Her amber eyes went wide. "Home? You mean

to Seattle? Are you sure it's Alistair who's sending for me?"

"Apparently your doctor wants to take a look at you and make sure you're all right." He knew this wasn't exactly what Sid had told him. But Joslyn looked upset enough without telling her that her guardian had threatened a court order to take her back to a mental facility.

He pushed away his plate and rose. "Thank you for telling me the truth last night."

She didn't look as if she'd heard as she rose. She looked like a woman who wanted to run.

"We should see what the sheriff has to say." Garrett motioned for her to lead the way. She hesitated but only for a moment, looking resigned. That's how he felt. Resigned to letting her go with her family. He didn't know where he and Joslyn went from here. Maybe nowhere. The thought was like a knife to his chest.

They walked out to the front porch as the sheriff got out of his patrol SUV.

Sid looked from him to Joslyn and back. "Did you tell her?"

"I told her that her guardian was coming to take her back to her doctor to make sure she was all right."

"That's not all, is it?" she asked Sid, her voice breaking.

Out of the corner of his eye, Garrett saw the ambulance come around the barn and head for the lodge. Joslyn saw it, too. Panic filled her face. She took a step back, the word *no* whispered on a surprised breath.

"Tell me what's going on," Garrett said, stepping to her and taking her arm. "You look as if you've seen a ghost. Tell me before it's too late."

"It's already too late," she said in wide-eyed horror as two attendants climbed from the ambulance and rushed toward her. She met his gaze an instant before they grabbed her. "You're not safe, Garrett. Don't trust anyone. No matter what happens, I'll always be your Joslyn."

The attendants grabbed her, pulling her away from him. She looked back at him, tears in her eyes along with terror.

"Hey, take it easy with her." He'd thought he could let her go. Now though, he wasn't so sure. He started down the steps after her, only to have the sheriff restrain him.

"What's going on?" he demanded of Sid. "You said they were taking her back, but not like this."

"They have a court order to take her," the sheriff said. "There is nothing you can do."

He watched in horror as one of the attendants pulled out a syringe and jabbed the needle in her arm.

Garrett pulled free of the sheriff's strong grip only to have Sid step in front of him, blocking his way.

"I don't want to have to arrest you," the sheriff said, keeping his voice down. "They have a court order to take her. Like I said, there is nothing either of us can do. Don't make me cuff you."

"They're treating her like…" He looked to the

sheriff. "She's not crazy." But at that moment, he felt as if *he* was. "We were just eating breakfast. She…" He couldn't continue as the attendants rolled out a gurney and placed her on it. He could see that the sedative was working. Her knees seemed to buckle as they lifted her onto it.

Garrett caught her gaze and tried to hold it, needing her to reassure him. But her eyes were unfocused. Whatever they'd given her was about to knock her out.

"She isn't who you think she is," the sheriff said, still restraining him.

"Joslyn," he called to her. Her eyes had closed, but she forced them open and looked right at him. For a moment he thought she no longer recognized him. Then, just before the attendants closed the ambulance door, she mouthed two words.

Help me.

CHAPTER EIGHTEEN

"Damn it, I have to do something," Garrett swore as he tried to push past the sheriff. The man was stronger than he looked. He heard the click of handcuffs an instant before one was snapped to his wrist.

"You settle down or I am going to take you in." Another *click*.

Garrett looked down to see that Sid had put the other cuff on his own wrist.

He let out of a howl of frustration. "You can't just let them take her. Sid, she doesn't want to go with them. You saw her reaction. She's terrified."

Sid shook his head. "Like I said, there is nothing I can do. Nothing you can do, either. I told you bringing her up here was a bad idea."

He looked to where one ambulance attendant had climbed into the back and was now closing the door. His last glimpse was of her strapped down in the back.

Garrett's voice took on an urgent pleading tone. "She told me everything. She really doesn't remember what happened with the man who tried to kill her on the ridge." The other attendant slid behind the wheel. He heard the ambulance engine rev and Garrett pulled hard on the handcuff.

"Listen to me, Garrett," the sheriff said, waving a hand in front of him to get his attention. "You've lost all perspective. You can't think around this woman. Apparently, she needs medical help or a judge wouldn't have sent a commitment order."

"She needs *me*," he argued as the ambulance pulled away. "You saw her when they drove up. She was scared stiff. She came up here with me because she felt safe."

"She could have killed you in your sleep and taken off with your pickup."

Garrett stared after the ambulance. Sid was wrong. All of this was wrong. He had to do something. He didn't know what, but his gut told him she was in trouble. Whoever those guys were, whoever had sent them, she shouldn't have been that terrified. He recalled what she'd said about not knowing whom they had to fear.

He felt light-headed from the anger, the confusion and a sinking feeling of dread. He kept his gaze on the ambulance, afraid to let it out of his sight.

"If you interfere with this court order, you'll get arrested. I don't want to be the one to lock you up, but I will," the sheriff said. "Listen, I spoke with Mr. Vanderlin this morning and—"

"Who the hell is Mr. Vanderlin?" Garrett interrupted as he lost sight of the ambulance, his panic growing.

"Her guardian and the person who has her power

of attorney," Sid said. "You need to calm down. I hope once you have time to think about this, you'll—"

"You know something is wrong with all this," Garrett argued. "What is she doing with a guardian at her age? She's not crazy."

The sheriff let out a sigh. "It's confusing and upsetting, especially given your relationship with her. But at least now you know her real name. Monica Wilmington. I stalled them as long as I could to give you the time with her. I shouldn't have even done that," he said. "You aren't going to like this, but you're going to have to accept that you don't know this woman."

The sheriff was right about one thing. He had to at least appear calmer or he would end up behind bars. He nodded, pretending to give in.

"WHY DON'T WE go inside and talk," Sid suggested. Garrett had been staring after the ambulance but now seemed to be resigned that there was nothing he could do. Once inside, he unlocked the handcuffs from their wrists before recounting everything that Alistair Vanderlin had told him about Monica, hoping he could get through to him.

"Split personality?" Garrett scoffed. "I don't believe it. No. There is no way she has multiple personalities."

"You don't think Joslyn Charles could have been one of them?"

The sheriff could see that his question took the

wind out of the rancher's sails. Garrett sat down heavily in one of the lodge's leather chairs and dropped his head into his hands. "She's not crazy. The guy's lying and you have to ask yourself why."

"He seemed pretty convincing," Sid said. "He's known her a lot longer than you have." He held up his hands when he saw Garrett's angry expression. "Just saying, what if you're wrong and it's true?"

"What if it's *not* true? What if she's in trouble? She thinks someone is trying to kill her? Well, I saw that man damn sure try and now two men just took her away in an ambulance after sedating her. What if she never makes it as far as Seattle?"

"No one but her knows exactly what happened on the side of that mountain and she says she can't remember. Memory loss is one of the symptoms, according to Alastair and he says—"

"Who has a name like Alastair Vanderlin anyway?" the rancher snapped.

"These memory losses are getting worse," he continued as if Garrett hadn't spoken. "Alistair said the first time she had a traumatic breakdown she wasn't able to communicate for weeks. Her memory loss is apparently getting worse and that's why he thinks it is urgent that she be taken to a place where she can get treatment."

Garrett raked a hand roughly through his hair in obvious frustration. "She's in trouble. I feel it." He shook his head and then stopped suddenly, a strange look coming to his face. "She was in the witness protection program but bolted because she said someone left her a photo of the two of us. She knew then that her cover was blown and that they knew about me. She'd thought she'd kept the two of us a secret. It was why she originally left me without a word—to go into the program. Don't you see? She doesn't know who to trust and now, who knows where they are really taking her?"

He didn't like seeing the rancher this worked up. He feared he'd do something stupid and end up behind bars.

Garrett was on his feet before Sid could stop him. "She's convinced someone is trying to kill her," the rancher called over his shoulder as he headed for the door. "How do we know it isn't the person who got the court order to have her brought back to Seattle? And you just let them take her."

"Damn it, Garrett," he called after him. But the rancher was down the front steps and almost to his pickup before Sid could get out the door. He heard the pickup's engine roar and had a bad feeling about where he was headed. "It was a court order. There was nothing I could do," he said under his breath as Garrett took off in a cloud of dust.

GARRETT KNEW COWS and grazing and ranching. He didn't know squat about any of the psychological complications of trauma or split personality disorder. What if he was wrong and she really did need medical help? That was the question that plagued him as he drove like a bat out of hell toward Whitefish.

Well, he'd been wrong before, he thought. Only

this time, it could get him thrown in jail—if not killed. He thought about what Joslyn had told him about why she'd left the safety of the government's witness protection program to come warn him that he was in danger. It had almost gotten her killed.

How could he stand by now and not help her? He thought of her mouthing the words, *Help me*, and was even more convinced he was right. He'd seen the look in her eye. She was terrified. She hadn't wanted to go with the attendants. There was no one else to help her. He had to save her.

He thought about calling his brothers because he was smart enough to know he would need help. But he was also smart enough to know that the last thing he needed was them trying to talk him out of this. Or worse, stopping him.

Reaching town, he whipped down an alley, stopped and threw his pickup into Park as he jumped out. "Don't shoot!" he called as he burst through the back door of Mitchell Investigations.

"Damn it, you crazy cowboy," Billy said, laughing. "You come back to find someone on Facebook again?"

"You're going to wish that was all I wanted," he said. "I have a huge favor, but I should warn you up front it's not just dangerous. It's illegal."

His friend laughed. "Don't sugarcoat it on my account."

"I can explain on the way, but at least this time I'm paying you for your services if you're interested."

"Great, that will make it so much better when

I'm standing before a judge at my sentencing hearing." He shook his head as he stood and grabbed his jacket. "Should I bring a weapon?"

"I'm hoping it won't come to that," Garrett said.

"Then I definitely better grab one." Billy stepped to a closet. Behind the door was a gun safe. He spun the dial, opened the door and pulled out a shotgun and two handguns. He tossed one of the handguns to Garrett, before grabbing ammo, which he stuffed into his jacket pocket. "So what's this one's name?" he asked as they went out the back door to the waiting pickup.

"Pardon?" Garrett asked as he climbed behind the wheel and Billy slid the shotgun on the rack behind their heads before jumping in.

"Tell me it's not that woman."

"It's Joslyn..." He glanced over at his friend as he started the engine and pulled out. "Or Monica Wilmington. Either way, she's in trouble."

His friend let out a low whistle. "Define trouble."

Garrett tipped his hat back and took a breath. It felt like his first since the attendants had closed that ambulance door. "Her guardian got a judge to write a commitment order on her. This morning two big burly dudes tossed her into an ambulance. They said they were taking her back to Seattle to what sounds like a mental hospital fronting as a five-star rehab. But I have a bad feeling that she'll never make it that far if I don't go save her."

Billy laughed. "So we're talking crazy trouble."

"She isn't crazy." He told his friend about what

Alistair Vanderlin had told the sheriff. "She doesn't have a split personality. Nor did she imagine that someone was trying to kill her."

Billy was quiet for a long while before he said, "I'm sure you have a plan."

He chewed at his cheek for a moment before he said, "I thought we'd break her out the first chance we get."

Billy said, "I see... So no plan. You sure about this?"

"I'm sure about *her*." One night after too many beers, he'd told Billy about the only woman he'd ever loved enough to want to spend the rest of his life with her.

Now his friend leaned back, settling in for the ride. "What do you know about this place they're allegedly taking her?"

"Nothing. That's another reason we have to catch the ambulance and rescue her before they reach wherever they are taking her." He could feel Billy's gaze on him but didn't dare look at him. He didn't want to see the incredulity in his friend's gaze. "Fortunately, the fastest way to Seattle from Montana is the interstate so I suspect that's where they're headed."

When he finally did glance over at Billy, his buddy was smiling and shaking his head. Garrett relaxed, knowing that the PI was in for long haul, whatever was ahead. Billy Mitchell had always been that kind of friend.

"Do they know your pickup?" Billy asked.

"No."

"Well, that's something. Try to keep your speed under eighty. I'll watch for highway patrol. Too bad we have a speed limit in Montana again. I liked it back when we didn't and if you got pulled over it would cost you five bucks. My old man used to carry a stack of fives when we crossed the state. Could cost us a lot more now if we get stopped, including valuable time."

Garrett shot him a grateful look. "Thanks. I knew I could count on you."

"Which is why you didn't ask your brothers for help," his friend said with a laugh. "I suspect they would have called the sheriff and there'd be a BOLO out on you."

"Probably will. When I left the sheriff… Well, let's just say he probably knows what I'm up to."

"Yep. Sounds like we're racing against the clock."

Garrett roared down the highway, trying to keep the speedometer hovering around eighty. He knew this was an ill-conceived idea, but Billy was nice enough not to point it out. All he'd thought about was finding Joslyn and rescuing her.

He could just hear what Dorothea would have had to say about what he was doing. Worse, he was dragging Billy into it. "You could lose your PI license if this goes sideways. I can let you out up the road if you want to change your mind."

Billy laughed. "And let you do something this stupid alone? Not a chance. I'm the voice of reason and I have a feeling you're going to need me. You might want to slow down up here. There's always a speed trap this time of year for the next few miles, then we should be home-free."

"Something is wrong with all of this, beginning with the guardian," Garrett said.

Billy pulled out his phone. "I agree. If they are so loaded with this massive fortune, then why not put her on a plane?"

"Because they immediately gave her something that knocked her out," he said.

"Okay, that would explain the ambulance. They can keep her sedated. You're right, that does sound suspicious. But they could also be worried about her hurting herself or someone else."

"So they want us to think."

"Assuming they want to get her back to the hospital as quickly as possible..." Billy considered the map on his phone. "Highway 2 down to the interstate, then a straight shot to Seattle. Depending on whether they turn on the lights and siren, I'd say it will take them about nine hours—if they don't stop for anything other than gas and coffee." He turned to Garrett. "How much of a head start do they have?"

"Thirty minutes to an hour, I'd say."

His friend laughed and put away his phone. "I've never seen a highway patrol on this next section of road. Step on it for a while."

He got the truck up to eighty-five, cruising speed. Unfortunately this was summer, tourist season, so they hadn't gone far when they were slowed down by a car pulling a small trailer.

He watched for a chance to pass, feeling Joslyn

slipping away. When the road straightened with no cars oncoming, he passed and got up to ninety.

"It's early enough that most of the tourists aren't on the highway yet," Billy said. "Also, most are headed the other way—toward Glacier Park, rather than leaving it this morning. We'll catch her."

Garrett knew his friend was trying to reassure him even though common sense told him this was a fool's errand. The ambulance might have dropped south to the interstate. Or it might not even be going to Seattle. Vanderlin could have lied. At this point, he didn't trust the man.

He drove, dodging in and out of the growing traffic on the two-lane highway until they reached the interstate and he could breathe a sigh of relief. Now, he would be able to make better time.

Billy leaned back in his seat and closed his eyes. "Wake me if you need me. I'm going to get a little shut-eye. I figure when we catch her, things could get busy."

THE SHERIFF PICKED up the newspaper and swore. The lead story was about the shooting, including that the gun had been used in another shooting two years ago in Missoula.

"Damn, Ward," he said under his breath. He knew where the leak had come from. His undersheriff had been buddying up to the press for weeks, thinking it would help him in his run for sheriff in the fall election.

Sid's first instinct was to fire him, but he couldn't

prove the man had been the leak. Ward had been with the sheriff's department for enough years that he would need more than suspicions to fire him.

Instead he had to solve this case and then retire and in that order. Let Ward run for sheriff. Hopefully someone better would run against him and win. But that wasn't his problem right now.

He crumpled up the newspaper and tossed it toward the trash. He missed, but his mind had already moved on. He was worried about Garrett Sterling. The damned fool had gone after that woman sure as hell. He'd thought about trying to track him down but had decided his time would be better spent solving this case and he couldn't bring himself to put out a BOLO on him. He needed to talk to the clerk from the convenience-store robbery. The gun was the key. If he could track down where it had been the past two years...

Now that he knew Monica Wilmington's past and her connection to Harvey Mattson, he had to assume that was who'd hired the stiff in his morgue. The only problem with that theory was the weapon used to kill the man. It was tied to the convenience-store robbery two years ago—and the woman Garrett knew as Joslyn Charles aka Monica Wilmington.

He needed to talk to the clerk to find out where he'd gotten the unregistered gun and where it had been. The only way he could sort this out was good old law-enforcement procedure, which was slow and often dull as dirt.

His phone rang. He groaned, afraid it would be more bad news.

"We got a match on that DNA sample you sent," the lab tech said without preamble. "We put a rush on it and got lucky. Matches a former inmate by the name of Leon Sheffield."

Sid had never heard the name before. After he hung up, he looked him up on the computer database and then called the warden at Montana State Prison. He told him what he had. "You familiar with him?"

"I'm sure you saw that he has a rap sheet longer than your arm. Most recently? A gun for hire."

"Are we talking hit man?" the sheriff asked in surprise.

The warden laughed. "Not a good one. He wounded the last person he shot, got caught and went to prison. He's only been out a few months."

Sid thought about how Joslyn—he couldn't help but think of her as Joslyn Charles—had managed to get the drop on Leon and put four bullets into his heart. "Well, his gun-for-hire days are over now. Send me what you have on him, especially any known associates there at prison. One in particular actually. Frankie Rutledge."

He explained that the gun from the convenience store robbery was the tie-in. Frankie's younger brother George had been killed with the same gun that killed Leon Sheffield. Joslyn had been at both crime scenes.

The warden made a surprised sound. "I can tell you right now. Rutledge and Sheffield didn't travel in the same circles. But I'll see what I can find out."

Sid hung up, disappointed. He thought he'd found a link. Garrett said that Joslyn had told him that she'd gotten a photo of both herself and the rancher and had recognized the threat. He could see where Frankie might blame the rancher for what happened. Garrett had been the one to knock Frankie out during the robbery, which in turn led to his brother being shot down by the clerk.

It was a stretch. What made his theory fall through though was that Frankie couldn't have known about Joslyn. Garrett had helped her get away while Frankie was out cold and his brother George was dead. Garrett didn't even know Joslyn's real name back then.

Well, he still had the clerk. It was a lead at least so he had to follow to see where it took him. It beat worrying about Garrett who was probably hot on the woman's trail thinking he was going to save her. Sid groaned, remembering what Alistair Vanderlin had told him.

Was she as unstable as her guardian believed? What worried Sid was that she might be guilty of more than just breaking Garrett's heart two years ago.

He agreed with the rancher at least on one thing. Something was very wrong with all of this. The lawman in him could feel it and that was what had him anxious.

CHAPTER NINETEEN

GARRETT LOOKED DOWN at the gas gauge and swore. "We're going to have to stop for gas at this next town."

"They're going to have to stop as well," Billy pointed out as he sat up from his nap, no doubt seeing how upset Garrett was.

Shouldn't they have caught up to the ambulance by now? What if it was behind them, had pulled off for gas and they missed the van?

He glanced over at his friend. "This is one of my more stupid ideas, isn't it?"

Billy laughed. "Would I be along if that was true?"

He laughed as well. "It's like looking for a needle in a haystack."

Nodding, his friend said, "When you're looking for a needle in a haystack, it all comes down to luck. Maybe you'll get lucky."

Garrett scoffed at that. He couldn't help feeling as if his luck had run out. To see Joslyn again, to get so close and then to have her snatched away before... Before what?

Last night, she'd finally told him the truth. He'd been so angry with her for not telling him what was going on at the time that he hadn't been able to forgive her. It had all come as such a shock, finding out about what had happened to her as a child and the life she'd led and then the whole going into the witness protection program and not telling him.

It had been too much. His biggest fear was that he might never see her again. He could admit that now as he sped down the highway that he'd wanted more than an explanation for what had happened two years ago. He wanted her. He wanted to turn back the clock, start over.

But what if Vanderlin had been telling the truth? What if the woman was more than flawed? What if Joslyn Charles had only existed in his mind—and hers?

He shook his head, reminding himself of what he'd seen in those amber eyes. She'd had her reasons for lying about who she was back then. What they'd had was real. And after their recent kiss? It was still real.

It was ten miles to the next town and gas. He tried to relax his hands on the wheel. But his mind was racing. There was so much he hadn't said to her last night. So much he wanted to say now. He'd been angry and hurt last night. Scared, too. He'd been afraid to trust her.

But seeing her taken away from him like that… He shook his head. He loved her. Had loved her for all this time. Whatever her problems, they'd work it out together.

He knew it was more complicated than that. Loving her was one thing. Really trusting her with his heart again…

First things first, he told himself. He'd find her. That's if he could find her. Find her before… That was just it, he thought, his pulse jumping at the thought. "I can't shake the feeling that Joslyn is in serious danger."

"That's reasonable since someone recently tried to kill her," Billy said.

"If we don't find her in time—"

"We'll find her."

"She said she didn't know who was after her. After the two of us." Billy said nothing. "Whoever hired the man will try again. But why? That's what's driving me crazy. Why does someone want her dead? She's never remembered who killed her parents. After all these years, that doesn't seem like a real threat. It's got to be the money."

"That's a shit pile of coin," his friend agreed. "People have killed for a lot less."

"But then that would mean that someone close to her was the attempted killer," he said. Isn't that what he feared?

"There isn't any chance that she's starting to re-member who she saw the night her father and step-mother were murdered, right?"

He glanced over at the PI. "She can't even remem-ber what happened a few days ago."

"Just a thought," Billy said. "You're right. It's probably family or someone close to her that has access to the money."

"That's why I'm acting like a crazy man by going after her. I don't trust these people and I don't think

Joslyn does, either." Even if he didn't catch the ambulance, he would go to every sanitarium in Seattle. He would find her.

The exit came up fast. He took it, looking for the first gas station. These towns along the interstate between Whitefish and Seattle were small. There was only one gas station, a large new convenience store slash casino slash fast food mart all rolled into one.

He pulled into the first open bay and started to get out when Billy grabbed his arm to stop him and let out a curse. "Like I said, it all comes down to luck, and buddy, you are one lucky bastard." Billy pointed to the ambulance that had just refueled and was pulling out, headed back to the interstate.

SID MADE A few calls and tracked down former convenience store clerk Jerry Fulton. The man had quit the convenience store after the robbery, gone back to college for a while and ended up working for a highway contractor. Right now they were putting up a new bridge down by Polson.

Grabbing his hat, Sid headed for the door. He wanted to talk to Jerry in person, get a feel for the now twenty-nine-year-old. He found the young man leaning on a shovel at the new bridge site as he waited for some heavy equipment to finish a job and move.

Sid flashed his badge even though he was in uniform and had driven up in a sheriff's department rig. "Can you spare a minute to talk?"

Jerry glanced at a man who was obviously in

charge of the job. The man motioned for him to go ahead and take his break. Sid and Jerry walked back to the patrol SUV but stopped short of climbing inside.

"What's this about?" Jerry asked, sounding scared.

"The convenience-store robbery and shooting."

The young man looked down at his boots, stalling. He dug the toe of his boot into the dirt and rubbed the back of his neck, clearly nervous. "I already told the cops everything I know. Why are you asking about it again?"

"You had a gun behind the counter," Sid said. "Where did you get it?"

Jerry's left eye began to twitch. "It was one I picked up. I hated working the night shift. It didn't feel safe and as it turned out…"

"Do you remember where you got it?"

"A gun show."

"Did you know it was unregistered?"

"You mean did the guy make me fill out some papers on it, no." Jerry rubbed his neck again, then stuffed his hands into the pockets of his jeans as if not knowing what to do with them. "Is that a problem?"

"Do you know what happened to the gun after the shooting was over?"

The young man frowned, looking down at his work boots again. "I just assumed the cops took it."

"Did you see it between the time you dropped it and when the cops arrived?"

Jerry shook his head, avoiding eye contact for a

moment. "Look, I don't remember much about that night. It was a nightmare I've tried to forget. I looked into that man's eyes…" He shuddered. "Have you ever looked into cold-blooded evil?" Sid had. "If that cowboy hadn't hit him… And then when his brother came charging in, I could tell he planned to kill every last one of us."

"That's when you pulled the gun you had behind the counter and shot George Rutledge," Sid said.

"I was afraid to go for the gun before that," Jerry said. "I'd never been so scared in my life. I just pulled the gun and started firing. It was so surreal. I couldn't believe when it was over that I was still alive."

"What about the woman?"

Jerry seemed to start at the question. "Like I told the cops, there was a woman in the store at the time, but I don't remember her."

"And a boy of about eight or nine? Did you happen to see him?"

Jerry frowned again. "I did see a kid. I'd been watching him when the crazy guy with the gun entered the store. Kids that age—ones that are alone…" He shrugged. "You have to watch them or they steal you blind."

It was clear that Jerry's experience as a convenience-store clerk had left him cynical. But it was also clear that he was more comfortable talking about thieving kids than the robbery.

"Did you see the boy leave?" Sid asked.

"Once the man with the gun came in… I didn't

see anything but the dark end of that barrel pointed at my heart."

"But it wasn't pointed at your heart the whole time. I believe when the robber grabbed the woman, he put the gun to *her* head," the sheriff reminded him.

"Yah," Jerry said and ducked his head. "I remember the guy saying he was going to kill her, but I was busy trying to get the money out of the damned cash register. I really wasn't paying any attention. The cops wanted a description of the woman but I couldn't give them one. My mind was a hamster going like hell on a wheel. I couldn't remember the combination for the safe and I knew that guy was going to kill me after he killed her."

Jerry had been twenty-two, still wet behind the ears, Sid reminded himself. "But you had it together enough that you grabbed the gun under the counter when the second robber came through the door."

"That was pure adrenaline. Like I told those cops, it was all just a blur. I would have shot my own sister if she'd come through that door at that moment holding a gun." He shook his head. "I never want to go through anything like that again." He glanced to where the other workers had taken a break but were now headed back to their jobs. "I really need to get back to work. You never said what this was about."

"The gun you used that night has turned up in another shooting."

All the color drained from Jerry's face.

"A witness said they saw you drop the gun on the

floor after you shot the second robber. But that witness didn't see what happened to it after that."

Jerry was shaking his head, eyes wide. "I have no idea. No idea at all." But he looked scared as he began to walk backward away. "Sorry I wasn't more help."

"Oh, you've helped more than you know," Sid said and tipped his cap before returning to his cruiser.

GARRETT GASSED UP the pickup quickly and then pulled onto the interstate again. He didn't slow down until he saw the ambulance ahead of them. Only then did he back off the gas pedal. He left enough room between the two vehicles that the ambulance transport driver wouldn't notice he was being followed, not with all the traffic on the interstate this summer season.

He and Billy had debated abducting Joslyn at the gas station before the ambulance could get away but nixed that idea. There had been too many people around not to mention security cameras. They felt that some people would get the wrong idea and things could go south quickly.

"So what is it about this woman? I have to ask," Billy said now that they were back on the road.

Garrett chuckled. "You're the only person I ever told about what happened two years ago." He shook his head. "It was bizarre the way we met. All of it."

"Which could have been a sign." He held up his hands. "Just sayin'."

"As it turns out, she was running from something back then. Maybe the same thing she was running from this time. That's the frustrating part. I have no idea what. I'm not sure *she* does. But it definitely appears someone wants her dead. I just hope it isn't the people who hired that ambulance in front of us."

How easy it would be to give her an overdose on the way to Seattle. He said as much to Billy who immediately shook his head. "Naw, I doubt whoever these attendants are, they weren't hired to murder her. If you're right, nothing will happen until they get her wherever they're taking her. So she should be safe for the moment."

Garrett held on to that as he watched the ambulance ahead of them. "What if I'm wrong about her?"

His friend laughed. "Doesn't matter. You're still nuts about her."

He laughed. "I am. I know Alistair Vanderlin wants me to believe that she doesn't know who she was or what she was doing those few months we spent together. But he's wrong. She was Joslyn Charles, the woman I fell madly in love with. And the other day when she looked into my eyes... It's still there, the way we felt about each other, the way we still do."

"What do you think about her so-called family?"

"I've only heard about them from her and the sheriff, but I keep thinking about the fear I saw in her eyes. I suspect they could be behind the attempts on her life even though it's clear to me that she doesn't want to believe it."

"Tell me about this family of hers," Billy said, taking out his cell phone.

Garrett listed them. "The guardian, Alastair

Vanderlin, the older stepsister, Amethyst, the older stepbrother, Peter, and the family lawyer, Benjamin Purdy and the psychiatrist, Neal Foster."

"Interesting family for a woman with a lot of baggage." He held up his hands again. "No judgment. Just an observation. None of them are blood relatives, not that blood relatives don't kill each other over all kinds of things, especially money."

"I keep thinking about how when the attendants had come for her, they immediately sedated her as if she was a danger. But to whom? Yes, there is a lot of money involved, but let's not forget Joslyn saw her father and stepmother murdered. If the man in prison really isn't the killer, then the real murderer has to have been worried all these years that she might remember. Maybe this recent memory loss is a precursor to her remembering what happened all those years ago."

DOROTHEA WAS GLAD no one was around when the sheriff called. Just the sound of his voice made her smile. She knew her delight showed on her face and she didn't want any of the Sterling brothers to see it. They'd tease her to high heaven and back.

"You have any plans Friday night?" Sid asked.

Her smile broadened. "Let me check my calendar." It was a joke and they both knew it and laughed. "Why, it seems I'm free. What did you have in mind? You said you wanted to see that new comedy that's out now."

"I do but I had something different in mind. I thought maybe we could go out to dinner, some place nice." He mentioned an expensive elegant restaurant uptown.

She felt her heart take off like a horse on locoweed and had to clear her voice before she spoke. "That sounds nice."

"Good. Let's plan on it then." Dorothea heard noise in the background. "I should go. I'm sure we'll talk before Friday night, but you might want to buy a new dress. My treat."

A new dress? Did she even own a dress? Her heart drummed so loudly in her chest that she thought it would bust its way out.

He disconnected before she could speak. She stared at her phone, her thoughts in free fall. Eleanor was right. Sid was going to ask her to marry him. Was she ready for this? Tears welled in her eyes and her smile was back, more bright and bigger than ever.

GARRETT DIDN'T KNOW how many more miles he drove before ahead of them, he saw the ambulance signal to leave the highway. "Looks like we're getting gas again," he said, nudging a sleeping Billy.

His friend sat up and looked around. "I don't think they could have picked a more isolated area." There was no town, just a wide spot beside the road that had a burger joint and two gas stations. The ambulance transport driver chose the gas station that was the least busy, an older one back off the road—with no obvious security cameras.

"Luck is smiling on you again," Billy said.

"Are you thinking what I think you're thinking?"

Garrett asked as he pulled into the other gas station across the road.

"As if we were both clairvoyant."

As the back of the ambulance opened, Garrett felt his pulse jump. He watched the attendant climb out, say something to the driver who was fumbling with a credit card at the pump, and stretched, then looked as if he might go inside.

"You walk over and do your thing," Billy said as he opened his door to get out. "I'll drive the pickup over and fill up the tank. If the attendant goes inside, you grab her. I'll keep the driver busy and buy you as much time as I can. Once you get her, go. Don't worry about me. I have friends out here."

As the attendant started toward the convenience store entrance, Garrett climbed out and crossed the road, keeping out of sight of the ambulance attendant filling the tank. As he did, Billy pulled the pickup directly behind the ambulance and, stepping out, began filling up the pickup's tank before striking up a conversation with the ambulance transport driver.

Garrett ducked between the front of the pickup and the back of the ambulance. When he tried the door, he was relieved to find it opened. He hurriedly climbed inside, knowing he had little time before the attendant came back—or saw what was going on from inside the station. His hope was that the man had gone to the men's restroom, but he could just as easily be buying snacks and watching from the front window.

Joslyn lay strapped down on the gurney. She

looked pale. There were faint bruises under her lashes. He hesitated for just a moment before he said her name. "Joslyn?"

Those amber eyes fluttered open. "Garrett." Her voice came out a hoarse whisper. He saw that she was having trouble focusing and keeping her eyes open.

"I'm getting you out of here."

She nodded as tears began to stream down her cheeks.

He quickly unstrapped her and lifted her to her feet. "Can you stand?"

She shook her head.

He managed to hold her up and open the door. He didn't bother to look to see if the coast was clear. He lifted her into his arms and, stepping out, carried her to his pickup. As he opened the passenger-side door, he set her down and reclined the seat. She slumped back without a word as he fastened her seat belt.

Slamming the door, he started around to the driver's side when he saw Billy. He was in the middle of an argument with the driver who had finished fueling the ambulance. Garrett quickly pulled the gas nozzle from the pickup's tank, replaced it and jumped behind the wheel.

But not before the driver spotted him. Recognition flashed in the man's expression an instant before he tried to get past Billy.

Garrett turned the key, the engine roared. He shoved the truck into Reverse. The tires squealed as he peeled out of the station. He hated leaving Billy, but he knew that the PI would wiggle out of the tight spot—and pay for the gas before the cops came. Garrett could always post bail for his friend, if it came to that.

As he was racing away, he saw the other ambulance attendant come running out of the station. The man appeared to be holding a large drink in one hand and a couple of hot dogs in the other.

He drove back onto the interstate headed in the direction of Montana. He had no idea where he was going or what he was going to do. But he had Joslyn.

Glancing over at her, he saw that she had fallen asleep. She looked restful. He just hoped he'd done the right thing. But at least he knew she was safe for the moment.

He hadn't gone far when his cell phone rang. Joslyn stirred but drifted off again. He hit Accept, seeing it was Billy.

"Everything all right?" his friend asked.

"I think she's okay. What about you?"

"You know me. Got in a little scuffle but I paid for your gas and slipped the net. I called a buddy. Might do some snowboarding up on Mount Hood before I head back. Unless you need me."

"Enjoy yourself. And thanks, Billy. For everything. You're sure you're all right?" A little scuffle with Billy could mean just about anything. "What happened when they realized she was gone?"

"Didn't stick around long enough to see." He laughed.

"Have fun snowboarding. And thanks, buddy." He turned off his phone as there wasn't anyone he

wanted to talk to right now besides Joslyn and he
didn't expect the sedatives to wear off for a while.

JERRY FULTON HAD been a lot more helpful than he'd
thought. Sid had watched him walk back to where
he'd left his shovel. He'd known Jerry would turn
and look back. The young man was as nervous as a
long-tailed cat in a room full of rocking chairs, as
his grandmother used to say.

Sure enough, Jerry had turned to glance warily
back, then had quickly lowered his head and had
kept walking.

Pulling out his cell, Sid had called Dorothea. He
wasn't sure why he'd needed to talk to her at that moment, but he had. Just hearing her voice made him
feel better about everything. He was also glad that
she hadn't mentioned Garrett. Apparently she didn't
know yet what had happened or that the rancher was
probably headed for some legal trouble—if not something worse.

He'd been a little surprised though when he'd suggested dinner at a fancy restaurant he'd heard about.
But now that he'd done it, he couldn't help smiling.

Not that he was through working today, he reminded himself. He disconnected after a little chit-
chat with Dorothea. This time he called the warden
at Montana State Prison. "I need to see Frankie Rutledge. This afternoon if possible." He felt the clock
ticking. He'd tried to call Garrett but it had gone
straight to voicemail. Not good.

The warden had been more than helpful. Getting what he needed, he disconnected and headed for Deer Lodge, Montana, and the prison. All his instincts told him he was onto something. Now if he could just find out who had hired the man in his morgue to kill Monica aka Joslyn, he could retire in peace.

Montana State Prison outside of Deer Lodge, Montana, sat up on a hill overlooking the small town. Sid was led into a room to wait as Frankie Rutledge was brought down. He didn't have to wait long.

Rutledge had a face that told of a hard life lived. He'd been thirty-seven when he'd pulled his gun in the convenience store in Missoula, Montana, that night. Two years later, he looked closer to sixty.

He walked with a limp, slightly dragging his left leg. His hair had grayed and there were deep wrinkles around his mouth and eyes. He had a badly done skull tattoo on his neck and numerous tattoos on his arms that made his skin appear bruised.

As he shuffled into the room, he seemed to be surprised to see a county sheriff and one he'd never met. "When I heard I had a visitor…"

Sid motioned him into the chair opposite the marred tabletop.

"What's this about?" Frankie asked, still standing.

"A woman, a convenience-store robbery and a clerk by the name of Jerry Fulton. Ring any bells?"

His hand went to the back of his head. "Rings a couple of bells. Or was it the canned beans that cold-cocked me that is causing the ringing in my ears still? But that's ancient history." Frankie was serving fifteen years for first degree armed robbery, not his first brush with the law.

"How do you feel about getting more added onto your latest sentence for attempted homicide?" he asked.

"What?" Rutledge looked confused.

"I know you didn't go to that convenience store that night two years ago to rob the place. You went there to kill the woman who was in the store. Did Jerry call you to tell you she was there? Or did you follow her?"

"I don't know what you're talking about," Frankie said, but he wasn't quite so cocky now.

"I know someone hired you to kill her and that Jerry was in on it." He didn't know it, but he suspected it, which right now was good enough.

Rutledge narrowed his eyes. "If that were true, you wouldn't be here telling me all this. My lawyer would be calling me to tell me the bad news. What is it you want?" He dragged a chair to him, and, turning it, straddled the seat so he could rest his arms on the back. One of the blurry tattoos on his arm read MOM, Sid noticed.

"There's been another attempt on the woman's life."

The prisoner looked surprised and then thoughtful before he let out a laugh. "And you think I had something to do with it." He scoffed. "Someone gave you the wrong information."

Sid could see the man's mind working. "Tell me who hired you to kill her that night at the convenience store. Maybe I can get you a deal."

"A deal, huh?" He broke into a lopsided grin as he rose and shoved the chair away. "I can get my own deal, thank you very much."

"Give me the name of the person who hired you to kill her the first time," Sid said. "Or you are going to be looking at attempted murder charges."

"I don't think so," the prisoner said. "But I will do this. I'll tell my lawyer that I might have some information. I get out of here early and in return, you get the name." His grin broadened, exposing dark holes where teeth were missing. "You'll find out who hates her so much that they would pay to have her gone."

"If she dies before you make the deal—"

"Then we are both out of luck, huh." He laughed and walked to the door to pound on it. A guard appeared at once. "We're all done here," Frankie Rutledge said to the uniformed man then turned to look back at Sid. "Thanks for coming by. Maybe I can return the favor when I get out."

It sounded like a threat, but Rutledge had confirmed what Sid had only suspected. If things went the way he hoped, the prisoner would be on the phone with his lawyer wanting to give up the name of the person who'd hired him to kill Monica Wilmington and it would be the same person who'd recently hired Leon Sheffield. In return Rutledge would try to get some time off his latest sentence; not that he would be out of prison long, given his criminal ways.

At least Sid hoped that would be the way it went down. There was always the chance that Rutledge would try to blackmail the person who'd hired him.

But that would mean contacting that person… He knew that was too much to hope for since there would be a record of that contact. Rutledge was too prison smart to make that mistake.

Sid just hoped it all went down quickly because he didn't know how much time Joslyn had. He'd almost reached his patrol SUV when his cell phone went off. He looked, not surprised to see that it was Alistair Vanderlin. He'd been anticipating this call and dreading it.

"Sheriff Anderson," he answered.

"Sheriff Anderson." In those two words he heard disappointment, anger and concern. He braced himself for the bad news. "Garrett Sterling and a friend of his have accosted my ambulance attendants and abducted Monica. Tell me one good reason I shouldn't call the FBI and have them arrested for kidnapping."

"Because you don't want the bad publicity or you would have already made that call." Sid sighed. "I've known Garrett all my life. He won't hurt her. Give me twenty-four hours before you do anything we would all regret. I can promise you that as long as she's with Garrett, she's safe."

CHAPTER TWENTY

GARRETT DIDN'T DRIVE FAR, wanting to get off the interstate as quickly as possible. He was both physically and mentally exhausted when he found an out-of-the-way motel. He registered under a false name, paid cash and parked his pickup behind the unit. With Joslyn still groggy, he had to carry her inside where he laid her on the bed and covered her with the comforter.

After tucking her in, as exhausted as he was, he got on his phone. He had to know everything he could find out about the woman he'd just abducted.

The story had gotten national news coverage. The murders of Horace and Thea Wilmington came up as the top story complete with a photograph of the husband and wife. He stared at the photo of the two. Horace T. Wilmington and his wife Thea Louise were dressed to the nines in the shot. According to the caption, they were at a charity benefit and were often seen at Seattle's upper-crust society gatherings.

Horace had made his money in luxury yachts. There was a second photo of the two of them on their yacht, the *Thea Louise*. With a start, Garrett noticed someone in the background. A small child with Joslyn's heart-shaped face. She appeared to be hiding. In front of her was an older blond girl in her teens with a typical sullen teenage look on her pretty face. According to the caption, the older girl's name was Amethyst, Thea Louise's daughter by her first marriage. The smaller child was unidentified. Garrett found that very strange, unless Joslyn's father had wanted to protect her from the publicity.

He read the entire article, cringing at the description of the murder scene. Both Horace and Thea Louise had been horribly battered to the point of being barely recognizable. The crime scene had been described as "grisly." The murder weapon was a baseball bat that was later found in the garage of a man named Harvey Mattson, an associate of Horace Wilmington's. He was convicted of the murders, received a life sentence and was sent to the state prison in Walla Walla. Mattson swore that the bat had been planted in his garage and that he was innocent.

Amethyst, then thirteen, hadn't been home at the time. Nor had her younger brother, Peter. But younger daughter from Horace's first marriage, Monica, then five, was found hiding covered with blood and no memory of what had happened.

That was the only reference to her.

He quickly read the other articles that followed. Much of it was repetition since the case had been solved quickly. Before that, there'd been an uproar from residents in the wealthy part of Capital Hill neighborhood in Seattle, demanding the killer be found.

Joslyn had seen the killer? And yet she still didn't remember? He reminded himself that her name was Monica, but he knew he'd never think of her as anything other than Joslyn Charles.

Eyes blurry, Garrett turned off his phone again and stretched. Getting up, he went in to check on Joslyn. She was sleeping soundly. He watched the rise and fall of her chest, stared at her beautiful face and felt his heart ache. She'd been through so much. And now someone had tried to kill her and, unless he was wrong, would try again.

He stood for a moment longer before going into the other room to crash on the couch, too exhausted to drive himself crazy over what he'd done by abducting her.

Garrett told himself that he'd saved her. At least he hoped he had.

"DID GARRETT GO back up to the guest ranch last night?" Dorothea asked as she came into the kitchen to find the two brothers eating bowls of cereal. "He didn't sleep here. I just walked by his room and his bed hasn't been slept in."

"The damned fool has gone after that woman after her guardian had her taken away by ambulance," Will said between bites.

"Joslyn?" Dorothea asked and couldn't help smiling. True, she'd been against Garrett taking her up to the guest ranch, fearing for his safety. But to go after her… "That's so romantic. Who knew he had it in him?"

"First, there is no Joslyn," Will said. "The woman's name is Monica Wilmington and second, there is nothing romantic about it."

"I'm confused," Shade said as he poured more cereal into his bowl. "*What's* going on?"

"I called the sheriff this morning when Garrett wasn't answering his cell or the landline up at the guest ranch," Will said. "Our brother and his sidekick Billy Mitchell kidnapped Monica from the back of the ambulance in the middle of eastern Washington."

Shade groaned. "Now that is a bad sign. You know what happens when those two get together."

"Sid said he's held Monica's guardian off for twenty-four hours from calling the feds and having Garrett arrested for kidnapping, but if we hear from Garrett, he wants us to call. At this point, Garrett is on the lam with a woman who is probably as crazy as he apparently is."

"So he rescued her," Dorothea said as she pulled up a seat at the kitchen table. "You have to admit, that's passion."

"Not if he gets himself arrested," Will snapped, then narrowed his gaze at her. "What's with you and stars in your eyes?"

Dorothea shook her head and busied herself with straightening the items on the table. Maybe Sid and their upcoming date did have a little something to do with her change of heart about Garrett and Joslyn.

"So who is this Monica Wilmington?" Shade asked.

"Garrett knows her as Joslyn," Dorothea said. "She's the woman who broke his heart two years ago."

"How do you—"

Will cut off his brother. "She's also a woman with a very disturbing history. She witnessed the murder of her father and stepmother when she was five but apparently has no memory of it. There have been other attempts on her life—enough so that she was in the witness protection program. At least until recently when she showed up on the mountainside with a man who wanted to kill her. Needless to say, our brother is neck deep in all of it now."

"So where did he and Billy kidnap her?" Shade asked.

Will groaned. "They jumped the ambulance attendants somewhere in eastern Washington at a gas station. The attendants were taking her to a mental hospital for observation out in Seattle, Sid said. The woman has…mental problems apparently."

"I'd have mental problems too if someone was trying to kill me," Dorothea said. "So of course Garrett is going to save her. What else would you have him do?"

Will huffed. "You can post his bail when he gets arrested then. But when he calls, I want to be the one to yell at him."

Poppy came into the room. She kissed her husband on the cheek and pulled out a chair. "I couldn't help overhearing this discussion," she said smiling at her husband. "I believe, Will Sterling, that you risked your life to save mine not all that long ago. I guess it runs in the family, huh."

JOSLYN WOKE TO sunlight streaming in the window of what appeared to be a motel room that had seen better days. Blinking, she tried to sit up. She could feel the sluggish effect of the drugs she'd been given yesterday. A dull headache throbbed behind her eyes as she tried to remember what had happened.

Rising, she saw that she was still wearing the dress that Garrett had bought her. But she had no idea where she was or how she'd gotten here. The last she'd heard, the ambulance transport driver said they were taking her back to Seattle.

As she stepped to the bedroom door, she remembered the dream she'd had though. Garrett had come to save her. The memory made her smile. But then the reality of her situation rushed back in. How could Alistair let his happen? Even as she thought it, she knew he had to be the one to sanction this.

That terrified her even more. Before, at least she'd always had him on her side. The thought of being locked up in some mental facility… Everything about this felt wrong. Especially now, so close to her birthday. She didn't want to believe that anyone in her so-called family would hurt her, but then again, there was all that money.

Her fear intensified as she realized something must have gone wrong for her to be staying in a shabby motel room. Had they reached Seattle? Or had the ambulance broken down on the way?

She slowly pushed open the door, telling herself that if the attendants were still asleep, she would slip out. She didn't know how she'd get away but she knew where she would go. Back to Garrett. He was the only one she could trust—even if he still didn't trust her.

Blinking, she couldn't believe what she was seeing at first. Garrett. He lay on the couch sound asleep. She stared at him. *It hadn't been a dream.* He *had* rescued her. An ocean swell of relief, gratitude and love nearly swamped her. She clung to the edge of the door as tears blurred her eyes. He'd saved her *again*.

Her heart beat faster at the sight of him. She'd never stopped loving him. But at this moment she loved him more than even all those months ago. She felt as if she would burst with the emotion.

He'd been so angry with her when she'd told him why she'd left him and why she hadn't given him the option of coming with her. But he'd still come after her when she'd needed him. He'd saved her. At least temporarily.

That's when she had a moment of clarity, when she realized there was only one thing she could do. She had to find out who was behind the attempts on her life. She had to put an end to this. Not just for her sake, but for Garrett's. She had to prove not to just Alistair and the others, but to the man she loved and even herself, that she wasn't crazy because there were parts of her life she couldn't remember.

His blue eyes fluttered open. He smiled as he focused on her face. "What are you doing?"

"Watching you sleep."

His smile broadened for a moment, then he sat

up, rubbed his hand over his stubbled jaw and said, "Did you see a coffeepot anywhere?"

She nodded. "Want me to make a pot?"

"While I shower?" he said, sitting up.

Joslyn had a sudden image of him standing under the spray, water droplets cascading off his hard, tanned body. "There was a time you would have invited me to join you."

He stilled, his blue eyes widening as he took her in.

She could see it was too soon. Might always be too soon. Her heart cramped as she tried hard not to let it show on her face. She swallowed the lump in her throat. "I'll see about that coffee." She turned quickly and went into the tiny kitchen. A moment later she felt him come in behind her.

"Joslyn?"

She silently pleaded for him not to say anything.

When he spoke again she could tell he was carefully choosing his words. "I can't just pick up where we left off. Not yet. I'm sorry. I don't mean to hurt you. Once we figure this all out…"

She continued making the coffee, unwrapping the foam cups, tossing the plastic wrap into the trash. When he'd backed away, she said, "I understand."

Out of the corner of her eye, she saw him reach to touch her shoulder, but pull back as if he'd changed his mind at the last minute. "We'll take the coffee to go. We need to get on the road as soon as possible."

She nodded without turning, fighting tears. "Do you know where we are?"

"Outside of Spokane. Why?"

"There's someone I need to see." She turned then to meet his gaze. "Harvey Mattson, the man who went to prison for killing my father and stepmother. He claims he didn't do it, that he was framed. I was told that he holds me responsible for his being behind bars for the past twenty-five years because I can't remember what happened that night. If anyone wants me dead, it is probably him."

GARRETT STOOD UNDER the warm spray of the shower wondering what the hell was wrong with him. Joslyn could be in here with him, the wall between them melting away as he took her in his arms. But he'd held back. Because he was scared that once they made love again, he'd really lose all perspective. What he'd told her was true. Too much was going on right now. Or was it because he couldn't be sure who he was making love with. Monica Wilmington or Joslyn Charles.

There was the sliver of doubt still embedded deep in his brain. His heart thought it knew exactly who she was. He wanted her, yearned for her, ached for her, but he had to know for sure what he was dealing with, he told himself.

He turned the water temperature to icy cold. It took his breath away but was definitely needed. How long could he keep holding her at arm's length when he wanted her so desperately it hurt? What was it going to take? He wanted her more than he wanted his next breath. But right now keeping her safe had to stay front and center, he told himself. He had to keep his priorities straight.

When he came out of the shower, dressed, his hair still damp, his body still chilled from his cold shower, he saw that she was waiting, ready to go. "Are you sure about visiting this prisoner?"

She nodded. "If he's the one behind the attempts on my life—"

"Sorry, but it seems a little naive to think that this man in a maximum security prison is going to tell you if he's trying to kill you or not."

Joslyn smiled at that. "I'll know," she said, hoping that was true. She'd never seen more than a photo of him and was terrified to face him, but what choice did she have? "I have to try."

Garrett raked a hand through his damp hair. "Where is he?"

"Walla Walla, at the state maximum security prison. How far are we from there?"

"A few hours to the south, but Joslyn—"

"I appreciate all you've done for me. I don't expect you to—"

"I'm going with you." He met her gaze and held it for a long moment. He was already in so deep, too deep. But he knew he couldn't walk away. Not now. Not ever.

It was only a matter of time before he'd be hearing from the sheriff. There was probably already a BOLO out on him and his pickup. He'd be wanted for abducting her, maybe worse, kidnapping especially since they'd crossed state lines.

He breathed in the smell of fresh coffee and reached for a cup. "You're sure about this?" She nodded and picked up her coffee cup. In for a penny, in for a pound, as Dorothea always said. "Let's go then."

It wasn't until they were on the road headed south toward Walla Walla that Garrett spoke again. He shot her a look and said, "There's something we need to talk about."

Joslyn held her breath. She told herself all that mattered was that Garrett believed that they were both in danger. His life depended on it. She couldn't bear the thought that she'd put him at risk. Being this close to him, not being able to touch him, to curl up in his arms, was killing her. Killing her almost as much as the doubt and distrust she still saw in his blue eyes.

"Your guardian had a long talk with the sheriff."

Was that what was bothering him? She could just imagine what Alistair had said. "Let me guess. He told him that I'm a troubled young woman."

"Apparently your doctor thinks your memory loss stems from a split personality."

"A split personality?" She scoffed at that. "You really can't believe—"

"It might explain why you became Joslyn Charles."

She sighed and had to look away for a moment. "The name Monica Wilmington comes with a lot of baggage as you can imagine." Turning to him again, she said, "I'd always hated the name Monica. When I met you, I desperately wanted a new beginning."

She looked into his eyes for a moment. "Joslyn wasn't just a name I picked," she said, her voice cracking. "It was someone I wanted to be—with you. I loved the name Joslyn Charles and who I was with you."

"Me, too," he said softly and seemed to be concentrating again on his driving. "But that seems like the behavior of someone with a split personality," he said.

True, but she could see him soften toward her as if a little of the anger and disappointment and distrust had fallen away. Her heart beat a little faster. If only she could reach him...

"Your doctor believes your memory loss and your use of other names proves that there is more going on with you," Garrett said. "Add to that the fact that you've been safe for the past eighteen months and you left that safety for a reason you didn't remember."

She shook her head, seeing why he was so worried that her. "I told you about the photo of the two of us. Someone put it under my door. I wouldn't risk jeopardizing your life unless I thought you were in danger. I wasn't acting irresponsibly. I came here to warn you that you were in danger."

He said nothing.

"This memory loss isn't from any emotional trauma. It's from the knock on my head because of the car accident. I know my psychiatrist in Seattle wants to make more of it than it is—"

"Why is that?"

She looked away. "I don't know. It could be be-

cause I'm about to turn thirty and then he and my
lawyer will have to get real jobs. On my birthday,
I'm free. No more guardian. I will no longer need
the services of my doctor or lawyer, who were both
hired twenty-five years ago to help watch over me."

"Joslyn, you were terrified to let those ambulance
attendants take you back to Seattle. What would have
happened if they'd locked you up before your birthday?"

She sighed. "If they could have proved that I
wasn't in my right mind…"

"You don't think that's motive?"

"Not to kill me. Neither my doctor or lawyer
would benefit if I died."

"Who would?"

She hesitated, hating to voice it. "My stepsister
and stepbrother, I would imagine. Maybe my guardian. I honestly have never asked."

"Joslyn, someone hired that man to kill you. I
think you're scared it wasn't Harvey Mattson, who's
serving time for killing your father and stepmother.
What if the person you have to fear is someone closer
at home?"

She rubbed her temples. She was still suffering
from the effects of whatever drug they'd given her.
"Let's start with Harvey, okay?" She looked to him,
pleading in her voice.

He nodded and gave her a pitying smile that made
her chest hurt.

"If I'm right about why I ended up in Whitefish,
then my car is somewhere in or around the town,"

she said needing to change the subject. She described it for him. "Which will prove that there is nothing wrong with my memory—until I was in an accident and hit my head. Maybe we can go look for it after we see Harvey."

He glanced over at her, his expression saying she was clutching at straws. Maybe she was, but it was all she had right now. Thanks to Garrett she wasn't strapped down in some mental ward in a hospital right now. She had a chance to try to figure this out. She wondered why she'd never considered talking to Harvey before. Because she'd been terrified as to what she would learn? Was it the same reason she couldn't remember who had killed her father and stepmother?

She pushed the thought away and looked out at the landscape as it rushed past. She saw Garrett watching the rearview mirror. How long before Alistair had him arrested and her sent to that mental ward? She recalled being strapped down and shuddered at the thought of what could happen if they were caught.

Glancing over at Garrett, she felt a rush of love for him. He thought this trip was a waste of time and yet he was taking her. She felt herself falling even deeper in love with him with each passing minute.

CHAPTER TWENTY-ONE

GARRETT WAS GLAD to be on the road again—even if they were headed for the Washington state prison on a fool's errand. At least they were moving and, right now, he didn't know what else to do. He'd hoped to work out some things in his head after he'd "saved" Joslyn.

But all of this felt too complicated to do any reasonable thinking. He could admit to himself that the sheriff was right. He was in over his head with this woman. The cold shower hadn't helped much. He was too aware of her next to him in the close confines of the pickup's cab. Her presence was messing up any thoughts he might have as to how to get them out of this.

They hadn't spoken the past hundred miles. Joslyn seemed lost in thought, her face turned toward the side window, the sun glowing on her cheeks. He couldn't help thinking about what she'd said about the name Joslyn Charles. It was the woman she'd wanted to be with him.

He hated to think what her doctor might make of that, but quickly shoved the thought away. Did he really believe that she might have more than one personality? That there might be more women inside her? He shook his head and tried to concentrate on his driving. They weren't that far from Walla Walla and the prison now.

"I need to know what you saw on that mountain before I ended up in the Whitefish hospital."

He glanced over at her, surprised that she'd not only broken the silence, but also that she'd done it with a demanding tone in her voice. "I have to know, Garrett. It was self-defense, wasn't it?"

JOSLYN COULD SEE that he was making up his mind, so waited, hoping he could provide the missing pieces and relieve her mind.

He took a breath and let it out before he spoke. "I was up at our family guest ranch in the mountains on a horseback ride when I spotted a man and a woman on the ridgeline across from a deep ravine. The man was forcing the woman through the pines. I pulled out my binoculars… The man had a gun on her, threatening her. She got away at one point and ran, but he caught her, struck her with the gun and then put the barrel to her head."

It surprised her that he was telling the story as if she wasn't that woman. But she said nothing, afraid he might stop.

"I reached for my holstered pistol, fired a shot in the air to let the man know I was watching all of this and then I heard four shots, in rapid fire."

He told the story as if he had recited it dozens of times. "I assumed the sheriff and I would find the woman dead. I had caught movement of someone escaping in a blue SUV, but thought it was the man. I was shocked to realize he was the one who'd been shot and died."

She'd somehow gotten the gun away from him and killed the man. The blood under her fingernails, the deputy outside her door. For a while, she'd let herself forget. *She'd killed a man.* The thought echoed through her, making her feel sick to her stomach.

"But you didn't see me pull the trigger?"

He shook his head.

"That explains why the sheriff said you saved my life." She looked over at him. "I owe you my life."

"That's a bit overly dramatic," he said. "You were the one who somehow got the gun away from him and fired the shots that killed him."

She looked away for a moment, feeling the weight of his words. "I was afraid that was the case when I noticed dried blood under my fingernails at the hospital."

"You still have no memory of any of it?"

Shaking her head, she said, "My last memory was getting up in the apartment where I lived as Krystal Bradley."

"But you remembered us."

"I told you. I could never have forgotten you."

He frowned. "There is one more thing. The gun that killed the man? It was the same one the clerk at the convenience store used to kill George Rutledge the night we met."

Joslyn felt the shock hit her like a slap. "How is that possible?"

"The sheriff has a couple of theories. One is that the youngest Rutledge, Nicky, was in the store that night and picked it up. The other is that you took it."

She felt her cheeks burn. He saw her reaction and swore.

"You picked up the gun!" He started to step away from her but she touched his arm.

"Please, let me try to explain. I was scared. I thought I might need it."

"And you've kept it all this time?" She nodded. "So how did the man on the side of the mountain get it?"

"He must have taken it away from me. I always carry it in my purse."

Garrett swore again. "I was so sure the Rutledge kid must have picked it up. But Sid was right. The easiest explanation was that you'd had it all this time."

She could see that she'd lost another piece of his trust. She felt the loss at heart level as the prison came into view.

The place was a huge complex of redbrick buildings. She felt her stomach churn. Was she really doing this? Coming face-to-face with the man who allegedly killed her father and stepmother? When she saw him would she remember? Would she remember it was him who'd committed the murder?

Her hands began to shake. She rubbed her palms down her legs and tried to calm her terror. The news of what had almost happened to her on that mountainside north of Whitefish had left her shaken enough. But realizing what she was about to do had her stricken.

She tried to hide just how nervous she was as they parked in the lot and made their way to the visitors' entrance only to find out that it was Monday. No visiting hours. Garrett asked to speak to someone who could help them. He explained the situation, telling them who she was.

Some phones calls were made and, after a while, they were shown into a private room and told there would be a guard in the room at all times.

All of it felt surreal as if in a bad dream.

She didn't remember the walk down the long hallway, the echo of their footfalls, the opening and closing of thick metal doors. Once inside, she sat on the cold edge of a chair in a small room with only a table and a few chairs, all bolted to the floor.

Her body trembled inside as she waited expectantly, her gaze on the door he would come through. While Harvey Mattson had apparently often been at their house before the murders, she had no memory of him. Her anxiety built at the thought that she would recognize him from the night of the murder—and he would see her expression and know that she'd remembered and his fate would be sealed.

There was a noise outside the door. The sound of keys rattling in a lock. From the chair beside her, Garrett reached over and took her hand in his large warm one. He gently squeezed it. "You can change your mind," he whispered.

She shook her head, unable to speak as the door began to open. She knew the expression *jump out of your skin*, but she'd never really understood it until the man walked in. He was shackled, the metal ankle and wrist bindings rattling as he entered.

Her heart lodged in her throat as she stared at him. He barely resembled the photo of the young man she'd seen in the papers. His wide face was pockmarked, his nose flattened to one side as if it had been broken numerous times and his brown eyes were deep-set like the wrinkles around them. He lumbered in and stopped just inside the door. His huge form seemed to fill up the room and suck out all the air.

Joslyn stared at the man she felt responsible for putting behind bars almost twenty-five years ago because she'd been unable to remember who she'd seen that night. Harvey might have just been in the wrong place that night—in the neighborhood where the murders had taken place. He'd been drinking and hadn't pulled over when the cop had flashed his lights and siren. He'd recently changed clothes and taken a shower, another red flag.

His connection with Horace Wilmington and other arrests in his past for violent behavior had been enough to convict him. When he'd gone in, he'd been only twenty and his nose hadn't been broken as many times, but he'd still had that thug-like look about him. She'd heard about her father's associates. She knew enough now to know that if Harvey had been one of her father's "associates" then Horace Wilmington had been into more than the yacht business, confirming the rumors about how he'd accumulated his fortune.

Garrett rose from his chair, ready for trouble if the prisoner decided to give them any even though there was a guard standing a few feet away just as ready.

Harvey Mattson's expression was unreadable for a moment, before he focused on her and suddenly broke into a huge smile. "I can't believe it," he said. "Mo, it's really you." He took a tentative step toward the table where the two of them were seated on the opposite side. The guard stopped him from coming any closer. He dropped into his chair across from them.

Joslyn was too stunned to speak. He'd called her by her father's nickname for her.

Harvey sat down heavily. "I'm sorry. I didn't mean to frighten you. I'm just so excited to see you. When they told me I had visitors, I never dreamed. But it is really you." He looked to Garrett before his gaze returned to her. "Tell me you're here with good news."

She felt confused. "Good news?"

Now he looked confused. "I thought maybe you remembered that night." He sounded so hopeful.

"I'm sorry," she said quickly and shook her head.

His disappointment was almost palpable. "I told myself when I saw you not to get my hopes up…" He wagged his big head and let out an embarrassed laugh. "But I couldn't help it." His gaze softened as he looked at her again. "But if that isn't why you're here…"

"Someone has been trying to kill her," Garrett said. "We thought you might know something about that."

True concern shone in the man's dark eyes. "No. You thought I... *No*," he said more firmly. He shook his head adamantly. "I need you alive. I wake up every day praying that you will remember what happened. Killing you would mean that this..." He glanced around the room. "Really is a life sentence." He shook his head again. "You are my only hope of ever walking out of here."

Tears burned her eyes as she looked at the man. He had spent all these years waiting for her to remember. "I'm so sorry," she said again.

He nodded and surprised her by smiling again. "You will remember, Mo. I know you will. I have to believe it. One day you will clear me. One day I will walk out of here a free man. Until you do..." He looked worried. Glancing at Garrett, he said, "You have to protect her. You can't let anything happen to her."

"I'm doing my best. But if you aren't behind the attempts on her life, then who?"

Harvey didn't hesitate. "The real killer. Who else?"

CHAPTER TWENTY-TWO

"HE WASN'T ANYTHING like I thought he would be," Joslyn said when they reached Garrett's pickup and were safely inside. "I felt...sorry for him. I want so badly to remember." She shook her head and looked over at him.

Garrett nodded. "I was surprised as well." He smiled at her as he reached for her hand. He was amazed by how well she'd handled herself back there. Harvey Mattson had been damned intimidating. At least at first. "You were awesome," he said and squeezed her hand before letting go.

"He called me Mo." Her voice broke and tears welled in her amber eyes. "That was my father's nickname for me." She shook her head. "I don't believe he killed my father or that he hired anyone to come after me."

Garrett agreed. "It's the who else that could be behind the attempts on your life that bothers me. There seems to be only one tie-in. The gun from the convenience store robbery in Missoula—the same gun Leon Sheffield tried to kill you with." He groaned inwardly. "The same one you made off with that night. We need to talk to that clerk." He pulled out his phone. "Are you still snowboarding?" he asked when his friend answered.

Billy laughed. "Not at the moment."

Garrett told him what he needed and his friend called back minutes later. "Jerrold Fulton. He's employed by Charlemagne Construction. Right now, they're building a bridge on the west end of Polson."

"You're amazing," he said and meant it.

"I just have friends in low places," Billy said. "How are things?"

"I haven't been arrested yet." He glanced at Joslyn. "We're good." Better, he wanted to say. Not fixed, far from it, but closer. Dangerously closer. He disconnected and drove toward Polson, Montana.

Several hours later, they found the bridge job. It was almost quitting time. They'd lost track of the day, but so far they hadn't seen a lawman looking for them. The sheriff had called a few times, leaving the same message. "Call me."

So far Garrett hadn't. He didn't need a lecture. Nor did he have words to come up with a reasonable explanation for what he'd done and was now doing. It was better that the sheriff didn't know, he told himself.

"Jerry looks nervous," she said as they watched the young man looking around as he quit work and started toward the parking area with the rest of the crew. "Do you think he was expecting us?"

"Expecting something, that's for sure. Let's see what's bothering him," he said and opened his door to step out. She followed.

Jerry was almost to his old sedan when he saw them. His eyes widened as he stumbled to a stop. He looked as if he'd seen two ghosts. Ghosts from his past, Garrett was betting he didn't want to see again.

The man also looked as if he might run. Garrett was ready if he did. Jerry must have seen that as well because he only took a step back as they approached and seemed to change his mind.

"I guess we don't have to introduce ourselves," Garrett said. Jerry's gaze jumped from him to Joslyn and back. "We need to talk."

The young man swallowed and looked around. "Not here," he said. "I live a couple of blocks from here. You can follow—"

Garrett was already shaking his head. "Hop into our rig." Jerry looked toward the king cab pickup. "This won't take long," he said.

Jerry looked as if he didn't like anything about it, but he walked with them to the pickup. "I already told the sheriff everything I knew."

Garrett wasn't surprised to hear that Sid had already been here. He was a good lawman. He'd be following up just as they were doing. Garrett said nothing until they reached the pickup and opened the passenger-side door. Motioning to the front seat, he said, "Get in." He could see that Jerry was considering telling him he didn't have to talk to him.

"Jerry, someone is trying to kill Joslyn and me so we really have nothing to lose. If I were you, I'd get in."

Reluctantly, Jerry climbed in. Joslyn got in the back as Garrett went around to slip behind the wheel.

"Tell us about the gun you had behind the counter," he said the moment his door closed.

"I already told the sheriff—"

"We don't want the version you told the sheriff," he said. "We need the truth. Who gave you the gun, Jerry?"

"It was mine. I picked it up at a gun show."

"You're not a gun show kind of guy, Jerry. What gun show was it?"

"I don't remember."

He grabbed the man by the collar and slammed him against the passenger-side door. "Jerry, let's cut to the chase. We have nothing to lose but our lives. You didn't get the gun at a gun show. Either you tell me the truth or so help me—"

"All right!" Jerry looked around outside the pickup.

"And Jerry, no more lies. I'm not the law. I just want the truth before they come gunning for Joslyn and me."

The man nodded nervously. "It was an old handgun my father picked up before guns were being registered. I took it from his house."

It still sounded like a lie. Or maybe he was lying about a lot more than the gun. "What did you think was going to happen that night that you had a gun behind the counter? I doubt you were planning to kill George Rutledge."

The man's face began to crumble. "That wasn't supposed to happen."

"But you knew Frankie was going to rob you that night." He could see that Jerry wanted to lie and realized it had never been about robbing the place. "How did they know Joslyn was in the store?" Garrett said and saw from Jerry's surprised expression that he'd hit paydirt. "You called them. You were hanging up the phone as I came in." He'd completely forgotten that until this moment, probably because he'd thought it hadn't mattered, that it had nothing to do with the robbery.

Jerry's Adam's apple bobbed for a moment. Tears welled in his eyes as he nodded. "Then all I had to do was empty the register and the safe. I didn't know what they planned to do. I swear." He turned to look at Joslyn in the back seat before he lowered his head to stare down at the floor. "I swear. I didn't know they were going to kill her."

"But you brought a gun so you knew something bad was going down. Don't lie to me."

The man began to cry in earnest. "He said he was just going to scare her, bring her back in line. I thought they were seeing each other. But then…" He looked at Joslyn again. "I realized you didn't look like the kind of woman Frankie could get. When he came in with the gun, I realized he was going to kill all of us. For a moment, I thought you had saved us," he said shifting his gaze to Garrett.

"But then George showed up armed."

Jerry nodded. "When George came through the door…" He wiped at his eyes. "If Frankie ever gets out of prison, he's going to kill me. He's crazy. If he finds out I told you…"

"Did he say who hired him for the job?" Garrett asked.

Jerry shook his head. "He offered me five hundred dollars to make the call and then let them rob the place. It seemed like easy money. I didn't know..." He put his head down again.

"Jerry, you couldn't have been that naive. Five hundred dollars to let them rob the store for chicken feed?"

"I swear I thought he just wanted to scare her."

Garrett couldn't hide his disgust. "Get out, Jerry." They had what they'd come for. More, in fact.

"I'm so sorry," the man cried as he turned again to look at Joslyn.

Garrett grabbed him, and with the other hand reached across the cab and opened the passenger-side door to push him out. The man stumbled and almost fell but caught himself before quickly scurrying away.

"How did you know?" Joslyn asked as she climbed in the front of the pickup cab again.

"I didn't. I was fishing, but when I started, I remembered him hanging up the phone as I came in. Also he'd seemed nervous before the robbery—just like he was today. I'd forgotten until I saw him again. At least now we know you were right. Someone hired the Rutledges to kill you."

"If you hadn't knocked out Frankie..."

"George was the backup. Jerry ended up saving both of our lives," he said, almost feeling sorry for the way he'd treated him. "So who hired them? I think we'd better pay Frankie a visit. Last I heard he was locked up again in Deer Lodge." He saw her recoil at the idea of visiting another prison, another possible killer. "You don't have to go in."

She shook her head. "I'm going with you. You know that by now they are looking for us?"

He laughed as he started the motor. "Another prison is the last place they will expect us to go." His cell phone rang. He'd forgotten to turn it off when he'd called Billy. He saw that it was the sheriff and decided maybe it was time to pick up. "Sheriff, good to hear from you."

SID SWORE. He couldn't believe Garrett. Was the man crazy? Crazy in love.

"What the hell do you think you're doing?" he demanded even as he tried to keep the anger and disbelief out of his voice.

"I'm just doing what I feel I have to do."

"Is Joslyn still with you?"

"Yes."

"I hate to even ask what you're up to now. I just talked to the warden at the Walla Walla State Penitentiary. He told me that the two of you visited Harvey Mattson."

"We were trying to find out who is behind the attempts on her life."

"Funny, that's the same thing I'm doing except I'm legally trained to do this." He gritted his teeth. "Have you figured it out yet?"

"It's not Mattson. He needs Joslyn alive to prove his innocence, hoping she remembers what she saw that night so she can get him exonerated and out of prison."

"At least that's his story."

"I believe him and so does she," Garrett said with so much conviction in his voice that Sid wanted to scream.

"Killers often lie, Garrett. Not that you're that familiar with killers. I am though." He sighed and tried to contain his frustration. "I also got a call from Alistair Vanderlin. I think I talked him out of going to the authorities and having you arrested for kidnapping. But just for twenty-four hours. Her doctor still wants her under observation at a hospital in Seattle."

"Thank you, for holding him off again."

"Garrett—"

"We just need to figure some things out for ourselves. I'll get back to you when we know more."

Sid stared at his phone for a moment. The rancher just hung up on him? He could have told him that he also spoke with Harvey Mattson and thought he might be right about the man. Not that it would help matters at this point.

Disconnecting, he knew there was no reason to call him back. Sid sat for a moment. They just wanted to figure some things out for themselves, huh? He shook his head and headed for his patrol SUV.

JOSLYN HAD BEEN quiet on the drive to Montana State Prison outside of Deer Lodge, Montana. She'd overheard enough of Garrett's side of the phone conversation to get the gist of it. The sheriff was upset and so was Alistair. She wondered what would happen next, but quickly pushed that worry aside as Garrett parked in the visitor's lot at the prison.

They now knew that Frankie had hired Jerry to let him know when she came into the store. Which meant it wasn't just the US Marshal she'd been working with from the witness security program who had known she was in Missoula. She lived in an apartment near the convenience store and often walked over to get a drink or a treat at night.

She hated to recall those days when she'd been on the run after almost being killed—and trying to decide if she was going into the program or not. One of the US Marshals had been trying to convince her it was the only way she would be safe. Alistair thought it would be best if she came home where he could keep her under lock and key. She definitely didn't want that.

Then that night at the convenience store, the handsome cowboy had handed her his pickup keys and offered her a way out.

She glanced over at Garrett as he turned off the engine. "Ready?" he asked and she nodded. Someone had hired Frankie. But if not Harvey Mattson... The thought struck her at heart level. Frankie hadn't known her before that night. He had no reason to want her dead.

Joslyn hesitated a moment before she opened her pickup door. Whatever Frankie told them, it would only confirm what she didn't want to believe. Her would-be killer had to be closer to home—just as she knew Garrett believed. But she'd known the people she considered her family all of her life. What if Frankie told them that one of them had hired him? Who'd also hired the man who'd tried to kill her outside of Whitefish? Was she ready to hear the truth?

Whoever wanted her dead hadn't given up. They'd gotten her to leave the safety of the witness security program by sending her the photo she'd remembered of her and Garrett. Whoever had taken the photo had known about the two of them. Had known that Garrett would be the weakness that could get her to break her cover to go to him to warn him.

"Why would Rutledge tell us anything?" she asked.

"I doubt he will, but we have to try. Right now, no one knows where we are. But eventually, when we surface…"

"Prisons give me the creeps," she said with a shudder as she looked at the hulking building with its razor wire and guard tower. "Or maybe it's the thought of seeing Frankie again. If you'd seen what I saw in his eyes that night…"

"You don't have to go in with me."

She shook her head. "Seeing me might help him talk."

Garrett smiled over at her. "It just might."

FRANKIE RUTLEDGE HAD only gotten rougher looking in the two years since they'd seen him. Garrett studied him as he limped into the room they'd been given. They'd barely made it in time to catch the last of visiting hours.

Frankie looked meaner and he'd clearly embraced the prison life if the crudely done tattoos showing on his neck and arms were an example.

Limping or not, he came into the room, all arrogance and attitude. But one look at Joslyn and he faltered. "What's this?" he asked. He clearly had not expected the two of them.

"It's been a while," Garrett said. "I'm surprised you remember us."

Frankie seemed to recover. His hand went to the back of his head. "I still remember you." This tone sounded threatening. Unlike Harvey Mattson, Frankie wasn't shackled, but there was a guard posted right outside the door who was watching all of them.

"Then you must remember me as well," Joslyn said, drawing his attention again.

He looked over at her and leered. "I never forget a pretty girl."

"I know you came into that convenience store that night to kill me."

Frankie laughed and shook his head. "Got a news flash for you two. There was a sheriff here earlier. We already had this conversation. My lawyer is working on getting me a deal as we speak."

"Really?" Garrett said. "Hope it's fast enough because if someone kills us before that happens—"

"The sheriff already stressed that point. I have it all under control."

"Just tell me this," Joslyn said. "How much were you paid to kill me?"

Frankie pulled back in surprise at the question.

He let out a bark of a laugh. "You just want to know what you're worth dead? Okay, sweetheart. Ten thousand dollars. But if I had to do it again I'd ask for five times that much." He winked at her. "I'm much smarter now."

"Is that what Leon Sheffield was supposed to get for the job?" Garrett asked.

Frankie frowned. "I wouldn't know. Leon and I weren't tight. But if he didn't get a bundle then he's a fool."

She stepped to the door and knocked on it. A guard appeared at once and opened it. She stepped out.

"Was it something I said?" Frankie called after her and laughed as the guard let Garrett exit before he motioned for the prisoner to come with him. "Seriously, come back and visit me. I don't get to see pretty girls in here. Maybe I'll give you a hint about the person you're looking for." His laugh followed them down the hallway.

"You already have," she called back.

Garrett turned to see Frankie's surprised face.

"I wouldn't be throwing any suspicions around about me," Frankie said as the guard unlocked the next set of doors at the other end of the hallway from them. "You could get me killed."

"That would be a shame," Joslyn said and the guard unlocked the door and pushed Frankie through it.

The last Garrett saw of the man was Frankie's worried look.

He waited until they were outside the prison before he asked. "Did I miss something?"

"The money," she said, sounding angry as she stalked toward his pickup.

He grabbed her arm and turned her to face him. "What are you talking about?"

Joslyn looked into his face, her amber eyes firing with fury. "Ten thousand dollars, but he would have asked for five times that much if he'd known. If he'd known what I'm worth."

He saw it then. Verification of what they'd both feared. "You're saying it had to be someone in your extended family."

She closed her eyes. "That's why they were in such a hurry to get me out of Montana, to take me back to Seattle, to sedate me, so they would finally have access to me. I played right into their hands and I've dragged you into it as well." Her eyes slowly opened, her gaze softening as she looked at him. "I was afraid this would be the case. It's someone close to me. Someone I've trusted all these years."

Garrett pulled her into his arms and stroked her long, dark hair. It felt just as it had all those years ago. Holding her felt right. He'd known that she didn't want to believe that anyone close to her could be responsible for the attempts on her life.

"We need to talk about what to do now," she said, her voice breaking.

He agreed. "For starters, let's get out of here." But as they turned again toward his pickup, Sheriff Sid Anderson stepped out from behind a prison bus.

"Going somewhere?" Sid asked. "Besides jail, that is. I've been waiting for you."

CHAPTER TWENTY-THREE

"I'M TRYING TO keep Joslyn alive and myself out of jail," Garrett snapped.

"So am I, no thanks to your interference," Sid snapped back.

Joslyn stepped between them. "We don't believe that Frankie or Harvey hired Leon Sheffield to kill me."

Sid sighed. "So who does that leave?"

She looked to Garrett, still hoping she was wrong.

"The clerk at the convenience store was in on it. He figured out that Frankie and George just might decide to kill him as well as Joslyn, so he pulled the gun and killed George," Garrett said to the sheriff. "We talked to Harvey Mattson. He has every reason to want Joslyn alive."

Sid nodded, but said, "Although her name is Monica Wilmington. I agree. While all that might be true, so far all you've done is gotten yourself into more trouble."

"So that leaves the person who killed my father and stepmother," Joslyn said.

"Maybe," the sheriff said.

"Or the person who doesn't want her getting her

inheritance in a few days," Garrett added. "The trail seems to lead back to her family and the money."

"Her stepsister and brother," Sid said.

Joslyn shook her head. "Not just them. My guardian, lawyer and doctor have also been like family for almost twenty-five years and I'm sure there is some monetary provision for them as well should I die before my birthday. Amethyst and Peter are related by marriage. But my lawyer and doctor have been on retainer for the past twenty-five years. That ends when I turn thirty which is coming up soon." Neither man spoke for a moment.

She saw it in their expressions. "I know what they write about me. Poor little rich girl. No one loves her."

"Someone does," Garrett said.

Sid sighed. "This is getting us nowhere. You two are on thin ice. Let me spell it out for you. Garrett, you're facing prison for kidnapping—since you've crossed state lines we're talking federal. Joslyn, your family wants you locked up and will be sending armed guards this time."

"So what are we going to do about that? You send her back and you know what will happen," Garrett argued. "They'll kill her. Make it look like a suicide or a drug overdose or—"

Sid held up his hand. "We don't know that, but I'm not sending her back unless I'm forced to."

"And you can't lock up Garrett. He saved my life and you know it," Joslyn said.

"Your birthday is only two days away," Sid said,

his voice more calm and understanding. "Let's assume you won't be safe until it's over. Maybe putting the two of you behind bars is the safest place for you both."

She shook her head. "I won't be safe until I get rid of that money. I have set up an automatic payout to numerous charities for the entire amount of my inheritance the moment that money goes into my account at midnight the night before my actual birthday—so the day after tomorrow."

"All of it? I'm assuming they've tried to talk you out of doing that," Sid said.

Her grunt tasted as bitter as it sounded. "You could say that. It's another reason Alistair doesn't think I'm in my right mind. But I've learned a lot about how my father made that money. I don't want any of it. I've been doing fine without it the past two years. What we have to do is draw the killer out before my birthday."

Both men erupted in disagreement.

"What if I invite them to Montana for my birthday and see who shows up?" she said as an idea took shape.

"We're not using you as bait," Garrett said. "We'll hide you away somewhere until—"

"No," she said firmly. "I'm through hiding."

"I'll go with you somewhere until your birthday," he said. "After that—"

She groaned. "I'm sick of running, Garrett. Anyway, if I don't do this, then I will never know which of them wants me dead enough to pay ten thousand dollars to Frank Rutledge. Or who knows how much for the other times I was nearly run down in the street or had a near accident in my car."

"You might find out just before they kill you," Sid interjected.

"We'll invite them out here to Montana to show them I'm fine," she said as if the sheriff hadn't spoken. "I know Alistair. He's worried about me. I'll tell him I want to prove that I've never been better. I suspect the rest will come. If we're right, one of them will show his or her hand before midnight when I turn thirty."

"I can't let you do that," Sid said, even though she knew he couldn't stop her. Only her family could with another court order. She couldn't let that happen. "I'll call a lawyer to deal with any order they try to get, but I don't think they'll try. I'll tell Alistair that if he isn't convinced that I'm fine, I will commit myself, *after* my birthday."

"What makes you that sure they will even come?" Garrett asked.

She turned to him and smiled sadly. "They'll come. It will be their last chance to talk me out of my plan for my inheritance—or to kill me."

He shook his head. "Do you have any idea what you're suggesting?"

"No matter what we do, they aren't going to give up," she argued. "If I'm right and all this has been about my inheritance, then one of them doesn't want me to see midnight on the day before my birthday. They will send someone after me or get another court order so they can get to me back home. Won't I be safer with me calling the shots?"

"Not necessarily," the sheriff said. "You're using yourself as bait. With the birthday deadline looming, one of them just might be crazy enough to try to kill you themselves."

"That person won't get much of a chance since the others will be there," Joslyn said. "They don't all want me dead."

"Let's hope not," Sid said.

"But if they try, I'll be ready. And come midnight before my birthday, the threat is over. The money will be gone to charities and I will finally be safe."

"*We'll* be ready," Garrett corrected. "She has a point," he said to the sheriff, with obvious reluctance. "She'll be safer on home court with me. We'll do it at the guest ranch. With it closed for the summer, it's the safest place."

Joslyn looked at him. "The guest ranch? Garrett—"

"Joslyn, I will be with you. It's the safest place if you're determined to do this."

"Safest? You're talking about inviting a murderer to your family guest ranch," the sheriff argued. "This person was desperate enough to hire a hit man. You think he or she won't do it again?"

"No, I don't. Not at the guest ranch," Joslyn said. "A hit man would stand out there. No, the person who wants me dead so badly will have to do the killing himself or herself."

"And that is supposed to make any of us feel better about this?" Sid demanded.

"You can lock me up and send Joslyn back, but you would be signing her death warrant if you do," Garrett said.

Sid rubbed his neck for a moment. "Your brothers aren't going to like this."

"I'll worry about my brothers. Just give us until her birthday. After that—"

"I'm not the one you have to worry about. Alistair could have you arrested and Joslyn committed. Or you could both be killed," the sheriff argued.

"He's right," Joslyn said turning to Garrett. "I've already risked your life and put you in danger. I can't ask you to—"

"The guest ranch was my idea," he said, meeting her gaze and holding it. She looked into his blue eyes and felt heat rush through her. "We're in this together."

She smiled and touched his stubbled jaw, wanting desperately to kiss him. When the desire became too much, she leaned into him and did just that. She heard Sid groan and say, "You two are going to be the death of me."

Laughing, she pulled back from the kiss. "I'll deal with Alistair. You're sure about this?"

Garrett's smile was sad and tender, but he nodded.

"Why didn't I retire last year?" Sid was saying to himself. "What was I thinking? I could end up behind bars for helping the two of you."

Joslyn came over and kissed him on the cheek. "Thank you. If you go to jail, I'll come visit you."

He laughed at that and blushed a little as Garrett handed her his phone to make the call.

"I just hope that Rutledge makes his deal and we find out who hired him in time," the sheriff said. "Otherwise, I want you both to know, I'm going to be at that guest ranch if you need me."

"Alistair," Joslyn said into the phone. "I'm so glad I caught you."

AFTER SHE HUNG UP, she realized how late it was. Garrett looked at his watch. "No way are we driving back tonight. We'll go in the morning. Your family isn't coming in until tomorrow late, right?"

She nodded, too exhausted after the day she'd had to think about tomorrow. The day had been one of emotional upheaval punctuated with moments of terror and she was feeling drained. She could see that it had taken its toll on Garrett as well.

"I'm going back to Whitefish now," Sid said. "Are you sure the two of you will be all right?"

"I'm not sure of anything right now," Garrett said. "But I'll get us rooms. With a good night's sleep, we'll be ready for tomorrow."

Joslyn caught the word *rooms*, not that she was up to anything other than sleep. True to his word, Garrett got them adjoining rooms. The moment she hit the bed, she was out.

"WHAT WAS IT you would have had me do?" Alistair asked the usual group gathered in his living room late that evening, drinking his expensive liquor and demanding he handle Monica. He'd called them after her phone call, asking them to come over. He'd had the chef make a few appetizers and broke out more of the good stuff for the bar, knowing they wouldn't take this latest request from Monica well.

"Have this man arrested," Amethyst cried after hearing that a cowboy named Garrett Sterling had abducted Monica from the ambulance that was bringing her back for observation. "Who is he, anyway?" she demanded as she took one of the large prawns wrapped in bacon.

"Apparently someone she knows since she went willingly with him to his guest ranch before all of this."

"Which shows that she isn't in her right mind," Neal pointed out as he rattled the ice cubes in his glass nervously.

"I agree with Amethyst," Rance chimed in, as if that was a surprise. He'd filled up his plate with appetizers and was lounging with his drink in one of the large leather chairs. "I'm amazed you've waited this long to call the authorities."

He'd been as shocked as anyone when Monica had called. He'd immediately contacted the sheriff, who'd confirmed that he knew about her plan and while he hadn't exactly approved it, he would be around if there was any trouble. He relayed this information to the group.

"Some backwoods sheriff?" Benjamin had scoffed. "That makes me feel *so* much better," he said, his voice dripping with sarcasm. He got up to help himself to the appetizers before Amethyst ate all the shrimp ones. Alistair knew this bunch so well. The only one who ever surprised him was Monica.

Since Monica was a teen, he'd been getting calls that surprised him, none more than this latest one. "She wants us all to come to this guest ranch in the mountains for her birthday."

"Ridiculous," Benjamin said.

"She's acting out because of her early trauma," Neal pointed out, not for the first time. "She needs more therapy."

But Monica had had enough "couch time," as she called it with "that snake-oil salesman." Alistair had found her take on the doctor amusing, though he'd never told her that. She reminded him so much of her father. He missed Horace and wished his friend were raising Monica. The thought filled him with regret.

"I don't care what she wants," Amethyst said as she popped another prawn into her mouth.

Alistair had questioned every decision he made involving Monica. He wasn't cut out to be a father let alone a guardian. He felt the weight of his job bending him into shapes he didn't recognize.

The sheriff had assured him that she was fine. That Garrett was a reliable protector. That having him arrested for kidnapping wasn't necessary.

He could admit now that the commitment order had been a mistake. He should have handled it differently. But Neal had been convincing and ultimately, Alistair's first responsibility was to Monica's well-being.

"I don't believe we handled this well," he told the psychiatrist. "So you can't blame Garrett Sterling for feeling as if he needed to save her. The sheriff tells me the man cares for her."

Neal groaned. "He cares for *one* of her personalities, not Monica Wilmington. I'm betting he's never met Monica and would be shocked if he did."

Alistair couldn't argue that, since apparently she'd gone by the name Joslyn Charles when she'd had a brief affair with Sterling two years ago—and was using it again now.

"I agree. What she's suggesting *is* ridiculous." Peter finally spoke up from his corner of the room where he'd been lounging against the wall. "I, for one, am not playing along. I'm not going."

"It's only for a couple of days," Rance said, surprising him. "We could all fly out tomorrow, celebrate her birthday at midnight and all fly back the next day. What would it hurt to indulge her for basically a day and then if you still think she's off her rocker, have her locked up and the man arrested for kidnapping."

Neal made a rude sound and started to argue, but Alistair cut him off. "Rance is right." He knew that had to be the first time he'd ever uttered those words. "We haven't handled this well with all the drama of having her sedated and taken against her will by ambulance. She's said that after her birthday, she will check herself into the hospital if we still think she needs it."

"After her birthday, she will be legally beyond

your control," Benjamin pointed out. "Your power of attorney will be null and void."

"He's never had her *under* his control," Amethyst quipped. "Monica has always done whatever she's wanted and none of you have been able to do a thing about it. This is no different."

Alistair ignored her taunts. They were true, so what could he say anyway?

What it came down to was that Monica was about to be filthy rich very soon. She'd threatened to give every dime of the money away. But would she? It was one thing to threaten to do such a thing and another to actually do it.

But unless she did need treatment, his job would be done. That thought should have relieved him. He'd lived up to his promise to Horace. He'd taken care of Monica, the apple of her father's eye.

"We could take my company's private jet," Alistair said and glanced at Peter. "At least the ones who want to go. She asked for all of us though." He knew what Benjamin was saying about the power of attorney and while he wouldn't admit it to this bunch, he was ready to let Monica go. He'd done what her father had asked. He was ready for this to end.

He thought about never seeing these people again and smiled. "So who wants to go with me in the jet?"

"I hate to fly and you know it," Amethyst snapped. He wanted to tell her that this wasn't about her, but that had been the case since she was thirteen. He didn't doubt that it was part of the reason that she felt like the abused stepchild even though she'd been far from abused.

Eight years ago when she'd turned thirty, she'd gotten a small fortune. Nowhere near as large as Monica's though. No, Amethyst had just never been the focus and still wasn't.

"I'm going to take the train," she announced. Rance groaned, since with no backbone to stand up to her, he would be forced to take the train as well.

"I'll call to see if we can at least get a room," he said. "I'm not going coach."

Peter pushed himself off the wall. "Have a nice time at the dude ranch. Don't forget to take your Stetsons and your boots, but I'm tired of all of this. I really don't give a damn what Monica or Joslyn or whoever she wants to be does." He started for the door. "Did Alistair mention that there is no cell service or internet at this…ranch? I just checked it out on my phone." He chuckled at Amethyst's horrified look.

"Yes, Sterling's Montana Guest Ranch is off the grid," Alistair said. "I guess I forgot to mention that."

Peter hesitated at the door before he turned. "You're getting forgetful, Al. Maybe you should have the doc here look you over." He opened the door and walked out.

"He was joking, right?" Amethyst demanded as she got to her feet. Alistair shook his head. She let out a curse and stomped her foot. "This is the last time for me. I will never be at Monica's beck and call ever again. Ever! I'll go just to put an end to this." She motioned to Rance that they were leaving.

Alistair turned to Benjamin and Neal. "What about the two of you?"

"As her doctor, I feel I have to be there." He looked to the lawyer.

Benjamin sighed. "I suspect I'll be needed for the legalities of signing over her inheritance when this is over. But I think I'll drive out early in the morning."

They rose to leave. Alistair thought it had gone well, all things considered. Sighing, he reached for his phone to arrange the flight to Whitefish. Did he think Monica was crazy for doing this? Maybe. Or maybe it was the only way for this odd-shaped family of hers to be together for her birthday. They'd missed so many other ones.

That she wanted to spend this birthday with them though did make him wonder. It also made him sad. She deserved better, always had. He felt as if he'd failed her in so many ways. But at least he could give her this one final request before his job as guardian was over.

He'd thought Amethyst had left until he heard her voice from the doorway. "You've spoiled her just like her father did," Amethyst accused, getting the last word in before she departed.

As the door closed behind her, Alistair knew it was true. He'd had a soft spot for that frightened traumatized five-year-old he'd inherited. He still did.

But this time he wasn't sure he would be able to save her from herself.

CHAPTER TWENTY-FOUR

"I'M GOING TO need your help."

Undersheriff Ward Farnsworth got up from his desk to close his office door so no one overheard this phone call. Since their last phone call, he'd tried to figure out who his benefactor was. He'd learned that the Jane Doe's name was Monica Wilmington and her guardian's name was Alistair Vanderlin. He'd looked him up online. The former businessman had done quite well for himself—as had Monica's father before he was murdered. Ward wondered if his caller was Alistair. He was looking forward to meeting him one day so he could find out, because he was pretty sure the soft-spoken voice was a man's. "Just tell me what you need."

"You said we could be honest? I don't have a lot of faith in your sheriff."

Ward couldn't agree more. "It's a good thing he's retiring. It's definitely time." He just wished Sid had retired last year. He knew he would be a better sheriff than Sid was right now.

"I'm sure you've heard that Garrett Sterling has kidnapped Monica. Do you have any idea where they might be?"

This was news to him. If it was true, then why hadn't the FBI been called in? Why wouldn't there be a BOLO out on Garrett? Because Sid was protecting him. Ward didn't have much respect for the man, but this proved it was time for a sheriff who didn't play favorites.

"The FBI needs to be called in," he said into the phone.

"I don't want to do that. I was hoping you could help me keep this out of the press. I'm sure by now you know that Monica…well, because of who her father was… You understand. We don't want the bad publicity. If you could just let me know if she turns up. I really want to try to keep this quiet."

"I understand," he said, even though he hated it. He would have loved to call the FBI, have Garrett arrested, have Sid removed from his position, become acting sheriff until the election.

"Also, let me know if the sheriff is still investigating this case. I feel like nothing is being done."

"I can certainly do that."

"You have been so helpful. I hope I can repay the favor. In fact, I'm even more convinced you should be sheriff. I'm going to send along some campaign contributions from some friends of mine. But I may need your help again soon."

"Just name it." Ward hung up, thrilled. Maybe being sheriff was too small a dream. Maybe he should consider getting into real politics, become a senator. With the right backing…

In the meantime, he had to do something. If he

was in charge, he knew he could solve this case. But Sid wasn't letting him near it. Then again if Sid had some reason to step down as sheriff...

"WELL, AT LEAST we know the law isn't looking for us—not yet anyway," Joslyn said the next morning as they drove into the outskirts of Whitefish. They'd both been exhausted last night and anxious this morning to get to the ranch to prepare for their guests who should be arriving this afternoon.

They hadn't talked much on the drive back to town. Garrett had worried about the plan Joslyn had set into motion. In the clear light of day, he had his doubts, but when he broached the subject with her, she'd made it clear that she was even more determined.

"It's the only way I will ever be free of Monica," she said, then grinned at him. "I don't have a split personality. But that name is so much about my poor little rich girl past that I've had to live with for twenty-five years. Who wouldn't want to shed it and start over fresh?"

He hoped that was what would happen after all of this. He wanted that fresh start as desperately as she did. But thinking of the countdown to her birthday and the people who were coming to the guest ranch today, he feared it might not be in the cards. Midnight wasn't that far away. They were taking one hell of a gamble. They'd been lucky so far. He just hoped that their luck held.

"I checked my credit card purchases on your

phone this morning," she said. "The last time I used my card was to refuel at a convenience mart not far from here. Can we swing by there? With my Jeep being red, it shouldn't be that hard to spot if it's around there."

"Good thinking," he said. Billy was right. He really did need to join this century. He'd mostly used the cell phone as a phone and little else. But then again, there still wasn't service at the guest ranch or a lot of other places in Montana so it was no wonder that he'd found the device fairly useless. "That means that your car should be somewhere around here, depending on where you crossed paths with Leon Sheffield."

"Yes. Before I killed him."

He heard the catch in her voice. "Leon was a hardened criminal. A man who'd burned his fingerprints off with acid."

She shuddered, no doubt realizing how close she'd come to dying. Garrett still saw it all in his sleep. He wondered if he could ever get the image out of his mind—even though it hadn't been the woman lying in the deep weeds. It could have been Joslyn he'd found dead on that mountainside. She could still end up dead and that was what haunted him in his dreams.

"It seems reasonable that I was abducted and taken into the mountains," she said. "Didn't you tell me that the sheriff found a map to your guest ranch in the wrecked car? Leon must have missed the turn and that's how we ended up on the ridge across from your ranch—instead of at your ranch." She shuddered again. "If he hadn't—"

Garrett reached over and took her hand. Squeezing it gently, he said, "We're going to get through this."

She nodded, but he knew she had to be as scared and anxious as he was.

Garrett wasn't sure what finding her car would accomplish, but he could tell that it was important to her. She was still trying to put the missing pieces of her abduction together. In the meantime, her family was on the way to the guest ranch. He wanted to get ready for them.

He glanced at his watch, assuring himself that there was time. Even if Alistair came on his private plane, he probably couldn't get to the guest ranch before late afternoon.

"There might be something in my car," she said, sounding as if she knew she was grasping at straws. He thought of the photo she'd said she remembered. If it didn't exist… He didn't want to think about it. There was little chance they would even find the car. They had no idea where she was abducted. Whitefish wasn't large, but the area around it was.

Again, it would be like looking for a needle in a haystack. Smiling to himself, he thought about what Billy said about luck. So far luck was with them. He was just thankful that she didn't drive a neutral-colored SUV because there were dozens and dozens of them.

After finding the convenience store where she'd

last bought gas, he drove around a few blocks and had started out of town toward the ranch, thinking if that was where she'd been headed, it would be the most likely place to find her car.

They hadn't gone far when she cried, "There it is!"

The red Jeep was parked next to an empty lot. As he pulled to a stop, she was already out of the truck and rushing to the vehicle. He saw her try the door. Unlocked.

Reaching in, she disappeared from view, coming up with her purse, which she'd retrieved from the floorboard. He was amazed it was still in the un-locked vehicle or that the vehicle hadn't been towed.

She seemed to be looking around for something else. He saw her disappear out of view again and come up with her car keys that had apparently fallen between the seats.

Whatever she'd found, she put it in her purse as she ran back to climb into the passenger side of the truck. "I was right," she said, sounding excited.

He waited as she opened her purse and pulled out an envelope. He saw that there was no stamp, no re-turn address, just a single word: *Krystal.*

The flap hadn't been glued shut, either. He watched her lift the flap and pull out a single item. He blinked as she handed him the photograph. Looking down, he saw it was of the two of them. Just as she'd said. Just as she'd remembered. "This is what brought you to Whitefish."

She nodded.

Had he believed there was a photo? Or was he

still worried that she'd lied about why she'd come to Whitefish. She'd come here to save him. The irony of it didn't escape him. She'd risked her own life for his—just as she'd said.

Garrett had to swallow the lump in his throat. How could he keep doubting this woman he loved? "You have no idea who left it?" he asked.

"None, but it looks as if it was taken with a telephoto lens from some distance," she said, excitement in her voice. "It's why I bolted, why I tried to get to you to warn you. They not only knew the name I was living under and where to find me, but also they knew about us. They wanted me to know that they knew about you. By threatening you, they knew I would bolt."

He stared at the photo for a long moment before looking up at her again. Someone had wanted her to head to Whitefish to warn him. They'd wanted her out of the feds' protection. They'd used him to get to her. And she'd risked her life in an attempt to warn him.

"I'm so sorry for doubting you." He turned to her, his heart breaking. He'd been afraid to trust her, trust what he felt for her. She must have gone for the gun in her purse and Leon Sheffield took it from her, planning to use it on her once they reached the guest ranch. Only he'd gotten lost and the rest was history. "I'm so sorry."

She shook her head, tears in her eyes. "You have nothing to be sorry about. I'm the one who brought trouble to your door. I thought I was protecting you but…" Her voice broke.

He reached over and pulled her to him. "Joslyn." He'd wanted, needed, her in his arms for so long. "Oh, Joslyn."

Emotion boiled over in her eyes. Tears began to stream down her face as he kissed her softly on the mouth. A pleasurable sigh escaped her. He dragged her to him, taking her mouth with a passion that had always blazed between them. He lost herself in her lips until a horn honked on the street and they jumped apart.

For a moment, he'd forgotten just how much trouble they were in. All he'd wanted was to take her somewhere the two of them could be together. For almost two years he'd yearned for this every day. Just being around her had stoked the flames of his desire. Kissing her… He didn't want to let her out of his arms.

But a sense of survival kicked in that was almost as strong as the desire he felt for this woman. He had to keep her alive. Keep them both alive until her birthday and right now, he had no idea how to do that.

"We need to get to the ranch."

"I'll follow you in my car." She was out of the pickup and running toward her car before he could answer. Reaching it, she turned to smile back at him. He felt an arrow of desire pierce his heart. All he could think about was getting to the guest ranch, the two of them alone, the two of them finally truly together. There would be time. There had to be time for them to be together before everyone arrived.

He watched her climb into the Jeep. A thought struck him like a brick. He threw open the door of his pickup, not realizing he was already screaming her name, as he ran toward the Jeep.

Reaching it, he threw open her door just as she was about to put the key into the ignition. He was screaming "NO!" as he'd grabbed her and tried to pull her out, but she'd already put on her seat belt. She was looking at him as the key went into the ignition and she turned it, looking at him as if he'd lost his mind, just moments before the first explosion.

CHAPTER TWENTY-FIVE

JOSLYN FELT HER seat belt release and Garrett's strong arms pull her out as an explosion rocked the Jeep. She saw flames shoot up from under the hood as he ran with her toward his waiting pickup.

Another explosion boomed, this one much louder and stronger behind her. She turned in his arms to see the Jeep lifted up off the ground for an instant before the entire vehicle turned into a ball of fire. She could feel the heat on her face as he put her down next to the pickup and turned to look back.

People came running from around the neighborhood. She saw some of them making calls on their cell phones, others videoing the burning Jeep.

Joslyn stared at what was left of her Jeep, her legs suddenly weak as she leaned against Garrett, realization hitting her. Smoke rose into Montana's big sky. In the distance she heard the sound of the sirens. Sid pulled up as the first fire truck arrived and motioned them over to his patrol SUV. She realized Garrett had called him.

"What was that?" he asked of the blackened shape now smoking in the side parking lot as firemen raced around to put out the last of the flames.

"It was my Jeep," Joslyn said, her voice cracking.

"Someone had rigged it with what sounded like two separate explosive devices," Garrett told him. "I should have thought of it before I let her get near that car, let alone start it."

"You see why I have to do this?" she cried. "I have to know who's trying to kill me."

Sid was quiet for a long moment. "I'm trying to imagine how Leon Sheffield could have done that the same day he abducted her."

Garrett shook his head. "He couldn't have. And we know he couldn't have come back that day to do it because he was dead."

"It wasn't him," Joslyn said. "Right before I started to turn the key in the ignition, I had a flash of memory. I'd pulled over to that spot because I had something dragging from my car. When I got out, I saw that someone had tied a tin can on the back. I untied it and was getting back into the Jeep when he came at me from behind. I dropped my keys between the seats as he shoved a gun into my back and forced me into his car. I remember starting to scream. That's all I remember until I woke up and he was pulling me out of the car again, only this time we were on the side of a mountain."

She saw Garrett and the sheriff exchange a look.

"If Leon didn't wire the Jeep with explosives…" Sid said. "The person who hired him? Not likely."

"That person must have known where the Jeep was," Garrett said. "When Leon bungled the job, they hired someone to make sure she never drove away. How did they know where the Jeep was though?"

She shivered. "They put a tracking device on my car."

Garrett put his arm around her and pulled her close. She breathed in the male scent of him. It mingled with the acrid smell of smoke.

"I hope this is a wake-up call for the two of you," the sheriff said. "Whoever wants you dead isn't giving up."

"We already knew that," Garrett said. "And we suspect why. We just have to narrow it down." He looked to Joslyn. "Unless you don't want to go ahead with our plan."

She shook her head, feeling anger replace her earlier terror and shock. "I haven't changed my mind. If anything, I am more determined to find out who is behind this. I've already talked to Alistair. He said he would do his best to get them all to come to the guest ranch."

Sid sighed. "I'll take your statements so you won't be held up at the police station." A police car had just pulled up to the scene. "But I think you're both making a mistake."

"At the stroke of midnight, every dime of my father's money will automatically go to the charities I've chosen," Joslyn said. "All I have to do is stay alive that long."

Sid shook his head.

"Are you sure about this?" Garrett asked. "We can still call it off."

"I've never been more sure of anything except..."

She met his gaze and smiled. "I just want it over. I don't want my father's money. I never have."

"Then why not give it to your family?" the sheriff suggested. "Let them kill each other over it."

She shook her head. "I have to do something good with it. They would blow it and then be miserable again. This way they can get right to the misery."

"You're joking," Sid said. "But this is serious. If one of them really wants you dead…" A weighted silence fell between them.

"I will be with her every minute," Garrett said.

"If you're able," the sheriff pointed out. "You have my cell phone number. Call from your landline anytime day or night. I won't be far away."

Garrett thanked him. "But like Joslyn said, there is safety in numbers. All we have to do is get to midnight and the money issue will be moot. There will be no reason to kill her. It will be over."

"I hope you're right." With Sid's help, they breezed through the report and once finally dismissed, they headed for the guest ranch, both somber and silent on the ride. Even with the sheriff's help, they'd lost valuable time.

"You saved my life. *Again*," she said as the full impact of what had almost happened hit her. "How can I ever thank you?"

"Don't thank me yet. But once this is all over…" He met her gaze, a promise in those blue eyes that gave her hope the two of them would make it through this and get their chance to be together at last.

CHAPTER TWENTY-SIX

THEY'D BARELY GOTTEN to the ranch when Alistair Vanderlin arrived. Joslyn had gone up to shower and change while Garrett was busy getting the cabins ready. They'd been all business, knowing what was at stake. They'd barely spoken, let alone touched. He told himself there would be time enough when this was over. He hoped.

Garrett had just returned to the lodge when Joslyn had come downstairs. They'd both turned at the sound of a car driving up. As they watched Vanderlin from the front window of the lodge, Garrett reached over and took Joslyn's hand. It was ice cold.

"Last chance?" he asked quietly.

She smiled over at him and shook her head. "You don't mind me giving up all that money? It's not like I'm broke. I had an allowance for years that I put away along with money I made when I picked up odd jobs. I built up quite a nest egg."

He smiled, hearing the pride in her voice. "It won't be long and your inheritance will be helping a whole lot of people—and unburdening you." At least that was the plan. He turned his attention back to the man getting out of the large black SUV he'd apparently rented when he landed, since he'd texted Joslyn that he would be flying in.

Vanderlin hesitated for a moment before he closed the SUV door. He stood looking around the place until his gaze settled on the lodge. Garrett figured that the sun off the glass hid his view of them because the man had no reaction until they opened the front door and walked out onto the porch.

"Monica," Vanderlin said, sounding disappointed. His tone matched his expression. "Was this really necessary?"

"I'm glad you came," she said and moved to him to kiss his cheek. "And the others?"

Vanderlin sighed. "They're on their way. Except for Peter. He refused to come."

One less possible murderer, Garrett thought, and realized that Peter not showing up didn't exonerate him. He could have hired someone to finish what he'd already started. It would just be hard for a hitman to get to Joslyn up here at the guest ranch.

Vanderlin's gaze shifted to him. He was a large, distinguished gray-haired man in a dark suit. Garrett could tell that the man was used to things going his way. "You're lucky you aren't in jail. But Monica has asked me not to do anything until after her birthday."

"Officially midnight tonight. By the way, we found my car earlier," Joslyn said. "It was rigged to explode when I started the motor. Fortunately, Garrett pulled me out before the Jeep turned into a fireball."

Vanderlin paled visibly. "Monica, what kind of trouble are you in?"

"Funny you should ask," she said. "I had a visit with Harvey Mattson at his prison yesterday."

Her guardian let out a gasp. "Why would you do that?"

"To find out if he was behind these attempts on my life. He isn't. I'm sure of it."

"You took his word for that?"

"I'm convinced that my would-be killer is much closer to home, so to speak. That's why I've invited you all to my birthday," she said. "By midnight tonight, I think we'll know who wants me dead."

The man looked aghast. "You can't be serious."

"Dead serious," she said.

Vanderlin's shoulders hunched for a moment before he straightened and said, "So that is what this... guest ranch birthday party is about. Oh, Monica. You do realize that Dr. Foster is even more concerned about your...mental health now. If he hears about this—"

"I don't want you to tell the others," she said. "Let it be a surprise to everyone. I probably shouldn't have even told you. If you're my would-be assassin, then I've spoiled the surprise, huh."

He shook his head, looking disappointed in her. "You're making me question if you're in your right mind if you think I would ever hurt you."

She said nothing.

"Why don't I show you to your cabin," Garrett

suggested, stepping off the porch. "We have every-thing ready for you."

Vanderlin glanced toward the cabins stuck back in the pines, then reluctantly pulled out his over-night case.

"Just this way," Garrett said and led the man to cabin number one, the closest one to the lodge. He opened the door. Vanderlin stepped in cautiously as if he thought it would be occupied by a varmint of some kind.

Garrett thought it almost humorous. He doubted the man had ever stayed in anything like the cabin—even though it was nicely furnished.

"There is a phone," he explained. "But it is only for calling the lodge or one of the other cabins. There is no internet, no telephones or television."

The man instantly pulled out his cell phone. "No service at all?"

"None." This was typical of what guests often did. He'd seen some wandering around trying to get at least one bar as if their lives depended on it.

"What if there is an emergency?" Vanderlin de-manded.

"There's a landline in the lodge, though it's not for guests to use."

"Seriously, what is the point of all this?" the man demanded. "I know you think you're helping her but—"

"This was all Jos—Monica's idea," he said. "I'm just providing the location."

"She really believes someone in her family wants to kill her?"

"So do I. And not just her family. That's why her doctor and lawyer were also invited."

The man shook his head. "It breaks my heart that she would even think such a thing let alone set something like this up, believing one of them is capable of murder."

"Food and drinks will be served up at the lodge," Garrett said. "You're welcome to rest here until the others arrive or take a walk. Perhaps you'll all want to take a horseback ride later."

Vanderlin looked appalled. "We aren't here to ride horses. We're here to see to Monica. I can't believe you don't realize what a troubled young woman she is."

"I guess I have to remind you that someone tried to kill her and we suspect will again. That is definitely troubling to me as well."

"Yes," the man said, eyeing him. "But what you're not taking into account is that she attracts trouble like metal to magnet. She's always associated with the…wrong people." His eyes narrowed. "Exactly what is your relationship with my ward?"

"I'm in love with her and if I have my way, I'm going to marry her."

Vanderlin scoffed at that. "I should warn you that no man can ever inherit her money married or not."

Garrett's laugh was bitter. "I expected you to think first of the money. That's very telling for a man who I'm told is wealthy in his own right."

"I don't want Monica's money," Vanderlin snapped.

"Neither do I. I didn't even know she had an inheritance when I bought the engagement ring for her." The man lifted a brow. "Two years ago when I first met her and fell for her, I didn't even know her real name. So you're the only one worried about her money." He started to turn and leave when he heard the sound of a vehicle. "Sounds like the others are arriving. When you're ready, come over to the lodge for refreshments before dinner."

He was anxious to get back to Joslyn. Not that he thought anyone would try to harm her immediately. But he wasn't taking any chances.

As he stepped out of cabin one, he got his first look at her stepsister.

JOSLYN HADN'T SEEN Amethyst in years and was surprised how little she had changed. She watched her climb out of a black SUV almost identical to Vanderlin's and wrinkle her surgically modified pert nose at what she saw. Her expression changed little when she saw Joslyn.

"Amethyst, I'm so glad you came," she said as she descended the steps.

"What choice did I have? Alistair said you'd lost your mind and that we had to come for fear of what you'd do next."

Joslyn doubted that was what he'd said. All he'd had to do was tell them that she was cutting off everyone financially and giving all of her inheritance to charities. That would be enough to send them all into a panic.

"It's good to see you," Joslyn said as Amethyst leaned in to give her an air kiss. "It's been too long. We really should keep in touch more than we do."

Her stepsister pulled back to give her a surprised look that asked why.

"We're the only family we have," Joslyn said.

Amethyst made a disgruntled sound. "We barely know each other."

"My fault since I've been…away."

Her stepsister laughed at that. "Wasting the tax-payers' money with your paranoia. At least that's what Alistair says."

She doubted Alistair said that either, but she was surprised that Amethyst knew she'd been in the witness protection program. Did all of them know that? "That sounds more like something your husband would say. By the way, where is he?"

Her stepsister waved a hand toward the SUV. "He and I took the train. Fortunately, Neal was flying in and Ben was driving, so he picked us all up."

Dr. Neal Foster, her psychiatrist, and Benjamin Purdy, her family attorney, emerged from the SUV. The last person out was of course Amethyst's husband, Rance. He looked as happy to be here as the others.

Joslyn was wondering if this wasn't a mistake, when Garrett appeared at her side and offered to see them to their cabins.

"Cabins?" Rance snickered. "How…quaint." The man moved to her to give her air kisses.

"I'm so glad you're here," she said and he grunted in response.

"You know Amethyst. She hates to go anywhere without me."

Joslyn looked up to see her stepsister roll her eyes.

"I'm sorry," she said. "I haven't introduced you to Garrett Sterling, your host and the man who saved my life earlier when my Jeep blew up."

"WHAT?" THEY ALL seemed to ask in a chorus of disbelief.

Garrett didn't believe any of their shocked faces.

"Someone had my Jeep wired with explosives," Joslyn said. "Fortunately, Garrett realized it and got me out before the explosion that destroyed my vehicle."

Amethyst looked skeptical. "That sounds like something out of a movie. Maybe you just flooded the motor and—"

"The sheriff and local police have called in investigators," Garrett interrupted. "They hope to find evidence to lead them to the person who tried to kill her, although we suspect someone hired the job done. But if they find the person who wired it, he could lead them to whoever hired him." It was a bluff, but he liked shutting up Joslyn's stepsister.

"Garrett," Rance said, raising his nose in the air. "You own this place?"

"With my brothers," he said taking in the expensively dressed man. Joslyn had told him a little about each of the people arriving.

"Rance Carrington," the man said with an air of superiority as he held out his hand. He was a slim man, who clearly worked out a lot, with a head of thick blond hair that he shook back into place with one smooth shift of his head. Beside him, Amethyst cleared her throat. "I don't believe you've met my beautiful wife, Amethyst."

Garrett turned to the woman after shaking Rance's hand. She was taller than her husband, with a pale surgically improved face and blond hair. Her eyes were a clear icy blue.

"The stepsister I've heard so much about," Garrett said and held out his hand.

Amethyst looked startled, her gaze going to Joslyn as she delicately shook his hand.

Joslyn had tried to say only good things about her stepsister, but in truth it was clear that Amethyst had never cared for the younger stepsister she'd inherited through marriage.

The other two visitors stepped forward then to offer their hands. Dr. Neal Foster was an attractive fiftysomething man who must have been hired right out of medical school by Alistair.

The doctor shook Garrett's hand, though his gaze was on Joslyn. And when he spoke, it was to her. "How are you, dear?"

"Fine," she said and smiled.

The other man stepped forward and offered his hand. "Attorney Benjamin Purdy."

"The family lawyer," Garrett said. "Welcome, I'm Garrett Sterling and this is my family's guest ranch. I hope you'll all be comfortable here."

As the attorney released his hand, Garrett turned to the group of them. "If you'll come with me, I'll get you settled in before supper."

Rance was looking around. "Are we your only guests?"

"The ranch is closed this summer for some construction. The crew working on the barn won't be back until Monday so, yes, it's just us," Garrett said. "Is that a problem?"

"Not at all," the man said and put his arm around his wife. "We like peace and quiet, don't we, darling?"

She shook his arm off and said over her shoulder as she moved away from him, "Get my bags."

Garrett repeated what he told the others about refreshments before dinner.

"I'll take a drink now," Amethyst said and headed for the lodge. The others agreed and followed. A few moments later, Alistair joined them.

Each had a drink and then Garrett closed the bar and offered again to take them down to their cabins, explaining he would ring the bell when dinner was ready.

JOSLYN FELT SICK to her stomach as she watched Garrett walk them down to their cabins. It was the first time she'd had a chance to catch her breath. She tried to relax but stiffened as she realized that she wasn't alone.

"Monica?"

She hadn't heard Alistair come up behind her and couldn't help starting as she spun around to realize he had left with the others and apparently doubled back.

"I do hope you know what you're doing," he said.

Joslyn smiled, hoping the same thing. He met her gaze and held it. He looked scared. He wasn't the only one. If she was right, one of these people wanted her dead. They were people she'd known all her life. People she'd trusted. She didn't want to believe it and yet...

She saw that he'd left the front door of the lodge open. She breathed in the sweet scent of the pines and reminded herself that this was her idea. If she was right, one of them would be coming for her in the next few hours.

"I want to help you," he said.

"Help me? Is that why you signed papers to have me committed?"

Alistair flushed. "I would never have agreed to that if I thought it wasn't critical for you to have the care you needed. I don't approve of the way Neal handled it."

"Really? Do I seem to need medical attention?"

His gaze softened. "You have to admit some of your recent decisions haven't been the most reasonable or sensible. Like leaving the witness protection program the way you did. You said yourself that you were almost killed."

"Exactly. Someone sent me a photograph of Garrett and me from two years ago. That's why I left the program. I had to warn him. But you wouldn't know anything about that."

He flushed again. "I knew nothing about you and this...cowboy."

"But two years ago you hired a private investigator to find me."

"Because I was worried about you. One minute you're talking to the feds about needing protection and the next you had taken off and I didn't know if you were alive or dead. What would you have had me do?"

"I was almost killed in a hit-and-run accident. That was after Neal said he thought I was remembering who killed my father and stepmother."

"You're remembering?"

"No, but it was like someone believed I was and wanted me dead. I did go into the witness protection program because the government believed I was remembering. Clearly they don't believe that Harvey Mattson was the killer."

Alistair let out a frustrated groan and started to turn away.

"Did you also hire the investigator two years ago to take photos?"

He stopped and turned back to her. "No," he said with a shake of his head. "I'm disappointed that you would think I was the one who lured you out so a man could try to kill you." He sighed. "I did my best with you all these years. You will soon be free of me and don't ever have to see me again."

His words cut her to the quick. He'd always been kind to her, always put up with her misbehavior, always seen that she had anything she needed or wanted.

"I'm sorry," she said but he'd already turned away and was walking out the open door and back to his cabin.

"Is everything all right?" Garrett asked as he joined her moments later.

She shook her head. "I hate this. How is it possible that one of the people I've known almost all of my life wants me dead?"

He put his arm around her and pulled her close. "We could be wrong."

She shook her head against his chest. "That's the worst part. I don't think we are." She felt close to tears.

"And by the way, you haven't known Rance all your life," he pointed out.

She drew back to look at him. "He'd sell his mother for one of his tailored suits. But murder?"

They both turned as another vehicle drove up. For a moment, Joslyn thought it might be her brother, Peter, who'd changed his mind about not coming. But when the car door opened, William "Billy" Mitchell climbed out.

GARRETT MOTIONED HIS friend inside the lodge. "I thought you'd still be out in Washington snowboarding."

Billy laughed as he said, "You must be Joslyn. I'm

glad we finally get to meet." He kissed her on the cheek and let himself be ushered to the lush leather furniture of the lodge. "When you called and told me what you two were doing…" He shook his head. "This gives a whole new meaning to crazy."

"You've brought us something," Garrett said, seeing the folder he was carrying.

"Nothing conclusive, but some definitely interesting stuff." Billy looked at Joslyn. "You sure you want to hear this?"

She nodded. "I have to."

"I had him find out everything he could about all of them," Garrett told her.

She seemed to brace herself. "So what did you find out?"

Billy looked around. "We can talk here?"

"They're all down at their cabins probably deciding how to have me taken back to Seattle in a straitjacket and Garrett put in prison for kidnapping," Joslyn said.

As they all sat, Billy opened the folder. "A whole lot of the money your father left has been keeping the people around you in style for years. Your guardian, lawyer and doctor are all on hefty retainers and have been for twenty-five years."

"That sounds a little excessive," Garrett said.

Billy shrugged. "To us, yes. But when you look at the fortune coming to Monica Wilmington when she turns thirty, maybe not so much."

"What about her stepsister?" Garrett asked.

Billy turned to Joslyn. "Your father left her a bundle that she didn't get until she turned thirty. She went through most of it in a year! Fortunately for her, your father set up a trust fund so she gets monthly checks, which she quickly spends."

"You're saying she needs funds," Garrett said.

"She's blasted through her inheritance and is up to her neck in debt. What is interesting is that about the time she began to get desperate for money was about the time someone tried to kill you—two years ago. Isn't that when the first attempt was made on your life?" Billy asked.

She nodded mutely. "I was almost run down in the street. There was no doubt that it was intentional. Then…" She glanced at Garrett. "We recently found out that the convenience store robbery where we met was really a hit on me that went awry, fortunately."

"So Amethyst is definitely a suspect," Garrett said. "What about Rance?"

"Ah, Rance," Billy said and grinned. "Grew up dirt poor. Went to Ivy League universities on scholarships. Became an investment banker. Makes pretty good money—just not enough to keep him and the wife in the lavish lifestyle they both want. I would keep him on the list."

Garrett shook his head in awe of his friend. "How were you able to find out all this financial stuff?"

"If I told you, I'd have to kill you," Billy joked. "It's my job, and in all modesty, I'm damned good at it. Anyway, the main question is who benefits most if Monica is dead. Amethyst is at the top of the list along with her husband and brother, but your guardian Alistair, along with your lawyer, Benjamin Purdy and your doctor, Neal Foster, would be impacted." Before Garrett could ask, he rushed on, "Your father set it up so that they would be there to take care of you, thus the retainer for each of them that made it possible for them to always be on call."

"You mean I was their only client and patient," Joslyn said.

Billy nodded. "But he also made it worth their while when their services were no longer needed. They get a bonus on your thirtieth birthday. It's not a lot in the grand scheme of things. Should you not reach your thirtieth birthday, they would share in your inheritance. Not as much as Amethyst and Peter, but all three, Alistair, Neal and Benjamin would receive a nice chunk."

Joslyn stood to walk over to the window and look out. "Was my father insane? Why would he do something like that?"

"He'd hoped, I would imagine, to pay them for their loyalty," Billy said.

Garrett shook his head in disgust. "All of these people have already been living off of her for twenty-five years."

His friend nodded and looked to Joslyn. "They all have motive and let's face it, there is a whole lot of money at stake here. The kind of money even rich people dream of having."

She turned back to them. "I've hated knowing about this inheritance since as far back as I can remember. It's been hanging over my head like a guillotine. I never wanted any of it."

"But one of *them* could want it enough to kill," Garrett said.

Billy agreed. "Maybe I should stick around in case you two need some help."

He shook his head, but Joslyn was the one to speak. "They need to feel safe. They made up their minds about me a long time ago. I'm just a spoiled rich girl and not very smart. Whichever one it is will be cocky with just me and Garrett up here. They'll see an opportunity and take it."

"That's what I'm afraid of," Billy said, and Garrett agreed.

Joslyn moved to the fireplace, where Garrett had started a crackling blaze. "There's something bothering me. If my stepsister is broke, how would she be able to hire a hit man?"

Garrett looked to his friend. "What does it cost to hire a hit man nowadays? Two years ago, whoever hired Frank Rutledge promised him ten thousand dollars."

Billy let out a whistle. "With inflation, I'd say you're looking at a lot more than that now," he joked.

"Wouldn't any large amount show up in someone's bank statement?"

"Not if they were smart and saved up a little cash at a time," Billy said.

"Or if they went in together," Garrett said and felt a chill run the length of his spine. He looked to Joslyn, suddenly not as confident about this plan. He reminded himself that the sheriff would only be a phone call away.

"You should stay for dinner," Joslyn said suddenly. She smiled at Billy. "I'd like your take on them."

"I'd be honored, but is Garrett cooking?"

"Funny," he said as he got to his feet. "I've had food delivered. Joslyn and I will be putting a few things together."

"Then count me in," Billy said. "I wouldn't mind getting a look at your...family."

"Brace yourself then," he said and went out to ring the dinner bell.

As Sid was about to leave his office, his phone rang. It never failed, he thought. Anxious to get up to the Sterling guest ranch, he'd considered letting the call go to voicemail. He'd already told his staff that he was taking the next twenty-four hours off. There was nothing more important right now than getting up into the mountains. He had a spot in mind where he could keep an eye on the ranch—and Garrett and Joslyn.

This whole plan was insane, but he couldn't stop the two of them. All he could do was provide backup if needed.

He saw that it was from Montana State Prison and answered the call. He had a bad feeling as he said, "Sheriff Anderson" into the phone and wasn't surprised to hear the warden's voice.

"It's Frank Rutledge. Someone shanked him earlier this evening."

The sheriff swore under his breath. "Is he—"

"He didn't make it. I spoke with his lawyer. He said Rutledge was going to make a deal, give up the name you wanted. I'm so sorry."

"Any chance he told his lawyer?"

"No."

So that was that, Sid thought. "You have any idea who killed him?"

"Rutledge didn't play well with his fellow inmates," the warden said. "Hard to say who was fed up with him. Of course, we're looking into it."

"Or someone could have been paid to make sure he didn't talk."

"There is always that," the warden said.

Sid doubted it was another prisoner with a grudge. Someone had heard that Rutledge was going to make a deal. Or maybe the damned fool had somehow reached out to the person who'd hired him with a little blackmail offer.

Either way, Rutledge was dead and he'd taken the name of the guilty person with him.

"There is something that might help in your investigation though," the warden said. "Rutledge made a phone call about an hour before he was killed. I can give you the number."

Sid wrote it down. "Thanks, I'll check it out." He disconnected and stepped to his computer to see if he could get a name to go with the phone number.

He couldn't remember the last time he'd been this

worn out. For days he'd been running on black coffee and adrenaline. Now he just felt dog-tired. But he felt an urgency to get up into the mountains close to the guest ranch. The fresh air would do him good. Joslyn's family would have arrived. He didn't expect trouble right away. More than likely they would strike tonight though. They would have to before midnight if they wanted to stop her from getting her inheritance.

His thoughts were on getting a catnap before he needed to be on lookout as he took a moment to cross-reference the phone number. The shock of the identity associated with the number took away all of his exhaustion. Hadn't Joslyn suspected that someone closest to her was behind this? But the problem had been how to prove it short of finding the killer standing over her dead body? Now he knew. He grabbed up his phone and called the guest ranch, his heart pounding.

"Answer, damn it," he said as he reached a busy signal. "Get off the phone!" He called the operator and asked that she interrupt the call. "It's an emergency."

She took the information and went off the line for a moment. When she returned she informed him that the phone was off the hook. "I'll report it."

Why would it be off the hook? Had something happened already? He had to get up there right away.

He hung up and left the sheriff's office. He had to warn them—if it wasn't already too late. His cell phone rang as he reached the middle of the street. Excited and scared, he picked up without seeing who it was from, thinking it could be Garrett. "I'm so glad you called. Is everything all right up there? I know who it is." He realized that the rancher hadn't spoken. "Garrett, are you there?"

Silence, then a cough.

He recognized that cough. He glanced at his phone. "Ward?" He hadn't realized that he'd stopped in the middle of the street until he heard the roar of the motor as it wound up.

Sid had only a moment to turn, to see the blinding glare of headlights, before the vehicle was on him. His feet seemed glued to the pavement. He felt the bumper connect with his right leg before he went airborne and crashed into the windshield. His head smacked the glass hard enough to nearly knock him out before he felt the pain.

He was still conscious though when he felt the vehicle stop. Sliding off the hood, he dropped in a heap to the pavement where he lay half expecting the driver to run over him. But still fighting the growing darkness behind his eyes, he heard the driver back up and speed away.

"Ward," the word came out on pained whisper. "Ward, I need help." But he realized the Undersheriff wasn't still on the line.

As the pain overcame him, Sid let the darkness come.

CHAPTER TWENTY-SEVEN

WHEN GARRETT RETURNED from ringing the dinner bell, he looked past her in surprise. Joslyn turned to follow his gaze. The landline phone was off the hook. "That's odd," he said.

"Do you think someone did that on purpose?" she asked, noticing that both Garrett and Billy were frowning in concern.

"It could have gotten knocked off the hook," he said as he stepped to the desk and replaced the receiver, then checked to make sure there was a dial tone. "It's fine."

"They're headed this way," Billy warned. As the three of them watched their "guests" file down from their cabins toward the lodge for dinner, Joslyn sighed. "They all look bored, angry and resentful. This should be fun."

"So much better than murderous," Billy quipped.

"You know they've all gotten together to discuss me," she said and braced herself for what she knew would be an uncomfortable meal as everyone entered.

"We'll give them all a glass of wine," Garrett said and went to the bar to begin filling glasses.

Amethyst downed her wine immediately. It was clear that she'd had more to drink than what Garrett had served her earlier. "It's not fair," she said, making them all turn to look at her in surprise.

She looked up, her blue gaze hard on Alistair. "I was his daughter, too. But all he ever cared about was Mo. Mo, this. Mo, that."

Joslyn felt the ache of the memory. When he'd called her that, she would giggle and he would chase her down and lift her high in the air. The memory came out of nowhere, startling her and dragging her away from Amethyst's accusations. She'd heard them all before anyway. That everything was always about Monica and not poor Amethyst.

"You came out just fine from the deal," Alistair said. "Just because you chose to blow all your money, you can't blame your stepfather or Monica for that."

Amethyst slammed down her wineglass. "And you always take her side."

Rance rose slowly from where he'd been sitting, looking pained. "You need something to eat, sweetheart." He touched her hand but she jerked it away.

"I hate to even think what you plan to feed us," Amethyst said.

"I'll see how dinner is coming along," Joslyn said and started for the kitchen as Billy was coming out. "If she's cooking, we're in real trouble," her stepsister said loud enough for her to hear. Then, seeing Billy, she added rudely, "Who's this?"

"My best friend," Garrett said, purposely leaving out the fact that Billy was also a private investigator. "He stopped by and we invited him to join us for dinner. Amethyst Wilmington Carrington, meet William Mitchell."

She gave him a dismissive nod as if he was of little concern. Joslyn thought how wrong she was about that as she continued on to the kitchen. She heard Garrett introduce Rance and Alistair and then Dr. Foster and Benjamin Purdy to Billy.

There wasn't anything to do in the kitchen. Garrett had planned a simple meal for tonight that took little more than heating it up. Right now they had pulled pork in the oven along with Mexican fixings. She knew Amethyst would turn her nose up at the meal since she went from being vegan to gluten-free to keto depending on the day of the week.

But Joslyn, even as nervous as she was, couldn't believe how good it all smelled. Garrett appeared at her elbow, making her jump.

"How is it out there?" she asked.

"Billy took over. I didn't want you being alone in here," he whispered and pulled her to him.

"I'm perfectly safe in the kitchen with everyone else in the other room," she said, smiling at his mock concern and the feel of his body against hers. It had been too long. She'd so hoped that they would find the time to be together before everyone arrived.

"Still, I don't want you out of my sight for a lot of reasons," he said and he kissed her.

She ached for him. Since they'd found her car and the photograph that had made her bolt to warn him, Garrett's attitude had changed. She could understand why he'd had trouble trusting her after everything she'd done. But now it was almost as if he'd forgiven her for two years ago. She could only hope, given the way he was looking at her right now. That look she knew only too well. He wanted her as much as she wanted him. Maybe they could take up where they'd left off.

"I see what's holding up dinner," Amethyst said from behind them, sounding disgusted as she slurred her words.

"I'm in love with your sister," he said, holding Joslyn tight even though she'd instinctively tried to pull back at the sound of Amethyst's voice and the reproach in it.

Her stepsister scoffed and turned to point. "Is this where we're eating?" She indicated the long farm tables and log chairs of the dining room, contempt in her voice and body language. Before Joslyn could say something, Amethyst left the kitchen, saying over her shoulder, "I'll tell the others."

"I'm sorry about her," she said to Garrett.

"Don't you dare apologize for anyone."

And yet she felt she needed to. She'd made excuses for her stepsister her whole life, taking up for her even when she'd heard some of the things Amethyst had said about her.

"Let's eat," she said and smiled at Garrett. He released her to help carry the food out to the largest of the tables she'd already set for everyone.

"Dinner is served!" he called.

FOR A WHILE, Joslyn thought they would be able to get through the meal without any outbursts. Everyone seemed to be enjoying the food. But she did notice that Amethyst was having trouble cutting her meat. How much had the woman had to drink?

As if sensing Joslyn watching her, she looked up, eyes narrowing. "Do you ever think about the night my mother and your father were murdered?"

She felt heat rush to her face. "You know I don't remember it."

Her stepsister scoffed. "But you were *there*. The police said you must have seen the killer, there was blood all over you."

"Amethyst," Alistair reproached only to have the older sister glare at him and snap, "Stay out of this, Al."

"I know you were five, but you were a precocious five, everyone said so," her stepsister persisted. "I've always wondered why you might lie about your so-called memory loss. Because you're covering for someone. Maybe Peter."

"Peter? He was eleven, Amethyst. *Eleven*."

"Strong though and in all those sports, including…baseball."

Alistair shook his head and said to Rance, "Don't let her have anything more to drink." As if Rance could stop her, Joslyn thought.

"Peter had lots of baseball bats," Amethyst continued as if no one else had spoken. "How would anyone even know if one was missing? Big, strong, athletic boy like Peter. And believe me, he was angry when mother remarried."

"Does anyone want more pork?" Joslyn asked, hoping to diffuse this.

"You know so much about the bats," Neal said, striking back. "You were a big thirteen as I recall and, as you just admitted, angry at your mother and stepfather."

The word *big* was like letting off a bomb in the room. Amethyst erupted. *"Big?"* She looked around for something to throw at the psychiatrist. She picked up the bottle of hot sauce and would have hurled it at him if Rance hadn't grabbed her wrist. She shot daggers at her husband with her eyes as he pried it from her fingers without a word.

"Psychoanalyze your patient, Doctor, and leave me to hell alone," she spat as she settled back in her chair.

"Does anyone want dessert?" Garrett asked.

The room filled with a dense, brittle silence. Amethyst pushed her plate away and got awkwardly to her feet. "You all act so sanctimonious." She let out a laugh. "Do you know why my mother asked me to stay at a friend's house that night? She said she and her husband wanted to be alone." Her voice broke. "She sent all the staff home early, even Ruth who always stayed the night during the week. She thought I didn't know what was going on, but I did." Her gaze raked the room, hesitating on Neal, then Benjamin, then finally Alistair.

Alistair got to his feet. "I think that's enough."

Her stepsister smiled and shifted her gaze to Joslyn. "She was cheating on your father. I was upset with the marriage at first. But we finally had a nice place to live, money, my own room and while he wasn't my father, Horace was nice to me. He said he wanted me to think of myself as his daughter. *His daughter.*" Tears began to stream down her face. "Even if he loved you more, I loved him. But my mother was going to ruin it all, just like she always did." She began to cry. "We could have been happy, all of us, but Thea Louise couldn't keep her panties on."

Rance rose from his chair to gently take her arm. Joslyn could hear her own heartbeat, the room had gone so deadly quiet.

Surprisingly, Amethyst let him help her out of the dining room. Joslyn could hear the woman's heart-wrenching sobs as she and Rance left. After a moment, Neal rose, tossing down his napkin and standing for a moment as if to say something. But he apparently realized there was nothing he could say and left.

"Monica, I think I'll pass on dessert," Alistair said. "But thank you both for a lovely dinner." He left, and Benjamin joined him, leaving only Billy, Garrett and Joslyn to stare dumbstruck after them.

"WELL, THAT WAS PAINFUL," Billy said of the dinner as the three of them began to clean up the kitchen together. "And enlightening." They all half laughed uncomfortably.

Garrett turned to Joslyn. "Did you know any of this?"

She shook her head, looking shocked by the revelation. "Remember, I was five. But this is the first time Amethyst has ever said anything like that about her mother."

"I wonder if it's true," Billy said. "If Thea Louise was meeting someone that night at the house…"

"Where was Horace?" Garrett said, finishing the thought as he turned to Joslyn. "And what about you? Wasn't there a nanny or someone to watch you?"

She shrugged. "I suspect I'd already been put to bed for the night. It isn't like my stepmother could have sent me off to a friend's for a sleepover."

With the kitchen clean, they moved into the lounge. Garrett poured them a much-needed drink from the bar while Billy stoked the fire. "This puts a whole new spin on things," he said. "I wonder if the police ever knew about this."

"If it's true…" Joslyn didn't finish.

Billy nodded as if they were all thinking the same thing. "Amethyst seemed to think her mother's lover was someone in the room."

"Makes sense," Garrett said. "Apparently the family doctor and lawyer and friend were around all the time."

"What was she suggesting? That one of them killed my stepmother?" Joslyn asked.

"Sounded like that might have been where she was headed, but it could have just been the alcohol talking," Billy agreed. "I suppose your father could have come home, caught them, a fight ensued…and it escalated to a tragic confrontation. Or Amethyst could have gotten one of her brother's bats and…" He didn't bother to finish.

She shook her head. "I've never seen them for what they are more than in these surroundings."

"They're just uncomfortable," Garrett said, hating that he was making excuses for them. "And they're all thrown off their game."

"Which is good," Billy said. "If one of them came here with a plan, he or she is no doubt revising it. They were probably expecting a hotel like the one at Old Faithful so they could merely sneak down the hall and do the deed. Getting to you here is going to take some imagination and planning abilities. Are you sure they have any?"

He was joking, but it was a good question. What if all of this was a waste of time? What if the would-be assassin had already given up? Garrett could only hope and said as much.

"You know, I thought I wanted to know which one of them I had to fear," she said. "But after that meal with them, I realized that I have no desire to ever see any of them after my birthday. Except Alistair. I can't cut him off completely. I've felt like he was the only friend I had."

Garrett's heart broke for her. Poor little rich girl. He promised himself he'd change all of that. If they lived past midnight.

IT WAS LATE by the time Dorothea got the call from a friend who worked at the fire department where the ambulance and EMTs were dispatched.

"It's Sid," the woman told her. "He was hit by a car."

The words didn't make any sense at first. Hit by a car? She'd been asleep and now reached over to turn on the lamp by her bed. "Sid?"

"I knew you'd want to know. He was taken to the hospital." Her friend seemed to hesitate.

Dorothea sat up in the bed, knowing she was about to be hit with even worse news.

"It's serious," her friend said.

She tried to catch her breath. The word *serious* and *hospital* registered like a clanging bell inside her head. "Thank you." She hung up and climbed out of bed, looking around for her coat, too panicked to think clearly. Sid. Not Sid.

Snatching up her coat, she realized that she was wearing pajamas. Her gaze went to the clock next to her bed. It was only a little after ten, but late for her. She was still trying to make sense of it as she stumbled to her closet for something to wear. It didn't matter what, she told herself. She just couldn't go to the hospital in her nightclothes.

She grabbed a sweatshirt and jeans, found undergarments and pulled them on with trembling fingers. Sid. Serious. Hospital.

Her mind screamed that this couldn't be happening. Not now. Sid was going to retire in the fall. They had a date Friday night. He was taking her to a nice restaurant. She was going to buy a special dress. Eleanor was convinced he was going to propose during their dinner.

She felt a sob rise in her throat and tried to swallow it back as tears burned her eyes. With trembling fingers, she pulled on her clothing, anxious to get to the hospital.

The knock at her door made her start.

"Dorothea?"

Shade. Someone must have called him as well. Montana was like a small town and they had a lot of friends here. He'd come from his part of the sprawling ranch house where they all lived seasonally down in the valley.

"I'm almost dressed." Her voice broke.

"You heard."

She couldn't answer. Her throat had closed as tears ran down her face. Sid. Serious. Hospital.

After a few minutes of fighting to get clothing on, she wiped her tears and opened her door.

Shade stood there, a big, strong cowboy she could depend on. He said nothing. He didn't try to tell her that everything was going to be all right. He knew better than to think he could comfort her with empty words. "I'll take you" was all he said as he led her out to his waiting pickup.

JOSLYN SAW SUCH love and understanding in Garrett's eyes. His gaze was an excruciating deep blue that ignited that old fire inside her. Soon they would be alone upstairs. His look said he was through holding her at arm's length. Tonight they would finally be together again.

Billy seemed to notice the different kind of tension in the room. He looked at the time, finished his drink in one gulp and said, "I should get going. If you need me, call."

Garrett didn't pull his gaze away from her. "Thanks, my friend. For everything."

"No problem." She felt the PI glance at them as he backed toward the exit. "I'll check in tomorrow. In the meantime…" Whatever he planned to say, he must have decided neither of them was listening anyway.

She heard the door close behind him. Without a word, Garrett moved to it and snapped home the lock. He hadn't had a chance to fix the broken window next to it, but he'd cleaned up the glass and secured a board over it.

Turning to her, he said, "Would you like to race me upstairs?"

Joslyn laughed. When she spoke, her voice was husky with desire. "What do I get if I win?"

"The same thing you get if you lose but the winner reaches my bedroom first."

She smiled. "Then I want to win." She turned and ran for the stairs. He was right behind her, his boots thundering up the steps, the two of them laughing as they reached the landing and ran down the hallway to his suite. She reached his door first. Out of breath and laughing, she turned to face him.

He stepped to her, cupping her waist in his large, rough tanned hands. "Joslyn." That one word said it all. She could hear the timbre of his desire and his disbelief. Neither of them had thought it was possible that the two of them would ever see each other again, let alone have the chance to make love.

Now within moments they could be naked, locked together in the throes of passion after all these months apart. Excitement seemed to fill the air as he pulled her to him and kissed her deeply.

At first she thought it was the pounding of her pulse in her ears. But just when Garrett was opening his suite upstairs, his lips never leaving hers, he froze as if to listen and then swore.

Someone was banging on the front door of the lodge.

CHAPTER TWENTY-EIGHT

IN THE GLARE of the porch light, a tall blond man was still pounding on the front door of the lodge. "It's my stepbrother, Peter," Joslyn said, sounding surprised and disappointed as the two of them made their way down the stairs.

Garrett frowned over at her, realizing that her disappointment was twofold. He hadn't completely written Peter off as a suspect but he'd hoped that his not showing up meant he wasn't interested in her money. And now here he was. On top of that, he'd interrupted them. "I thought he wasn't coming."

"He must have changed his mind."

They reached the door together. As he unlocked it, he took in the man's appearance. Agitated. But that could just be because they hadn't opened the door quickly enough for him, Garrett thought.

Then he looked past Peter Wilmington to the expensive black sedan he'd arrived in. The front right of the vehicle was smashed in, the hood dented and in the porch light he could see something dark. Blood?

"Bloody hell," Peter said, looking shaken. "I had no idea this place was at the end of the earth on top of a mountain full of wild animals."

"What happened?" Garrett asked, looking from Joslyn's stepbrother to the damaged car and back.

"I hit a damned deer. Ran right out in front of my rental car. I was almost killed."

Garrett wondered about the deer. He couldn't stand the thought of it lying injured beside the road. "Do I need to go down the road and take care of it?"

"It's dead." Glancing past them, Peter said, "But I'll take a drink." Garrett stepped aside as the man pushed his way into the lodge. "You do have alcohol up here since you bloody hell have no cell phone service."

He was going to tell the man to help himself but he need not have bothered. Peter made a beeline for the bar and was already pouring himself a glass full of bourbon by the time they closed the door.

The man downed the drink and poured himself another. Garrett saw that his hands were shaking.

"I THOUGHT YOU couldn't make it," Joslyn said, sounding sorry that Peter had shown up. Clearly she had already ruled him out as an attempted murderer.

Peter seemed to have calmed down some after his second drink. His gaze locked on Joslyn. "I wasn't going to come. But it's your birthday party, right? Although I have to ask why you couldn't have thrown it somewhere less…isolated." He smiled then and stepped to her to kiss her cheek. "I didn't want to miss your birthday. You are finally free of everyone. That's cause for celebration."

She smiled. "Not quite. I still have…" She glanced

at the clock on the wall. "Over an hour to go. Then you can wish me a happy birthday."

"On some god-forsaken mountain top, huh?"

"Why not? It's beautiful here."

"And this is the hero cowboy I keep hearing about?" he asked.

"Garrett Sterling, my stepbrother, Peter." The two men shook hands.

"Your cabin isn't ready, but can be quickly enough," Garrett said.

"A cabin?" Peter echoed. He glanced toward the stairs. "Where are you staying? Isn't there room here?"

Garrett had readied just enough cabins for the group he knew was coming. He hadn't planned on Peter so the bed in another cabin wasn't made up yet. But she knew he wasn't about to let the man stay just down the hall from them.

She could also tell that he didn't want to leave her alone with Peter, but she signaled that it was all right. "Peter, you'll be in cabin five. I'll leave the outside light on so you can find it." He turned to Joslyn. "Lock up after your brother leaves," he said and she nodded.

"Are you hungry?" she asked her stepbrother when Garrett still hesitated. "I can get you something to eat while Garrett checks your cabin."

"Check it for what? Bears?" Peter demanded, clearly only half joking.

"I just need to make sure it meets your standards," Garrett said.

Her stepbrother let out a bark of a laugh. "Good

luck with that," he said under his breath as he finished his drink and turned to Joslyn. "Something does smell good."

"Come into the kitchen and I'll dish you up a plate," she said. "I'm glad you came." It wasn't quite true and yet she'd always liked Peter. She couldn't say *love*. He'd been eleven when she was five, so by the time she was in junior high school, he was in college. But he'd always been kind to her.

She hoped that hadn't changed as she led him into the kitchen.

DOROTHEA LOOKED UP expectantly from where she sat in the hospital waiting room. She'd hoped it was the doctor with news about Sid. But she was happy to see Will and Poppy come through the door. She rose to let Will engulf her in his strong arms.

"How is he?" Will asked as he held her.

She shook her head, unable to speak for a moment around the sob caught in her throat. "He's still in surgery." Poppy rubbed her back and asked if she knew what had happened. She shook her head again.

The door to the waiting room opened and Shade came in with two cups of vending machine coffee. Dorothea stepped out of Will's arms to take her coffee. She cupped it in her hands, needing the heat to defrost her chilled body. She was so scared and yet she didn't dare voice her fears that they might come true.

"Do we know any more about what happened?" Will asked.

"Hit-and-run," Shade said and offered Poppy the

coffee. She shook her head and stood next to Dorothea to put her arm around her. "Ward's looking into it."

"Ward?" Will swore. "I can't understand how this could happen in Whitefish. Has anyone heard from Garrett?" When no one spoke, he said, "He probably doesn't even know since the last we heard, he'd kidnapped a woman and was on the lam. I tried his phone. It went straight to voicemail."

"Sid was worried about him, but now Sid—" Dorothea said as the door opened and Dr. Bullock stuck his head in the door. They all turned to him. She felt her heart in her throat and said a silent prayer.

JOSLYN STUDIED HER stepbrother as he devoured the pulled pork sandwich she'd made him. They were sitting at the end of one of the tables in the dining room. He seemed oblivious to her and everything else, eating as if he couldn't recall his last meal. His earlier agitation seemed to have either been dulled by the two drinks he'd consumed or the food.

"So what's up with you and the cowboy?" he asked after finishing the sandwich and wiping his hands on the napkin.

"I'm in love with him."

Peter quirked a brow. "I find that hard to believe."

"Why?"

"You can do better," he said bluntly. "Once you have your birthday and get your inheritance, men will be beating down your door. You can have anyone you want."

She sighed and sat back. "Because I'm coming

into a lot of money? So I can buy myself a more appropriate husband like Amethyst did?"

He snorted at that. "Rance is an imbecile. Believe me, she regrets marrying him. I would just hate to see you make the same mistake."

Joslyn shook her head. "Garrett isn't a mistake. And anyway, I'm not keeping the money."

He scoffed at that. "You'll change your mind when the time comes."

"No, I won't. At the stroke of midnight, all of it goes automatically to the charities I've chosen to support." Unless she died before then, but she didn't say that. Didn't want to think it.

Peter stared at her. "You're serious." She nodded. "And how will you live?"

"I've been working off and on for years and unlike the rest of you, I've lived very frugally. I'll be fine."

He shook his head as if he couldn't believe it. "I hope you don't regret it."

"I won't. I've always seen that much money as a burden, one I don't need."

"Except for the fact that you had everything you wanted growing up, thanks to Alistair. He wasn't quite as generous with me and Amethyst."

"I'll admit it, I was spoiled." She knew that was putting it mildly. Still, she hadn't cashed a lot of the checks he sent even then because she wanted to be independent.

"Spoiled and rebellious, and always in trouble, and a real pain in the ass." He smiled as if to soften his words. He seemed to study her for a moment. "I admire you. There is no way I would give away that kind of money. No way." His eyes darkened for a moment. "No, I'd have a ball with that much money. I would be able to buy anything I wanted."

"Can't you now?" she asked, surprised he felt that way. She knew that Peter only dated older women who did most of the paying.

He shrugged. "I'll admit, it makes me nervous when my bank balance falls even a little. I'm afraid of being broke like Amethyst. It terrifies me."

She felt sorry for him. But she also worried about what she'd seen in his eyes. Money meant a lot to him. Enough to kill for it though?

"Did you know your mother was having an affair?" She saw the answer in his eyes. "You don't really think Amethyst…" She couldn't bring herself to make the accusation.

He chuckled. "She was angry enough at Mother to…" He sighed and shook his head. "I guess we're all capable of murder." He rose. "I'm dead on my feet after hitting that…deer."

She walked him to the door, unlocked it and watched as he walked in the direction of the cabins until he disappeared into the dark. Back in the dining room, she began to clean up and was almost finished when she noticed the time. After eleven. In less than an hour she would turn thirty. If she was still alive.

Where was Garrett? She was starting to worry about him. What if the killer jumped him and—

She heard someone at the front door of the lodge and spun around, realizing she'd forgotten to relock the door.

CHAPTER TWENTY-NINE

DOROTHEA PRESSED HER face into Sid's bare shoulder, needing to feel his heat, needing to know he was still alive inside his broken body.

She tried to stem the tears but felt them cascade down her face to moisten his bare shoulder. Hastily wiping at them she lifted her head and was shocked to see him looking at her.

"Sid?"

He gave her a weak smile but it was the most beautiful thing she'd ever seen. "You're crying on my shoulder."

She laughed and cried at the same time as she pushed to her feet. "I'll tell the doctor that you're awake."

"Don't leave." He reached for her hand and squeezed it weakly. "I thought I'd never see you again."

She couldn't speak around the lump in her throat so she only squeezed his hand back. "You're going to be all right," she said when she could. "Do you remember what happened?"

"Vaguely."

"A hit-and-run driver mowed you down in the street."

He gave her a slight nod and then his eyes fluttered closed and his hand went limp in hers. For a moment... No, she wouldn't let herself even think it.

She stared at his chest, holding her breath, until she saw the reassuring rise and fall of his breaths. Letting go of his hand she left to find the doctor and tell him that Sid had awakened after his surgeries.

Down the hallway, she saw the undersheriff talking with the doctor.

"I'm sorry, but only immediate family can see him," Dr. Bullock was saying.

Ward turned as Dorothea approached. "*She's* not immediate family. I need to see the sheriff." He looked pale and upset.

"He's still in recovery. Come back later," the doctor said, clearly annoyed with the man.

Dorothea waited until Ward stormed off before she told the doctor that Sid had awakened for a few minutes.

"How did he seem?" Dr. Bullock asked as he walked her back to the sheriff's room.

"Good. He knew me. He said he was a little vague on everything that happened."

"That's to be expected." He pushed open Sid's hospital room door. Dorothea followed and watched while he checked over the sheriff, seemingly pleased by his progress.

"Let's let him sleep," the doctor said, steering her out of the room. "You look as if you can use some as well. Go home. I can call you when he's awake again."

Dorothea shook her head. "I won't bother him. I'll just sleep in the chair next to his bed, but I'm not leaving."

Dr. Bullock seemed to study her for a moment before he said, "I'll have a nurse bring a rollaway bed into his room for you." He left her, shaking his head and smiling as he went down the hall to make the arrangements.

GARRETT WAS SURPRISED when Joslyn rushed into his arms the moment he stepped through the door.

"I was worried about you," she cried as she pressed her face to his chest.

He held her tight as he tried to still her trembling. "I'm sorry it took me so long. Once I got your brother settled in, I checked on the way back to make sure everyone was in their cabins." He could see that the stress and fear was getting to her. "Are you all right?"

She nodded and stepped from his arms to walk over to the fireplace. The logs had burned down to glowing embers. "Fortunately, we have less than an hour to go. You said everyone was in their cabins?"

"They were. I could hear your stepsister and her husband arguing. There was a shower going in the doctor's cabin. The lawyer had his curtains open. I could see him apparently unpacking his suitcase. Alistair was sitting outside admiring the starlight."

"What if we're wrong?" she whispered. "Once I turn thirty, all of this will be moot. Maybe Harvey Mattson lied to me. Maybe it's been him all along."

In which case, she might not be safe after all.

"I believed him. If he truly is innocent of the crime, then his only hope *is* you remembering. With you dead…"

"But maybe he did it. Maybe he's guilty and when I remember…"

"Joslyn, he was sentenced to life. If you remember and it was Harvey who killed your father and stepmother, it wouldn't make any difference to his sentence."

She knew he was right. "That just leaves Frankie Rutledge."

Garrett was still shaking his head. "Someone hired him. Someone with money. He was ready to give up the person's name. Do you really think he would do that if Harvey Mattson was that man? You said yourself that Alistair told you that Harvey was no angel. One look at him and you can see that he's had a violent past."

"I know you're right," she said. "It's someone on this guest ranch. But what if they aren't planning to do it themselves? What if they've hired someone?"

Garrett had thought of that himself. "The doors are locked. If someone breaks in, we'll hear them. I still feel this is the best place to take a stand."

"I'm sorry for—"

"Don't. There is no need."

She smiled at him. "When this is over—"

They both turned at the sudden loud banging on the door. Through the window that hadn't been broken, they could see the attorney. He was waving frantically. "Come quick!" he called through the door. "It's Amy."

SID HURT ALL over but he didn't want to press the medication button just yet. He'd awakened to find Dorothea dead to the world in a bed next to him—and his undersheriff standing at the end of his bed.

"Ward," he said, startled. He'd caught the undersheriff with a strange look on his face. Ward stood holding his Stetson by the brim and looking down at Sid as if…

"Come to see if I'm still alive?" he asked the man.

Ward blinked as if lost in thought. "It's worse than I was led to believe."

Sid knew his body was badly broken by the cast on his right leg and arm as well as the wrap around his ribs that made even shallow breaths hurt.

"At least I didn't break my hip," Sid joked. It was a bad old joke that went right over Ward's head even though he was only a couple years younger.

"I thought I'd fill you in on what's going on," Ward said, puffing out his chest. "This situation with Garrett Sterling and—"

"That's taken care of," Sid interrupted.

"What? He *kidnapped* her."

"I've spoken with her guardian. It was just a misunderstanding."

Ward ground his teeth, his jaw muscle working. "Just because you're friends with the Sterlings—"

"I said it was taken care of." Raising his voice had hurt his ribs. He sucked in air, wondering how Ward had gotten into his room. Fortunately Dorothea was still out. He lowered his voice. "You just tend to what you usually do and stay away from the press."

His undersheriff had the good grace to color. He started to open his mouth to say something more, when Sid asked, "Why did you call me last night?"

"What?"

"I was crossing the street when you called."

Ward shook his head, avoiding Sid's gaze. "You're sure? I mean after being hit by a car—"

"There is nothing wrong with my memory. It was you on the line when I was hit."

Ward shrugged. "If you say so."

The man was calling him a liar. But that wasn't even the disturbing part. His undersheriff was hot to arrest Garrett Sterling for kidnapping but had said nothing about finding the driver of the car that had run Sid down in the middle of the street.

"You're fired."

"What?"

"I said you're fired pending an investigation."

"Investigation of what?" Ward demanded.

"My hit-and-run."

The man advanced on the side of his bed, anger turning his beefy face a bright red. "Have you lost your mind? You're accusing me of running you down?"

"You called me. I remember stopping to take the call. I was having trouble hearing you. Then you coughed."

Ward was shaking his head. "You heard me cough?" He had a distinctive smoker's cough.

"Then I looked at my phone and saw it was you."

"You can't prove anything."

This just proved what a lousy lawman Ward was. "There will be a record of the call, Ward."

All the color drained from the undersheriff's red face. "Maybe I did call you, but with everything going on, I guess I forgot."

"Get out," Sid said between clenched teeth. "Turn in your badge and gun to Lizzy."

"Lizzy?"

"Deputy Conners. I'm making her temporary sheriff until I return."

"You can't be serious. She's...she's..."

"A woman?"

"That, and she doesn't have the kind of experience that I do."

"I certainly hope not. Now get out before I call her to have you thrown out." Sid had raised his voice to the point where a nurse and Dr. Bullock had rushed in. On the bed next to his, Dorothea had awakened with a start and was now staring at the two of them.

"What's the problem in here?" the doctor demanded.

"Ward was just leaving. Please escort him out of the building and don't let him in my room again," Sid ordered. "Call Deputy Conners for me, please. I need to speak with her."

"Okay, calm down," Dr. Bullock said to him, then turned to Ward. "You're leaving."

"This is crazy. You can't fire me."

"I just did. These people are my witnesses."

Ward reluctantly let the doctor see him out of the room, but not before he said, "This isn't the last of it. You might be able to fire me, but I'm running for sheriff this fall. There is nothing you can do about that."

"We'll see," Sid said before the door closed behind the man. In an instant, Dorothea was beside him.

"What is going on?"

"Ward was involved in my hit-and-run. He called me and when I stopped to take his call… That's when I heard the engine rev and the next thing I knew I was struck. I think Ward was driving the vehicle that hit me. When he first saw me, he said he didn't think it would have injured me so badly. I need to call Lizzy and have him arrested before he destroys any evidence."

CHAPTER THIRTY

THE BLOW CAME out of nowhere the moment Garrett stepped out on the porch. The back of his head felt as if it exploded, knocking him to his knees. As he fell, he knew he should have been expecting it. Time was running out. He'd been lured into thinking that he and Joslyn had been wrong, that whoever had tried to kill her was either dead or didn't know about her birthday deadline.

He felt the darkness close in as he dropped, but before he could hit the floor, strong arms grabbed him on each side and lifted him. He could hear Joslyn screaming for the person to stop, yelling that it was her they wanted and to not hurt him.

Someone was holding her back, he couldn't see who in the darkness as his vision blurred. All the fight had gone out of him with the stunning blow. He could feel them drag him back inside the lodge and dump him unceremoniously on the floor by the fireplace right before everything went black.

JOSLYN BROKE FREE of Amethyst's steely grip and rushed to Garrett. "You've killed him," she screamed, seeing the blood matting the hair on the back of his head.

"He's not dead," Dr. Foster said. "He'll be fine."

She swung around to glare at him. "Is that your professional opinion, Neal, because I know what that's worth."

He seemed to take the words as a glancing blow. "He shouldn't have interfered."

"He saved my life not once, not twice, but three times," she cried.

"I wouldn't count on the fourth time being the charm," her stepsister said lazily. "Can we please get this over with? I'm sick to death of listening to her."

Joslyn stood staring at the two of them, Amethyst and the psychiatrist. So where were the others? Were they in on this as well? She opened her mouth and let out a bloodcurdling scream that should have been heard all the way to town. "Alistair! Peter!"

"Shut up," Amethyst snapped and slapped her hard across the mouth.

She let out a cry and tasted blood.

"Try not to get violent," the doctor said with contempt. "Remember what we need to accomplish here." Turning to Joslyn, he said, "Anyway, it's a waste of breath. No one is going to come help you. After Peter arrived, we all met up to talk in my cabin. We doctored their drinks so they will be sleeping like babies. Didn't want any interruptions."

She felt her heart hammer against her ribs. They were really going to do this. Kill her. For the money.

"I knew you were greedy," she said as she looked at them. "But I never knew what coldhearted lowlifes you really were."

Amethyst stepped to her so quickly, her arm going back for another slap, but Neal caught it. Her stepsister let out of a cry of pain.

"I told you not to hit her again," Neal said through gritted teeth.

"You don't tell me what to do," Amethyst snapped back at him, but lowered her arm when he released it. She swung around to face Joslyn. "Don't you ever call me a lowlife. You think you are so much better than me. You always have. I wasn't anything to you."

She rubbed her inflamed cheek, realizing the drunken scene at dinner had been a ruse. Her stepsister was as sober as a judge. "That's not true. I wanted a sister. You didn't. You wanted it all from the very beginning. Peter better watch his back or you'll kill him to get his share." She glared at Neal. "Did she promise to share with you? Newsflash, Amethyst doesn't share. Look how short a leash she keeps her husband on. I'm betting he has to beg for every cent he gets."

Amethyst tried to strike her again, but Joslyn was ready this time. She caught her arm, digging her nails in. Her stepsister cried out and the two of them struggled until Neal separated them. Joslyn knew she could take Amethyst in a fair fight, but she couldn't take the doctor as well.

"So what are you going to do? Shoot me? Bludgeon me to death? You should know that the sheriff is in on this. He knows the real reason I invited you all here. He'll be after all of you for murder."

"I don't think he'll be after anyone," Neal said. "I

doubt he can even walk. That's if he hasn't already died. He's been…taken care of."

This was the last thing Joslyn expected. The doctor's cold-blooded look of satisfaction shocked her. She'd never liked Neal, never thought he was much of a doctor. But she hadn't expected this. She thought of Sid. "What did you do to him?" she said, her voice breaking.

It was Amethyst who answered. "He was hit by a car."

Her first thought was Peter. He'd said it had been a deer, but…

"A stolen car, one that will never be traced back to us. No one is coming to save you."

Not Peter, she realized. He really had hit a deer. Joslyn glanced over to where Garrett lay bleeding. Her heart lodged in her throat. She didn't care what they did to her. But not Garrett. She had to stop this. She had to find a way.

"So what is your big plan?" she asked, hating that her voice wavered a little.

"Suicide," Amethyst said, almost with glee. "Everyone knows you're unstable. You'd be in a hospital, safe, if this stupid cowboy hadn't interfered. I think I'll sue his family when this is all over. I'll end up with this ranch—at least long enough to hire a Realtor to sell it."

So they weren't going to hurt Garrett. Her relief weakened her knees, but it was short-lived.

"It's going to be a tragic love story," her stepsister continued. "You attack him then overdose and die in his arms."

Out of the corner of her eye, she saw Garrett move slowly, carefully, just enough that she was sure no one else had noticed. They were too busy watching her.

"You really think anyone is going to believe that?" she demanded.

"Probably not," her doctor agreed. "But they also won't be able to prove any different. I don't believe even you realize how sick you are. There is no happy ending for you. If I had my way, you'd be in a padded room under my treatment for years."

She let out a bitter laugh. "You just can't bear the thought of the money coming to an abrupt stop tonight at midnight."

"I've spent the best years of my life taking care of you," Neal spat, anger like a loaded syringe in his tone. "I could have spent those years helping families in need. Instead, I did what your father asked. I took care of you."

She shook her head. "And were paid handsomely for it." She shot a glance at the clock on the wall. If she could keep them talking… "Sorry to have wasted your time. But not your money, huh. I've been to your house, Doc," she said, turning on him. "You've lived off of me and now you dare to blame me for how it's turned out? Is that what you tell yourself?" She scoffed. "You have no conscience, either of you. But I can tell you right now, this money you want so badly? It will only bring you grief. I'll see to that."

Her stepsister laughed. "How will you do that? You'll be dead."

It hadn't been her imagination. Garrett had opened

his eyes and looked right at her before quickly closing them. Was he trying to tell her that he was regaining consciousness? She told herself to stall as long as she could.

"The money is cursed. Don't you realize that? Has it brought any of you happiness? It's because of the way my father made it," she said.

Amethyst laughed. "Cursed. Sure."

She lifted a brow. "It's dirty money. It's why I don't want anything to do with the inheritance. It's bad enough that it has helped support me the past twenty-five years. I just want to be free of it. And so should you. Look how unhappy you are married to Rance. He married you for the money and when it's all gone, he'll be gone too and you know it."

"That's ridiculous," her stepsister snapped, but turned to the doctor to back her.

"She's just trying to rattle you," Neal said and scoffed. "Let's just get this over with." He looked at the clock on the wall and picked up his bag from where he must have dropped it earlier.

Joslyn had stalled as long as she could. She had no idea if Garrett was pretending to still be knocked out or if he was too weak to do anything but lie there. She hoped he was only waiting until the right moment. Otherwise, they were both in terrible trouble.

GARRETT KNEW HE was weak, but he could feel his strength growing. Joslyn was stalling them and doing a damned good job, but time was running out.

Earlier, he hadn't seen a weapon on the two. But

he wasn't sure what he'd been hit with. His head felt as if there was a bass drum inside it beating wildly.

Neither of them seemed like gun people. No, they were likely to hit a person from behind. Or hold a person down and inject them with enough drugs to kill them.

He couldn't let that happen. Somehow, he and Joslyn had to get the better of these people. Both the doctor and Amethyst looked as if they worked out daily.

"Rance loves me," Amethyst said, her voice cracking. "He can't do any better than me." She sounded unsure, worried.

"Keep telling yourself that," Joslyn said, looking at her stepsister. "But isn't this why you have to have my money? Otherwise, why would you stoop to murder to get it? Murder, Amethyst. You think that won't bring you the worst kind of luck?"

"Enough of this foolishness," Neal snapped. "There is no such thing as luck."

"Are you sure about that?" Joslyn asked. "Ever heard of Pandora's box?"

"Please, you might be able to scare Amethyst with your hocus pocus, but it's wasted on me," her doctor said. He set his bag down on the coffee table, opened it and began to take out syringes and bottles of both liquid and pills.

"Are they going to suspect something if a needle mark is discovered during the autopsy?" Amethyst asked, sounding worried. Joslyn had gotten to her stepsister, at least a little. Just not enough.

"You want to try to get a dozen pills down their throats?" Neal snapped. "I'll leave the syringes close by. It won't be the first time she got into my bag and took something."

"Alistair will know," Joslyn said, but not even she sounded like she believed any of them would ever be arrested for their murders. "You need to spare Garrett," she said, her voice breaking as she walked over and knelt down beside him. He caught her fingers for a moment, letting her know he was ready. She got to her feet. "He was just trying to save me."

"Save you from yourself," Neal said with a shake of his head. "It's what I have been trying to do for years." He squirted a little from the syringe and took a step toward her. "I promise that you are finally going to find peace in death."

Not if I have anything to do with it, Garrett thought as Neal approached. Joslyn had backed up against him and the couch as doctor approached, holding out the syringe as if offering her candy.

"It would be best if you used it on yourself, Monica," Neal said.

She pretended to be thinking about it until he was close enough.

Garrett swung a leg out, catching the man directly on his left kneecap. The doctor let out a scream as his leg caved and he toppled to the floor. The syringe went flying.

Expecting Amethyst to attack, Garrett swung around. But instead of coming for him, she went for the syringe—and so did Joslyn. He saw what was happening but couldn't help as Neal managed to get to his one good leg. He looked around for a weapon, grabbed up an agate figurine from the coffee table and hurled it at Garrett.

Garrett was still weak from the blow to the back of head. His movements were slowed because of it. He ducked, but the heavy figurine clipped his shoulder. Out of the corner of his eye, he could see Joslyn grappling with her stepsister for the syringe.

Neal barreled into him. Garrett went for the man's already wounded leg. The doctor's scream of pain was so loud that for a moment, Garrett didn't hear Amethyst.

Then her words grabbed all of his attention. "Say goodbye to your sweetheart." With Neal down, he swung around to find her holding the syringe. She had Joslyn in a headlock, the tip of the syringe just a breath away from her jugular vein.

THE FRONT DOOR burst open, making them all turn. A dark tall figure appeared framed in the space. There was that moment when everyone seemed to freeze.

Then Peter stepped in through the doorway, a gun in his hand. "What the hell is going on?" he demanded as he looked at the scene before him.

The doctor lay on the floor at Garrett's feet. Amethyst still had a headlock on Joslyn but she'd moved the point of the syringe farther from her neck.

For a moment no one spoke. Then Amethyst said, "Peter, I thought you'd gone to bed. You are just full of surprises. You didn't drink the cocktail I made you, did you? That's so like you." Her words seemed to tumble all over themselves.

When Peter spoke it was slow and measured. "What are you doing?" he asked her.

She made a whimpering sound as if beseeching him to understand. "It has to be done. You know it does."

Peter seemed to sway in the doorway. Garrett remembered what they'd said about doctoring everyone's drinks with sleeping pills. Had he been drugged?

Only seconds had passed since the door had opened. Garrett saw that Amethyst wasn't paying any attention to Joslyn and knew he might not get another chance—especially if Peter sided with her. His only chance was to get Joslyn away from her stepsister and that syringe.

He launched himself at her. The force broke the hold Amethyst had on Joslyn enough that he could drag her off to the side.

But as he swept past Amethyst, he saw her thrust the syringe at his hip as he passed. He felt the force of it strike something in his pocket, heard the needle break and Amethyst let out a cry an instant before he heard the deafening roar of the gunshot.

GARRETT WRAPPED JOSLYN in his arms as Peter hurried to his sister. He dropped to his knees and began to cry. Amethyst lay on her back, a dark hole just off center of the middle of her forehead.

Peter dropped the gun as he cradled her in his arms, pressing her face to his chest. "Why? Why did she have to take it this far? I begged you not to do this. I pleaded with you. Why?"

Garrett let go of Joslyn to limp over, pick up the gun and point it at the doctor. Neal Foster looked in shock as if realization had set in as to where he would be living soon.

Joslyn had gone over to the phone and was now calling 911. "We need law enforcement and the coroner," she said into the phone. "Sterling's Montana Guest Ranch."

Garrett reached into his pocket and felt the stone Dorothea had given him to protect him and smiled as he realized that was what the syringe needle had struck and broken on.

As Joslyn hung up the phone, Garrett moved to put an arm around her. She didn't know how long they stood there like that, but in the distance there came the sound of sirens, and soon the lodge window lit with the flash of lights and wail of sirens.

She glanced at the clock on the wall. After midnight. It was only then that she could let herself breathe. It was finally over.

The rest of the night was a blur of law enforcement, sirens and flashing lights. She answered their questions. At some point, Garrett wrapped a blanket around her shoulders. She hadn't realized that she'd been shaking.

Her stepsister was dead. The coroner had taken her away in a van. Officers had taken Dr. Neal Foster away in handcuffs, Peter too, which she knew must just be procedure. Peter had saved her life and Garrett's. She knew now why he'd come to the guest ranch. He'd known what his sister might do.

The officers had awakened the others and brought them into the dining room to fill them with hot black coffee. She'd heard Peter say that he hadn't finished his drink—the only reason he hadn't been as out of it as the others. Joslyn counted her blessings for that.

Everyone seemed in shock. Rance was beside himself, crying. "My wife is dead. I can't believe my wife is dead."

Alistair seemed in shock as he sipped the black coffee. Across from him, Ben shook his head and muttered. "It's over. Twenty-five years." He looked sick as he glanced at the clock. "What am I supposed to do now?"

Dr. Neal Foster had been muttering to himself as well as he'd been taken away. "One hundred million dollars. Gone. What a waste."

When the officers finally let the rest of them go, Garrett drove her down to the family ranch in the valley. He put her to bed, saying he had to go check on Sid. "Tell him I'm thinking of him," she said and closed her eyes, too exhausted to argue about going along.

The next thing she remembered was waking the next morning, sun streaming in Garrett's bedroom windows.

CHAPTER THIRTY-ONE

THE SWEET SCENTS of summer blew in the window, the dawn breeze caressing her naked skin. She breathed in the wonderful fragrance of pine-and-sunshine-kissed earth.

Joslyn opened one eye and smiled as she saw that Garrett was awake. His blue gaze was as warm as his smile.

"Happy birthday," he said, a little hesitant as if he feared it was the wrong thing to say after everything that had happened.

She'd dreaded this birthday from the time she'd heard she would be getting an inheritance. She'd watched her stepsister squander hers. It had been like a burden hanging around her neck.

And now it was gone. All of it had disappeared at the stroke of midnight, as if it never existed. She thought of the charities and hospitals and research it would fund and felt a swell of relief. The money would do good. She wished she could have done it years ago.

Her smile broadened as she looked at the man she loved. "This is the best birthday I've ever had."

He laughed. "It's only just begun."

"What will I do?" she joked.

Garrett pulled her close. "I have some ideas."

"I can't wait to hear them," she whispered, feeling the sweet chemistry between them arc hot as a flame. It vibrated through her, filling her with excitement. Just his touch sent delicious shivers racing up her spine.

She'd never wanted anyone the way she did him and couldn't imagine ever getting enough of him.

"I just realized something," Garrett said as he trailed his fingertips along her bare arm. "If Amethyst hadn't found out about the private investigator Alistair had hired to find you two years ago and paid him to take a photo…"

She shivered at the jolt of electricity that moved across her arm at his touch. "And paid to have a copy of that photo left for me, I might never have bolted from my hiding place." She frowned. "But how did my stepsister know where to send the photo? I was in the witness protection program. No one knew where I was."

"Obviously, someone knew. But if she hadn't seen that photo, I might never have seen you again."

"Because I would be dead."

His gaze met hers, the seriousness of what had almost happened to them still frighteningly fresh. "Do you believe in luck?"

"I do now." If he hadn't been at the guest ranch that day… If he hadn't gone for a horseback ride and fired that shot… If he hadn't saved her life two years ago. "Was it luck? Or destiny?"

He laughed. "You're starting to sound like Dorothea." He'd told her all about the woman who'd helped raise him and his brothers after their mother died. "You'll like her and she'll like you."

"I hope so," she said, worried since she had yet to meet his family. "I almost got you killed."

"They'll all love you, I promise." He lifted his hand to brush his thumb pad over her lower lip, making her shiver. His blue eyes held hers as he slowly lowered his head to kiss her. Sparks flew, her lips tingling until he deepened the kiss.

"Do you have any idea what I want to do with you for your birthday?" His words were as rough as his thumb pad had been against her lower lip and just as provocative. She felt her center turn molten.

"But first, I want to give you your birthday present." He reached into the drawer next to the bed and pulled out a velvet box.

She felt her eyes widen and burn with tears as she sat up in the bed, too excited to wait.

"If the timing is wrong. If it's too soon…" His voice was deep with emotion as he sat up in the bed to face her.

"It's perfect timing," she said, her own voice cracking. "I don't want to lose any minute."

He opened the dark velvet box to reveal the beautiful diamond engagement ring he'd bought for her all those months ago. She began to cry as he said, "Joslyn Charles, will you marry me?"

She nodded as tears streamed down her face. He reached up with his thumb to brush them away before he slipped the ring on her finger. "Oh, Garrett, it's more beautiful than I remember."

Removing the ring, he slid the band around her finger before tossing the velvet box aside. He then pulled her to him in a searing kiss. His mouth moved from her lips as he pushed back her head and began a slow exploration of the tender skin of her throat. His lips and tongue left a trail of goose bumps along her flesh as he made his way to the hollow between her breasts and the two of them plopped back on the bed.

Last night, he'd slipped her into one of his worn-soft T-shirts to sleep. Now he tore the thin fabric easily to free her breasts. She leaned back, her pulse a thunderous throbbing just beneath her skin as he worked his way down to one aching nipple. His lips tugged at the tender hard throbbing tip until she cried out with need. She cupped his face in her hands, drawing him back up to her as she breathed his name.

She felt as if she would die if he didn't take her. She wanted to rip off his clothes, but he stilled her hand as she reached for the opening on his shirt.

"Not yet," he whispered against the rosy glow of her skin as he lowered himself again to suckle at her breasts, making her moan and grind against him.

"Please," she begged as his hand slid under her panties to her wet center. She arched against him. The moment his fingers touched her, she came, crying out with a release that felt years in coming.

He drew her into his arms and held her as waves of pleasure coursed through her, then as her breathing began to slow, he slipped off her panties as his eyes and hands caressed every inch of her.

She grabbed his shirt in both hands. The snaps on his Western shirt sang as she flung the fabric open to reveal his hard, tanned chest. Planting her palms against his warm skin she let out a sigh. It was like coming home.

He grinned at her as her fingers dropped to the buttons of his jeans. She wanted him naked, needed to feel every part of him against her. Inside her.

As his shirt and jeans and Jockeys dropped to the floor, she flung herself at him, catching him off guard. He laughed as they were propelled backward. They fell on the bed, both of them naked, both of them wrapped in each other's arms.

"I love you, Garrett Sterling."

He smiled and kissed her. "And I love you, Joslyn Charles."

She laughed. "I think I'll hire a lawyer to change my name to Joslyn Charles, so it's all legal and binding."

"You won't be Joslyn Charles for long," he said, "Since I'm planning to change your last name as soon as we can get married."

She certainly hoped so. Joslyn Sterling. It had a nice ring to it. She glanced down at the diamond on her finger. It twinkled in the bedroom light just before Garrett rolled her over onto her back and began to make love to her all over again.

CHAPTER THIRTY-TWO

THE WEDDING WAS SMALL, only family and friends. Joslyn had insisted on waiting until Sid was out of the hospital and ambulatory. Garrett had been right about his family and Dorothea. She'd fallen in love with them—and them with her. For the first time in her life, she felt as if she had a real family.

Marrying Garrett had been her dream come true. While he had a lot of friends, she had only invited two people. Peter had thanked her but turned her down. He apologized, but said everything was too fresh. He'd had Amethyst cremated and would be taking her ashes with him on a long ocean cruise.

The other person she invited was Alistair. "I wouldn't miss it for the world," he'd said.

"I'd like you to give me away," she'd told him and heard the emotion in his voice when he'd said he would be honored.

Everyone at the reception said the wedding had been beautiful. But Joslyn only had eyes for Garrett. He'd been so handsome in his Western attire. She'd chosen a simple dress. When he'd seen her—they'd been married at the ranch—his gaze had told her everything she'd needed to know.

Their first dance had been magical. Now the reception was winding down. She headed for the sitting room where she'd prepared for the wedding. They would be leaving soon for their honeymoon. She hadn't realized that Alistair had followed her until she dropped the "something blue" pin Will's wife, Poppy, had given her before the wedding.

"Here, let me help you," Alistair said.

She'd already leaned down to retrieve the pretty blue pin, but now froze. Something about his words made her stare up at the man standing over her. As she looked up at Alistair, her throat closed. Blood drained from her head.

The memory came in a rush. *"No."* The word came out a whisper as the memory knocked the air from her lungs even as she fought to push it away as she had for so long. *"No."* Even as she told herself it couldn't be, she knew. She knew so deep inside her that she felt again like that five-year-old girl she'd been.

He must have seen her expression as she slowly rose, the pin biting in the flesh of her palm. The change came over him slowly as if he too wanted to keep denying it. Twenty-five years of holding so tight to his secret seemed to drain from him. He suddenly looked twice his age.

Stumbling back, he sat down hard on one of the chairs in the sitting room. He looked broken, as if it took all of his energy to raise his head to meet her gaze.

She felt her heart break. "You." It came out on a

ragged breath followed by a sob. He'd always been so kind to her. She remembered that even before her father's death how Alistair never failed to bring her a small gift when he returned from one of the business trips her father sent him on. He would sneak her chocolate and small trinkets that made her laugh. He used to say he loved her laugh. He would lift her up and spin her around until she burst into a fit of giggles.

"How is my Mo today?" he would say and then squat down to her level to listen. He'd seemed fascinated by her stories of finding a grasshopper or scraping her knee or eating something yucky that her sister, Amethyst, bet her she couldn't eat.

A sob escaped her throat. He'd made time for her when her busy father and uninterested stepmother hadn't. He would tell her how much he wanted a little girl just like her and she would laugh and tell him he should get his wife to make one for him.

As young as she'd been she'd seen how sad it made him not to have a little girl of his own. "I'm afraid that isn't going to happen," he'd said only months before his wife died.

She took a step back only to stumble into the chair opposite him. She dropped into it as she remembered how he'd changed after her father's death. He no longer spun her around or brought her trinkets. He had seemed...wary of her.

He was looking at her now with that same wariness, his eyes hangdog sad and full of regret. She pressed her back to the chair as if to distance herself from it, the memory floating around her like the smell of blood.

"I'm so sorry," he choked out.

She shook her head. "You and my stepmother?" Even though she could now understand what she'd seen that night, she still didn't want to believe it.

"Thea." He said it like a curse. "I can't even explain it after all these years."

"You always said that my father was your best friend."

He nodded, his eyes wet with unshed tears.

She saw it all after twenty-five years of locking the memories away, unable to face them. "He caught the two of you together."

Alistair raked a hand through his gray hair and looked past her as if seeing that night as clearly as she did now. "He suspected. Thea's doing, I'm sure now. I realized too late that she was only using me to get back at him because he worked so much, she felt neglected."

"I heard raised voices," Joslyn said more to herself than to him as she remembered waking up and getting out of bed to walk to the top of the stairs. Her father had a baseball bat in his hand and was threatening Alistair. She closed her eyes for a moment remembering the fight, her stepmother screaming, her father and Alistair fighting over the bat. Alistair taking it away from her father and swinging it. Thea jumping on his back. Him throwing her off and then…

She opened her eyes to stare in horror at Alistair,

realizing why she'd never been able to remember. It was as if Alistair had lost his mind. He attacked them both, screaming in what she now knew had to be pain. She couldn't bear what she'd seen. Still couldn't.

"You…" She couldn't say the words.

"Thea set me up. I lost control. I was so ashamed of myself. I'd betrayed my best friend, but I felt betrayed too, not just by Thea but Horace. I can't explain it and I've tried for the past twenty-five years. I had the bat in my hands…"

She felt a shock move through her. "You framed Harvey Mattson."

He colored at her accusing tone. "The man is far from innocent. But you're right. This was one crime he didn't commit."

She felt sick and was glad she was sitting down. Otherwise, she felt as if she would puddle to the floor. "You took care of me all these years knowing that I might remember."

He nodded slowly. "I'd promised your father, but I would have taken care of you even if I hadn't. Monica, you were the daughter I never had. I know you never thought of me as a father. I'm sure that's my fault because often when I looked at you I saw…" He let his head drop into his hands for a moment before looking at her again. "I did my best."

She knew he had and that made it hurt all the more. "I have one question. How did Amethyst know where to send the photo of me and Garrett?" She saw the guilt stain his face red. "You found out where the witness protection program had sent me." Sometimes she forgot about the power Alistair wielded and then there was all that money to grease the wheel. "You told her?"

"I let her discover the truth," he said, his voice breaking. "You know how nosey she always was when she visited my house. The feds thought you were remembering. I… I…" He buried his face in his hands, his body heaving with sobs. "I'll never forgive myself for it."

"Joslyn?" Garrett stepped into the room and stopped. She looked up at him and said, "Please call the police."

He glanced at Alistair who was sobbing loudly, his face still buried in his hands.

Garrett pulled out his cell phone as he stepped to his wife. He pulled her to him as he made the call. She began to cry, clinging to him. Her heart was breaking but she knew with Garrett's love she would get through this. She would undo the wrong Alistair had done. Harvey Mattson would go free.

"The police are on their way," Garrett said and looked to Alistair.

He'd pulled himself together, calling up what dignity he had left. "I'll admit to all of it," her former guardian said.

She nodded, knowing she would ask for leniency for him, but doubting he would get it.

Garrett wiped at her tears. She looked into her husband's handsome face, felt his strength. This cowboy would get her through all of it. She smiled through her tears, feeling her troubled past slipping away. With Garrett's love she was going to be fine. More than fine. No longer was there a darkness inside her that she had to fear.

He pulled her closer with the promise of the future they would share, the family they would make, the memories they would collect. New memories, happy memories.

* * * * *

The moment Fiona found the letter in the bottom of Chase's sock drawer, she knew it was bad news. Fear squeezed the breath from her as her heart beat so hard against her rib cage that she thought she would pass out. Grabbing the bureau for support, she told herself it might not be what she thought it was.

But the envelope was a pale lavender, and the handwriting was distinctly female. Worse, Chase had kept the letter a secret. Why else would it be hidden under his socks? He hadn't wanted her to see it because it was from that other woman.

Now she wished she hadn't been snooping around. She'd let herself into his house with the extra key she'd had made. She'd felt him pulling away from her the past few weeks. Having been here so many times before, she was determined that this one wasn't going to break her heart, Nor was she going to let another woman take him from her. That's why she had to find out why he hadn't called, why he wasn't returning her messages, why he was avoiding her.

They'd had fun the night they were together. She'd felt as if they had something special, although she knew the next morning that he was feeling guilty. He'd said he didn't want to lead her on. He'd told her that there was some woman back home he was still in love with. He'd said their night together was a mistake. But he was wrong, and she was determined to convince him of it.

What made it so hard was that Chase was a genuinely nice guy. You didn't let a man like that get away. The other woman had. Fiona wasn't going to make that mistake, even though he'd been trying to push her away since that night. But he had no idea how determined she could be, determined enough for both of them that this wasn't over by a long shot. It wasn't the first time she'd let herself into his apartment when he was at work. The other time, he'd caught her and she'd had to make up some story about the building manager letting her in so she could look for her lost earring.

She'd snooped around his house the first night they'd met—the same night she'd found his extra apartment key and had taken it to have her own key in case she ever needed to come back when Chase wasn't home.

The letter hadn't been in his sock drawer that time. That meant he'd received it since then. Hadn't she known he was hiding something from her? Why else would he put this letter in a drawer instead of leaving it out along with the bills he'd casually dropped on the table by the front door? Because the letter was important to him, which meant that she had no choice but to read it.

Don't miss
Steel Resolve by B.J. Daniels,
available July 2019 wherever
Harlequin® Intrigue books and ebooks are sold.

www.Harlequin.com